PRAISE FOR *SIN*

"Urgent, haunting, and fearless."

—Megan Abbott, author of *Beware the Woman*

"Pochoda demonstrates keen insight into the minds and hearts of desperate people . . . She never misses a shot."

—Lisa Levy, *The Washington Post*

"A haunting noir thriller stretching from Arizona up to the California coast, *Sing Her Down* . . . [is a] hot, propulsive new book."

—Lauren Puckett-Pope, *Elle*

"A wild, revelatory ride, one that's rich with complex characters and an acerbic social critique that won't soon be forgotten."

—Dwyer Murphy, *CrimeReads*

"Ivy Pochoda writes with style, and often with nuance. *Sing Her Down* is . . . a fast, stylish read."

—Doreen Sheridan, *Criminal Element*

"*Sing Her Down* is a real accomplishment, a novel that interrogates the violence inherent in both the American carceral system and society as a whole. It places Pochoda squarely in the ranks of Los Angeles crime writers such as Raymond Chandler and Walter Mosley, although her style is all her own."

—Michael Schaub, *Alta*

"I read everything Ivy Pochoda writes. Her capture of the complexities, diversities, and insanities of today's life and culture is next to none. I loved *Sing Her Down*. The world will too."

—Michael Connelly, author of *Resurrection Walk*

"Gripping, relentless . . . *Sing Her Down* is brutal and chaotic and entertaining." —Patrick Rapa, *The Philadelphia Inquirer*

"Pochoda's tour de force."
—Oline H. Cogdill, *South Florida Sun Sentinel*

"A gritty thriller with a fiery heart, *Sing Her Down* is a pulse-pounding western with a devastating message about the oft-forgotten explosions made by women the world tries hard not to see."
—Alice Martin, *Shelf Awareness*

"Visceral descriptions of everything from the proliferation of homeless encampments to the simmering emotions of her characters distinguish Pochoda's latest, intense novel."
—Kristine Huntley, *Booklist*

"In muscular prose, Pochoda plumbs the psychological depths of her fascinating characters and extracts high drama from their shifting allegiances. This searing, accomplished page-turner deserves a wide audience." —*Publishers Weekly* (starred review)

"*Sing Her Down* is that rare novel that explodes your expectations from the very first page and goes on doing so until the end . . . and the entirety has the epic intensity of a murder ballad."
—Jonathan Lethem, author of *The Arrest*

"*Sing Her Down* is an incantation, a hallucination, a fiery odyssey of women taking back the power stolen and leached from body and mind, while their souls get harder and harder—like diamonds."
—Susan Straight, author of *Mecca*

Maria Kanevskaya

IVY POCHODA

SING HER DOWN

Ivy Pochoda is the author of the critically acclaimed novels *Wonder Valley*, *Visitation Street*, and *These Women*. She won the 2018 Strand Critics Award for Best Novel and France's Prix Page / America, and has been a finalist for the Edgar Award and the Los Angeles Times Book Prize, among other awards. For many years, she taught creative writing at Studio 526 in Los Angeles's Skid Row. She is a professor of creative writing in the low-residency MFA program at the Palm Desert Center of the University of California, Riverside. She lives in Los Angeles.

ALSO BY IVY POCHODA

These Women
Wonder Valley
Visitation Street
The Art of Disappearing

SING

HER

DOWN

SING
HER
DOWN

IVY POCHODA

MCD · PICADOR

FARRAR, STRAUS AND GIROUX | NEW YORK

MCD
Picador
120 Broadway, New York 10271

Printed in the United States of America
Originally published in 2023 by MCD / Farrar, Straus and Giroux
First paperback edition, 2024

Background texture by Guenter Albers / Shutterstock.com.

The Library of Congress has cataloged the MCD hardcover edition as follows:
Names: Pochoda, Ivy, author.
Title: Sing her down : a novel / Ivy Pochoda.
Description: First edition. | New York : MCD / Farrar, Straus and Giroux, 2023.
Identifiers: LCCN 2022057864 | ISBN 9780374608484 (hardcover)
Classification: LCC PS3616.O285 S56 2023 | DDC 813/.6—dc23/eng/20221202
LC record available at https://lccn.loc.gov/2022057864

Paperback ISBN: 978-1-250-33579-1

Designed by Gretchen Achilles

Our books may be purchased in bulk for promotional, educational,
or business use. Please contact your local bookseller or the Macmillan Corporate
and Premium Sales Department at 1-800-221-7945, extension 5442, or by email at
MacmillanSpecialMarkets@macmillan.com.

Picador® is a U.S. registered trademark and is used by
Macmillan Publishing Group, LLC, under license from Pan Books Limited.

For book club information, please email marketing@picadorusa.com.

mcdbooks.com • Follow us on social media at @mcdbooks
picadorusa.com • Follow us on social media at @picador or @picadorusa

10 9 8 7 6 5 4 3 2 1

For Louisa Hall—fierce, wise, and loyal beyond measure

And bad people cant be governed at all. Or if they could I never heard of it.

—Cormac McCarthy, *No Country for Old Men*

But that was just a story, something that people will tell themselves, something to pass the time it takes for the violence inside a man to wear him away, or to be consumed itself, depending on who is the candle and who is the light.

—Denis Johnson, *Angels*

PROLOGUE

KACE

Let me tell you a story.

I know everybody's story. Been collecting them for years—a goddamn library of voices filed away in my head. Sometimes there's not much to tell.

But you'll want to hear this one.

It's about two women, two women in a world of women, cut off from a world of men until they weren't.

You won't believe what women can do.

These women—their mistake was in thinking they burned with their own unique rage. Something deeper, darker than what the rest of us feel.

Let me tell you—inside we all rage the same. It's how we let it out that differs.

This story ends seven hours west of here but a few miles short of the ocean. Like the women in it, ran but didn't make it all the way. Ran from this desert but failed to find the water. That's some raw luck to fall before you catch the ocean breeze. Gotta suspect that shit can wash away some sin. Couldn't hurt to try.

But maybe they didn't want to make it that far. Maybe that wasn't part of their plan. Part of their story.

To each, you know.

Now, I don't know what-all happened between here and there. I only know what I've been told.

What I've been told about is a mural.

You probably think that's some bullshit, that I'm wasting your time talking about something spray-painted on a wall in a city I've never even been to. But I'm telling you—I've heard it's a real *something*.

I'm gonna see it one day. Fly this coop and check it with my own eyes.

So, this mural's painted behind a gas station at the corner of Olympic and Western in Los Angeles. Until recently those street names meant nothing to me. But they're coming into focus.

As far as I know, it's just another intersection of bad and worse—trouble running in either direction.

And far as I can tell, it's where this story ends.

Thing is—this mural isn't just any mural. People say it's alive. People say it jumps and moves. People're always saying crazy shit. People always thinking I'm saying crazy shit. After all, I got the voices in my head and I'm not going to lie about that.

You know what I thought when I first heard about this living mural, this paint job that moves? I thought motherfuckers been so cooped up, so safer-at-home, flattening-the-curve that they've gone out of their minds.

Motherfuckers been breathing through these fucking masks so long they've oxygen-deprived themselves.

A living mural, my ass.

But then I realized it makes sense.

All these voices in my head—the victims dropped by the women in here, they live on in me. So why the fuck couldn't that mural be alive? Why couldn't that story keep telling itself?

Over time, I've seen a lot more that's made a lot less sense.

My girl Cassie finally sent me a photo. Been asking her for a month now—wasting stamps and phone time getting through to her.

Told her, *Next time you're in Los Angeles, you got to get me a picture of this thing, this mural.*

The fuck you want a photo of a wall for? she asked me.

The least you could do for someone stuck inside like me, I told her. *The least you could fucking do. Just take a goddamn fucking picture.*

So she did it. Got her ass over to that intersection and snapped a photo on her phone. Like I said, the least she could fucking do.

Took ages for these assholes to print that shit out and show it to me.

By then I'd already reached Cassie on the phone to ask where the fuck my photo was.

Bitch, she says to me, *you won't fucking believe it. I thought you were crazier than crazy sending me to chase down a painting middle of a fucking pandemic. But that goddamned mural moves. My photo doesn't capture shit. But I swear one of those women keeps walking toward the other.*

The next day they handed me the printout. Blurry as fuck, but still.

I only know Los Angeles from movies, but in the mural it looks like a ghost town. Fucking dead. Empty. "Hollow" is the word I'll use. Even blurry, you can just tell.

How the hell art can capture what isn't there instead of what is, I don't have a clue.

And let me tell you, you can almost hear that emptiness. A sound of blowing trash and echo. A sound of nothing.

Plus there's all these masks and crap swirling up the street like tumbleweed. My granddad used to watch that John Wayne and Henry Fonda shit, so I know what I know.

As I said, a ghost town. That's what the artist painted.

Listen, I don't know how this shit works, but even in the bad copy the photo seems to move.

At first I thought it was the light in my cell.

Then the shifting light in my scratched window.

But it's the goddamned photo. I'm sure.

I'm sure, I'm sure. I might be a killer. I might hear voices. But that doesn't mean I'm crazy.

There are two people in the mural, two women. Dios and Florida. You're going to hear all about them.

That intersection is the end of their run.

Florida is striding north up Western. Up ahead, plastered on a hillside, the Hollywood sign watches the scene unfold.

Dios stands in her path, blocking it. She's got her hands on her hips. Her coal-black hair is plaited and slicked. I've been on the receiving end of that look. She means business. She means don't fuck with me or fuck with me and find out.

Look close and you can see the wind lift a stray hair. Promise.

Dios's eyes are snakelike, unblinking. That's something that doesn't move no matter how long I look at the picture. That stare is fixed. Stone-cold stone.

It's Florida who is on the move, coming up the street, straight down the middle. No cars. No people. Just these two women. Like the city has made way for them and what is about to happen.

You see Florida in profile. Her face looks off, like she's wearing Halloween makeup. Her hair is pulled back. But you can tell that it's still bleach-frizzled.

Now, I've known Florida for coming up on three years. Lived with her for nearly twelve months. And I've never seen the look on her face that's captured on that wall.

Part of me wants to think the painter fucked up.

And this other part—well, that part guesses this side of Florida has been there all along.

It's surprising how long it takes for us to know ourselves. Often takes until it's too late.

Me, I'm not really a murderer, although I killed someone. Still, people—so many people—tell me that's exactly what I am. That and nothing else.

Florida—well, I'm not exactly sure who she is. But the woman in the mural sure seems to know.

In the painting, she's still wearing her state-issued boots.

You can almost hear them strike the asphalt.

She takes one step.

Another.

She's got something in her hand, but the mural doesn't show it.

All I see is the coming standoff. The endless approach. The last gasp. The final moments of Dios and Florida.

PART 1

DIOS

See your tree, Florida. See it bowing and bending under the smothered sky. Wind-whipped and swaying. See it through the scratched glass—the work of blades and nails and night after night of desperation. Rain hammered and storm tortured.

You got the white-girl blues again, Florida. I know. I can tell through these walls. I can *feel* from my own cell next door. I can vibe you vibrating with your hurt—a deep chord that shakes the cinder block like the bass on a car radio.

You're heavy into that *I don't belong here* shit.

But this is exactly where you belong.

Rich girls like you, Florida—blinder than the rest by far.

Yours is not one of those hard-pity tales that make the privileged feel as if they've moonlit in a rough world. Yours isn't the story that makes women like your mother shed phony tears—if only for a moment—at the injustices in the world.

You don't need a good look to know that that particular song has been sung in here too many times—nearly every bunk filled with a woman wronged on the outside, wronged by the system, wronged on the inside. Wrong begetting wrong like dominos on their way down.

Who will tell *our* stories, Florida?

Who will listen to the song of a cold heart?

Who will sing, "Pero nunca se fijaron / En tan humilde señora"?

See your tree bowing down until it nearly breaks. Marking time and passing the seasons, budding and blooming and shedding. See your tree for two years and five months, twenty-two days and a handful of hours. Your sentence ticking away until completion.

And tonight, in the throes of the storm, in the arms of the kind of violence that fills your dreams, see your tree battling the wind, rain, and sand that rip through this flat desert state. Like Daphne, rooted strong against the assault of her unwanted lover.

"You still watching? You still watching, Florida? You still . . ." I can hear Kace's rambling from here. "Because Marta says it's no good to watch. Marta says that's how the devil gets in. Marta says he's watching you from the tree. Marta says you're inviting him in. You want the devil, Florida? You want him?"

"Enough about Marta," you tell her.

I can hear the heavy thud as Kace pounds the bunk with her fist, punching you through the springs and flimsy mattress. You recoil to the wall. I feel the bang.

Now listen.

Listen to Kace hearing voices. Listen to her talking back and talking for them. For part of the night or, worse, the whole night. Listen until you know those voices too, like they're your friends. A crazed chorus wailing at the walls of a fallen city. A whole bunch of mad Furies.

So listen to them and her and miss them when they're not around and she's deadly quiet, scary in her silence. Listen to them because you think it's better than listening to me.

I fear women with nonlinear anger, you told me, back when we lived together. Before you moved out and your old cellie Tina moved in.

You think anger moves from point A to point B like a formula? I asked. *You think there's always derivation.* "Derivation" shut you right up.

You had imagined you were the educated one in here.

Kace is anything but linear. So let her talk all night if she needs. I'm just next door and it drives me crazy.

But that was the transfer that was available, so you took it. Anything to create space between us, you thought. Anything to rip you from me—from the you you saw in me.

You should have paid more attention to the old stories. Fate is fated.

Nothing you can fucking do about that.

We will meet at the crossroads.

You think you are unique in your appreciation for the finer things—contrails that cross-streak the sky at sunset, a scattershot of buds erupting on your tree, the soft swallow as the desert rain hits the dry earth.

I know how close you hold them because I listened to you go on and on about how this place was not your place. How you can't breathe, can't feel, can't sense properly—as if your senses are keener. I know you think these people are not your people and your crimes not your crimes. I listened to you make everyone else's excuses for what you did.

Except I know that your guilt runs deeper than the story crafted for you. A small detail no bigger than a matchbook. I know because Tina told me. And I know more than that.

You're no victim, Florida.

There was the summer you spent in Israel that you paid for by smuggling diamonds into Luxembourg. And the year abroad in Amsterdam, where you fraudulently signed your name to mortgage papers that secured bad loans for grifters.

Then there was what brought you in here—accomplice to murder after the fact. Drove the getaway car from a fire that left two bodies burning in the desert. Like you didn't know.

Inside, they call you Florida because of the color you dye your hair—jailhouse blond.

Florence isn't a name for in here. So you keep ruining your hair with the cheap bleach.

It's raining a hard desert rain, a monsoon so powerful you can almost feel it through the thick windows—a rhythm so fierce that it's inside us. The storm surges like an advancing battalion, cleansing the air of the nightly noise of everyone up and down the block. A purge.

Kace is talking. Marta is talking back. The tree is swaying silent.

Lightning splinters the sky, cracking it like a rock kicked into a windshield, x-raying the yard and the fence.

Now, I can barely hear you two above the storm. I close my eyes and lie back on my bunk, thankful I don't have to listen tonight.

———

SING HER DOWN

In the morning the storm has left a low-slung sky. Because of the rain, we all slept well, able to forget one another for a second.

We wake to the regular sounds, to women hollering down the halls. Calling from bunk to bunk and cell to cell. The coughing too—we wake to that.

The window is dirt-streaked and spattered with water stains.

The yard is mud.

The tree is gone.

I'll let you tell the rest.

FLORIDA

Last night's storm raised hell. The electricity from the lightning lingers in the blocks and coils around the bars of each cell Florida passes, ramping up a tension that you can almost see vibrating down the line. More cells than normal remain occupied at mealtimes—more and more older women are hanging back from group activities, buying their meals in the canteen and eating on their bunks.

But even at reduced capacity, the cafeteria is charged with a current that reveals itself in spikes and ripples of activity, small explosions of noise, dropped trays and spilled drinks. As Florida fills her plate, she notices the room has grown strangely silent, the customary chatter receding to nothing. Only a cough breaks the calm.

At the sound the women flinch and scatter like they've heard a gunshot. Then it is still again—a sure sign of a quiet storm brewing.

Florida's eyes shift, careful to land on no one and nothing. Head down. Business to herself. She slides into a seat next to

Mel-Mel, a woman innocuous except for her size, and occupies herself with the nothing-doing of her breakfast.

"Unsex me now, bitch!"

Diana Diosmary Sandoval jumps back from her seat, arms wide, stomping her foot for the room's attention. The guards lift their eyes at trouble on the boil, but no sooner has she assumed her stance than they look away.

What happens next will be swift and painful. Dios has barbed wire in her veins one second, mercury the next.

"I said, unsex me now, motherfucker."

Florida is too close to this action. Dios's eyes land on hers.

Then Dios smiles, mean and mirthless, a quick flash of her perfect teeth. If it weren't for her regulation orange, it would seem as if Dios has wandered in from a different world—a place of cleanliness and order and the luxury to focus on the superficial details. Beneath her obsidian hair, her high forehead is a polished orb. Her eyebrows are painted arches. Her eyes are cold green stones. Her skin glows golden with an inner heat.

She steps toward Florida's table, positioning herself just behind Mel-Mel. Florida flinches at the sight of the fork in her grip.

At least the mountain of Mel-Mel is between them—an undulation of soft peaks in bright orange, a physical manifestation of Mel-Mel's personality, malleable and gullible, a pawn, never a player.

Florida knows some of the COs aren't paying attention or are looking away on purpose in deference to a deal sealed in the kitchen or chapel with a handshake, a trade-off, a handoff, a dirty exchange. Some might even be looking on with perverse pleasure, eager for the fight, aching to seeing Diana Diosmary Sandoval in her element.

They can't hide that they love it when the women throw down, especially when it's a woman like Dios—someone who outclasses them on the outside but whose status in here forces her to bite her tongue at their rude talk. They permit her to fight, Florida thinks, because it reduces her to their animal level.

Dios raises the fist with the fork. She feints toward Florida, lurching over Mel-Mel's head. Then she cracks her nasty smile again. Florida doesn't flinch.

You take your beatings when they come. Sometimes you only discover their reason later.

How badly will this hurt? Will it be as bad as the beatdowns Florida took when she came inside—the poundings that left a watercolor of blue and purple cascading from neck to hip? Will it pulse and ring for weeks, resonate with its own throbbing sound, a brutal, percussive cacophony, like the concussion she received at the hands of a guard in the shower? Or will it be its own sort of art? A contrast in metallics, the cold, sharp tines of the fork in her skin and the iron taste of blood on her tongue.

But then, there's a moment, a hairsbreadth passage between Dios and Florida, when Dios relaxes her grip on the fork, when it hangs loose in her grasp, when she turns and fixes her stare on Mel-Mel and when Florida knows what's coming isn't coming for her.

Then Dios holds out the fork toward Florida. In Dios's eyes, a challenge to take up the mantle, to finish what she is about to start.

"Come on, Florida," Dios says, her voice the sharp suggestion that inflicting pain is pleasure. "You know you want to."

Florida keeps her face blank.

"Have it your way," Dios says. A quick upward flicker of her painted eyebrows and Dios's hand is tight on the fork again. With her eyes locked on Florida, Dios reaches around Mel-Mel and plunges the fork into her cheek, instantly reaping furrows of blood. She presses down, punctuating her strike. Then she rakes the tines toward Mel-Mel's jaw.

Florida imagines the sound of ripping flesh like tearing fabric, a gruesome pop-pop of stitches bursting. But she can't hear it over Mel-Mel's brief scream, which is quickly muffled as Dios covers her mouth with her free hand. Then she twists the fork, twirling the shredded flesh into a mangled spiral.

Mel-Mel's blood rushes over Dios's hand. Dios keeps twisting like she wants to pull all the loose skin of Mel-Mel's cheek into a bloody whirlpool, drawing her eye bags and second chin closer and closer to the gory core.

Dios lets go, leaving the fork in Mel-Mel's cheek. She steps back from the table. Mel-Mel raises her hand to her mauled flesh, her mouth flopping open and closed like a fish gasping for air.

Dios's eyes remain on Florida's. "Next time," she says.

Florida lies on her bunk. It's a few weeks out from the longest day of the year. The sun's sunk out of sight, turning the clouds from yesterday's storm a menacing black shot through with shocks of orange.

"A devil's sky," Kace says. "Desert rain is a clear sign of the devil. He leaves his mark when he's done, so don't forget."

Florida squints at the sky. It sure does look like hell or maybe hellfire.

You don't have to work hard to see the devil in here. There's a devil in everyone and everything.

"You think everything is a sign of the devil," Florida says. "Sneeze three times and he's got you."

"That's what Marta thinks. That's her thinking," Kace says, pacing the room in a ten-step beat that Florida knows will stay with her for years to come.

Florida knows better than to question Marta. The unseen woman behind Kace's most violent violence is best ignored.

"You gonna climb a tree when you get out? I bet you're gonna climb a tree first thing," Kace says. "Climb a whole gang of trees."

Less than a year until her first chance at parole—time enough to make plans and revise them and then reverse.

"I don't climb trees," Florida says. "And I'm getting out of state the minute that gate clangs."

Ten steps—a full lap. "So what then?" Kace pounds the top bunk two-handed.

Florida sighs. "I'm going to California," she says.

"Florida heading for California," Kace says. "Shame you'll be paroled here."

"I'll put in for transfer before I get out," Florida says. "Get a PO in Los Angeles." She meets the criteria—suitable residence, treatment plans for a problem she doesn't really have, financial support.

"Then what?" Kace asks.

"I'm going to get my car."

"You think you got a car waiting for you after all this time? You think someone hasn't up and sold it for cold hard cash? Taken it for a drive? Crashed it? Repoed it? You forget they forget us when we're gone."

"The car's waiting," Florida says.

"And you think that shit still runs?"

That shit—it better run. A 1968 Jaguar E-Type Florence's mother inherited from her own father when he died. The same year that she stopped driving the freeways, then stopped driving altogether. Her therapists told her it was a temporary paranoia, that her fear of crashing, losing control, jamming the accelerator to the floor, or forgetting to brake, would pass. They told her it happened to some women in middle age. They told her she'd ease back in.

Instead, her mother sold her Mercedes and her BMW and she never drove Florence anywhere again.

The Jag sat idle, forgotten in the six-car garage, gathering dust, until Florence, unlicensed and unsupervised, began to drive it to school. Her mother hadn't cared as long as transporting Florence didn't become her problem.

Florida stares at the ceiling, at the map of cracks spidering without purpose. Squint and these transform into the freeways of her teens, not the main arteries through Los Angeles—the 10 to the beach, the PCH along the coast, the 101 from Echo Park to Santa Barbara, the 405 from the west side to the OC. But the ones her friends and mother didn't dare—the 105, 710, 605. The freeways that led from her acceptable Los Angeles to Vernon, Commerce, Bell, and Carson—small cities swept up in the metropolitan area and ignored by everyone from Hancock Park to the west side. What started as shortcuts and work-arounds to avoid traffic became destinations of their own, where Florence, only fifteen, could veer and weave on the narrow freeway, hit the gas as the Jag streaked by casinos, power plants, racetracks, and gravel yards, the unfamiliar surroundings soon becoming as familiar as the curves and bends in the road.

Where do you go all day after school? her mother once asked, less concerned than curious.

Nowhere, Florence told her.

As far as her mother was concerned, this was good enough.

"What you gonna do with that car? Where you gonna go?" Kace is asking.

"Everywhere," Florida says.

"You watch the news? No one's supposed to be going anywhere. We're all supposed to be safer at home."

But by the time Florida's up for parole, that should have

changed. And first thing, she'll head west to her mother's house, grab the car, and then drive.

So, you're the kind of girl who can't leave the scene of the crime, Dios said when Florida told her about the car. *You're the kind of girl who heads back to the eye of the storm. After all this time inside, you're hunting for trouble, heading straight for your getaway vehicle.*

It's just a car, Florida said.

You're one dark bitch, even if you pretend otherwise. Then Dios had laughed her sharp, cold laugh. *Bet that Jag is worth bank. Better to sell it than drive it.*

At least 200K, Florida guesses. She didn't tell Dios that. She didn't have to. Dios just knows shit.

"Just drive," Florida says aloud. The same words her accomplice, Carter, had said a few moments after he'd hurled that homemade pipe bomb into the trailer. He didn't have to tell her twice. She was flying high on MDMA, her foot already teasing the accelerator.

"Who the fuck are you talking to?" Kace says.

"No one."

"Girl, this place is cracking you up." Kace side-eyes Florida. Ever since the riot, ever since Tina, Kace has been side-eyeing her. "You cool, Florida?"

"I'm cool."

"You just driving away in your mind?"

Florida wiggles her toes, trying to feel for the pressure of the accelerator going down, down, down as the speed increases and the vibration in the steering wheel makes her palms itch. Even now, even after all that happened with her and that car—even after racing the Jag away from that exploding trailer—she still wants to feel that pressure in her calf and the acceleration that rises from her feet to her chest, nearly taking her breath away.

"Tell me where you'll take me, Florida. Tell me where we'll go in that car."

"You ever been to Los Angeles, Kace?"

"I don't do big city."

"Then we'll head out of town," Florida says. "I'll take you out of town."

The 110 to the 105. The 105 to the 605 passing through Norwalk, Bellflower, Los Alamitos, before rejoining the 405 near Seal Beach.

"I like the beach," Kace says. "Now that sounds just right."

Florida can take the beach or leave it. It's the drive that matters, the journey through a web of freeways, instead of the destination. The first time she drove to the OC and back without taking the 5 or the 405 she felt like she'd cracked a code to a secret city. She felt like she'd cracked the code to herself. Like she could see how she worked on the inside instead of how she looked in the mirror.

She ran different from everyone else.

She closes her eyes, feels the car reverb up her leg, the slight muscle ache in her left wrist when she exceeded seventy. She steadies her hand on the invisible wheel, reaches for the shift as she presses her other foot for the imaginary clutch.

Even after everything—just drive. Because what else is there?

But then there's a shift in the room, Kace sliding into a different gear.

"You were front and center for that shit that went down today. What the fuck was Dios's message? Bitch always needs to prove herself. We know what brought her inside. Not much. Assault. Simple self-defense gone wrong."

Florida puts a finger to her lips, points to the vent through which Dios can hear them. But it's too late. There's a pounding on the opposite wall.

"Always got to prove yourself, Dios. Always got to let the rest of us know that your fucking crime could have been as hard as ours. 'Cept it wasn't. Run-of-the-mill assault. And not even half-bad at that."

"Ssshh," Florida insists.

Kace rolls her eyes. "Fuck do you care if she hears us? Anyway, what's Mel-Mel done to her? Cutting Mel-Mel is like cutting the sad-ass zoo elephant. You can't blame a lady for being dopey as fuck."

"You can if you think dopiness is a crime."

"But it isn't. A crime's a crime. If we could avenge people for their personalities, we'd all be in trouble," Kace says. "That would fill up the prisons so fast there'd be no more prison." She pauses and inclines her head toward the wall, giving Florida a view of the cobra tattoo that climbs from her neck into her mess of curly brown hair. "I know you're listening, *Diana*," Kace continues, drawling on Dios's Christian name. "Marta told me." She pounds the wall. "She can hear you even when you're not talking."

"We're cool, Kace," comes Dios's muffled voice. "Just keep talking."

Kace takes a lap, then lowers her voice. "Did you see her after? Did you see Mel-Mel? Did you see her face?"

Florida had. But she'd seen something else—the challenge in Dios's eyes. *Finish what you started*.

"I was right there, remember?"

"You know what Mel-Mel told them happened? She told them she tripped bussing her tray. Told them the fork was sitting there like a bear trap, waiting for her. And they believed that shit. They believed that shit."

Before Florida can reply, a bark-like cough, a desiccated animal hacking, fills the hallway. Kace freezes, her face contorted. Then her expression relaxes as the coughing fades away. "Mel-Mel didn't even let them take her to the infirmary. Said she was all cool. But did you see her?"

"It was bad, Kace. Really bad. Her cheek was like spaghetti. It was all ribbons and sauce. And you could see that white part, that underflap of the skin. The part you aren't supposed to see."

Florida knows Kace loves this stuff. Not the pain but the details. "That's what I'm talking about," Kace says. She takes a deep breath, drinking this all in, letting it relax her.

Too soon her reverie is splintered by another explosion of coughing on the block.

Kace stamps to the door. "Quiet!"

"Easy," Florida says. "Easy."

The cougher doesn't heed Kace's command.

"I said be quiet."

"Easy."

"No, you be quiet. You shut your fucking mouth," someone calls down the line.

Kace roars back. But the beef is drowned out by a fresh volley of coughing.

"God-fucking-damnit," Kace shouts. "Shut the fuck up." She pounds the walls with her fists.

"Easy," Florida repeats. "Easy, easy, easy."

But Kace is too far gone and fired up. Her voice is sinking into a new register. "You want to kill us all. Shut the fuck up with your coughing. You goddamn fucking murderer. Murderer."

A moment of silence falls. Florida can sense everyone holding their breath, a strangulated tension that catches the block in its death grip and is only punctured when another attack of coughing arrives.

Kace raises both fists to the wall. "There's murder in your

breath. Death inside of you. You keep it in there. You keep it, or I'll steal your breath for good. Lock it deep inside you. So deep you won't goddamn need it ever again."

Florida lies as still as she can, as if she can shrink away from all of this. She hears boot strikes in the hall, then pounding on the other side of their door.

"Baldwin! Cut it."

Kace takes a step back from the door at the sound of the CO's voice. She cocks her head, thinking, thinking.

"Cut it, Baldwin," the CO repeats, rapping on the door again.

Kace jerks toward the door, like she's going to fight the officer through the small window.

"Baldwin."

Kace cracks her neck and rolls her shoulders and steps farther back from the door. Soon the CO's footfalls recede down the line. "Fucking asshole." She turns and faces the bunks. "Asshole," she says, pounding her fists on Florida's mattress.

"Who was it?" Florida asks.

"Bergman. He lets Mel-Mel suck his shit. Wonder if he cares her face is like fucking spaghetti. Probably likes it. The sick fuck. Marta says men like him will receive their punishment in hell. Marta says the devil has plans for them. Marta says—"

She's interrupted by an explosion of coughing. Florida rakes her fingers through her hair as Kace bolts to the door.

"Shut up," she screams. "Shut up."

But her cry is interrupted by another, louder voice, one that insists above the coughing and clamor, "Woman down."

Woman down. The phrase echoes up and down the hall—everyone at their door, chanting, bellowing, using two words to condemn the CO and the whole system for everything that's wrong.

Soon a stampede of boots comes down the line. Florida looks out the door in time to see three guards in masks blow by.

She hears a cell door open. The prisoners quiet. The line is silent except for the crackling of walkie-talkies, then the rattle-roll of a stretcher.

The women usually defer to emergencies, refraining from adding their noise and anger to the crisis.

This time is different. The banging starts somewhere far down from Florida and Kace's cell—a one-two beat. A heartbeat.

Bam, bam.

Bam, bam.

Another cell takes it up. And then another. Soon the whole line is hammering in time. Kace and Florida position themselves on either side of their door, one palm pounding the metal.

Bam, bam. Bam, bam.

Florida can hear the stretcher come down the hall, the wheels rolling more slowly now. The women still pound, as if they can strengthen the patient's pulse with their hands.

Bam, bam.

Florida knows this is supposed to be a sign of solidarity. But it sounds like something else.

She's heard how male prisoners hold a death vigil on execution nights—marking time with their fists, voices, or some kind of light, keeping the condemned alive as long as they can, keeping his soul and spirit strong until the inevitable.

The stretcher passes her cell, the patient's identity hidden under an oxygen mask.

"Death march," Kace says. "She's not coming back. They don't come back."

———

The sky is all heat shimmer—a blistered blue that hurts. The sun stings, cooking the hairs on Florida's arms. The yard is busy with women keeping away from one another even though they are all going to be breathing the same air soon enough.

Florida watches Mel-Mel sitting on a bench opposite, her cheek poorly patched with bloody gauze.

"Baum."

Florida startles at the sound of her name buzzing across the loudspeaker.

"Baum. Report."

Florida glances around at everyone looking at her, then looking away as if the trouble she's caught is catching.

She pushes off the bench, dusts the desert sand from her seat and thighs, and heads indoors.

Kace scoots along the bench.

"Florida," Kace calls as Florida heads off. "They don't come back. Marta wants me to tell you."

A sergeant is waiting at the desk, his face an unreadable death mask. "Baum, let's go."

"Go?"

"You want to obey an order or ask a question?"

Florida follows the sergeant to the section of the building where classes and specials meet. "Sit," he says, indicating a bench where two other prisoners are waiting. "They'll call you."

"What's this about?" Florida asks.

"I get orders. I give them to you. You take them."

Florida finds a seat on the bench. She knows the two women next to her by sight only. Mavis Jackson is a real old-timer, a poster woman for compassionate release, someone who has done her time, and everyone else's too—her face is on the fliers and websites of several different activist organizations. Twenty-six years and counting for killing her trafficker—one of too many like her inside. Less guilty than Florida in everyone else's eyes.

The other is a new girl, too much high shine and polish, as if the outside hasn't fully rubbed off yet. Bad checks, identity theft, some kind of skim game, if Florida had to guess. She's young, mid-twenties, with an infuriating freshness Florida wants to slap off her cheeks.

"You know what this is all about?" the new girl asks Jackson.

"I don't know," Jackson says, her words drawling with frustrated patience.

The new girl whirls round so she's up in Florida's face. "What about you? Do you know?"

"What do you think?" Florida snaps, sliding down the bench.

They are sitting opposite one of the all-purpose classrooms for everything from parenting to creative writing to office training.

"So what? What is this?" the new girl says. "We in trouble. What'd we do? I didn't do shit. I didn't do anything."

"You're in prison," Jackson says. "You did something."

The door to the classroom opens and a CO pokes his head out. "Baum?"

Florida rolls her eyes. Last to arrive, first on the chopping block.

"You worried?" the new girl says. "You think it's going to be bad?"

"Shut the fuck up," Florida says. "Wait your turn."

Marta wants you to know they don't come back.

Florida heads for the open door.

Before she can enter, she comes face-to-face with another prisoner on her way out. Dios.

Florida freezes and takes a step back. Dios stays put. She cocks her head, giving Florida the once-over, top to toe. Her lips are pursed with amusement, fury, or frustration, it's hard to guess.

She relaxes her mouth into a wide, cruel smile. "Florida," she says. "Guess we both got them fooled."

Her black hair is slicked back into a ponytail, curls slithering over her shoulders as she towers over Florida. There's a flicker in her cheekbones, a slight muscle twitch—some barely suppressed emotion that's rippling to the surface.

"I'll be seeing you, you know, out and about." Dios jerks her chin slightly, then shapes her thumb and pointer finger into the shape of a gun and places it at Florida's temple. Florida steps aside as Dios pushes past her with a shoulder check just because.

"Baum," the CO barks again, as if she's at fault for not entering sooner.

The room has been cleared. All but one of the desks have been pushed to the edges. A single table sits in the center of the room. Behind it is Officer Markum, the lead CO for the unit, staring down at the top folder on a small stack of files. Next to the stack is a telephone, its cable stretched to the max from the jack on the wall.

The door shuts behind Florida. The other CO stands guard, as if Florida might make a break for it.

"Number," Markum barks. He's middle-aged with the moon pallor of someone who has spent his life indoors. His face is cratered with pits—a permanent dark-side shadow cast—deepening his hostile lunar appearance.

Florida spews out the digits that have become her surrogate identity.

"Sit," Markum says.

The walls are papered with materials for different classes. A faded poster with a poem by Langston Hughes. Another with Walt Whitman's words in fussy cursive. Opposite these is a diagram showing simple yoga positions. There's a whiteboard on the back wall with half-wiped figures probably left over from a basic accounting or business admin certificate program. In the top left corner of the board is a single word: *Trust*.

Florida slumps into the hard plastic chair. Markum looks up from the file. "Florence Baum?" His voice is weary and worn, as if whatever business is in front of him is unpleasant and exhausting.

Florida grips the edges of her seat. She can feel her palms start to slick with moisture.

"Do you know why you're here?"

Florida holds Markum's gaze. But she's not seeing him, not really. Instead, it's Tina's battered face—a rotten, trampled eggplant—staring back at her.

Fucking Dios. Always fucking Dios.

Florida counts back—more than seven months since the night of the blackout and the only fallout is people giving Dios wider berth than before. Until—

"Baum? Do you know why you are here?" Markum reaches for the phone on his desk. He waits for her reply, his hand hovering over the telephone.

"Do you know why you're here?" This time his voice is strained.

Florida blinks, trying see Markum behind the scrim of Tina's death mask.

"I-I-I made a few mistakes," Florida stammers. "I haven't been perfect. But I've done well here. I've—"

Markum holds up a hand, silencing her. Then gives his head a hard, swift shake, as if Florida's response is so off base it hurts. He lifts the receiver to his ear and repeats her DOC number. "Baum, Florence," he adds, with a look at Florida like she has to confirm this information. "All right," he says into the receiver. His eyes meet hers. "I have a representative from the governor's office on the line. Because of the ongoing health crisis, I have been instructed to inform you that you meet the criteria for early release. As of today, May 19, 2020, your sentence is being commuted."

Florida stares at him, thoughts breaking so hard and fast she feels like she might pass out.

"Do you understand what I'm telling you?"

"Yes," Florida says. She's heard his words, but she's not exactly up to speed.

"Accepted," Markum says into the phone, and replaces the receiver.

"Why me?"

Markum makes a note on the file before him and shuffles through the paperwork. "Does it matter?" He glances at her file. "Background, ease of reintegration. It's a formula. Your name came up. Upon release you will be required to quarantine for two weeks. If you do not have a place in state to do that, a motel room will be provided to you."

"I don't have anything in state."

"If you cannot afford accommodation when your quarantine period is over, you may move into a state-run group home."

"I'm from California. I can't quarantine here."

"The conditions of release stipulate that you remain in the county for the quarantine period. If, after two weeks, you move to another county, you will be assigned a new parole officer in that county. All of this will be explained to you in the next few days."

"And if I want to leave the state?"

"You will need to apply through Interstate Compact for a transfer."

"Can I do that before I am released?"

Markum slams his pen down on the desk and closes Florida's file. "I wouldn't bet on it." He nods toward the CO standing by the door. "Send in the next one."

"So I have to remain in Arizona?" Florida sputters. "I don't know anyone here. I don't have anything here."

Markum looks down at her file, scanning for her name. "Baum.

I have twenty of these to process today. Just count your blessings. You'll receive further instructions tomorrow—your condition-of-release paperwork and so on."

"When am I getting out?" Florida asks.

"That's the first reasonable thing I've heard come out of your mouth," Markum replies. "Seventy-two hours. Enjoy the rest of your stay."

He looks away. Interview over.

Florida staggers into the hallway. There are tears rolling down her cheeks. Six months of her life handed back in an instant.

"What the fuck?" The newbie is up on her feet and face-to-face with Florida. "What the fuck is all of this? What did they do to you in there?"

Florida blinks, trying to figure out what just happened.

"What the fuck. What the fuck. You better tell me what's up," the woman says.

"Get your ass away from me," Florida says, shoving past her. Who the fuck is this woman? A few months in and already she's getting out?

"Oh shit, I'm not going in there," the woman pleads. "I didn't do shit. I didn't do fuck-all."

There's nowhere to be alone but in her cell and she'll have enough of that later, so Florida goes to the common area, which is less used these days due to everyone trying to keep their distance. When she can make calls she'll try her mother first, then her father. But she knows she'll fail to reach them and if she does, they'll be of no immediate help. Her father is off the grid in New Mexico and her mom is probably in Oman or Thailand, pretending to help others while indulging herself.

There are about twelve women scattered around the twenty

tables, in groups no larger than two. Florida finds an empty spot and sits. She keeps her back to as much of the room as she can, holding on to this moment, saving it for herself before it becomes community property of gossip, whispers, speculation, and lies.

"Florida, did you ever wonder why you're so lucky?"

Dios swings into the empty seat next to her, her high forehead looming over Florida. "Did you ever take a moment to consider that you are one lucky-ass motherfucker? A real lady of fortune?"

Florida glances around the dismal common area and the two levels of cells that rise above it on three sides. "Some luck," she says.

"Tick-tock," Dios says. "Soon the lucky bird gets to fly the coop."

"You're getting out too."

"Stopped to wonder why?" Dios's green eyes are inches from Florida's face. Despite the harsh light, her skin has a golden glow. "Have you, *Florence*? Or are you just racing ahead to the next thing, like none of this matters? Like it didn't happen at all?"

Dios yanks Florida by the shoulder and spins her around so she's facing the room. "Look at them." She points at the women scattered about the tables, her other hand still digging into Florida's arm. "How come it's you and not them?"

"I don't need your shit."

"You assume everything just goes without saying? Play the state's game and claim your reward just because you're *you*." Dios tugs Florida's frizzled blond ponytail, yanking her head side to side. "It. Doesn't. Work. That. Way." A final tug, this time pulling Florida's head back so far she's staring at the ceiling.

"This is over, Dios. Three more days and this is over."

Dios leans close to Florida, her nose inches from Florida's own, her breath hot on Florida's lips. "It's never over. It just is."

Florida feels the tight inhale-exhale of Dios's restrained fury.

"How come you haven't learned that? How come you still think one day you'll just return to your comfortable house, your comfortable life, your precious car, and all of this will be a memory that belongs to someone else? Do you actually still think after everything you've seen in here that your mommy can just pay the past away?"

Florida feels the heat rise in her like a fire tearing through a canyon—ripping, destroying, devouring. She clenches her fists, then rolls her shoulders, trying to find a sliver of cool calm. "I don't think—"

"Oh yes you do. I know exactly what you think. I didn't spend a year sleeping below you for nothing. *This world is not your world and these women not your women. And your fucking crimes have nothing to do with you.* But this *is* your life, Florida, even if you've spent nearly three years pretending otherwise." Dios wraps a hand around each of Florida's wrists. "Imagine," she says. She pulls in opposite directions. Florida's skin burns. She feels Dios's fingers pressing down to her bones. "Imagine," Dios says, her lips pressed to Florida's ear as the pain in her wrist ignites, her thumb working between tendon and sinew. "What if I didn't fucking stop? If I keep pressing and pulling."

Florida squeezes her eyes shut to block out the pain. But it comes hard and fast, swamping her rage with white-hot hurt. She can feel Dios's fingers in her wrist, digging, worrying the cords that hold her together, feeling for a fault line that she can use to snap Florida in two.

"Imagine if I kept pressing, freed your hand from your body, got down to the gory pulp of your wrist with all its dangling veins and tendons, and the only thing you said was—*she was high*," Dios says. She lets go.

Florida grabs her wrist, cradles it to her chest, assuring herself it's intact.

Sweat has exploded on Florida's brow. Her pulse thumps in her throat. Her chest burns. Florida swallows hard. "So what? I've been lying to everyone because they took into consideration that I was under the influence when I drove away from the scene? You think they should keep me in because of *that*? Everyone in here is a liar, Dios. You included."

"Florida—I don't care whether you get out or not. And I don't care who you lie to in order to do it." Dios's eyes are glittering menace. "All I care about is you stop lying to yourself. You're not rehabilitated. You don't want to be. That's another lie you tell yourself." Dios gestures at a table of women across the room, both past middle age, both inside paunchy and pale, probably doped on the state-issued meds that make all the days seem the same. "Look at them. Look how numb they are. They've been drugged and fooled into submission. They've accepted that they are exactly who the state has made them—addicts, victims, whatever. They've let themselves be told they weren't fully in control when they did whatever they did on the outside. And that's the story they're going to tell everyone forever and always." She raises her voice. "Look at all of you. Look at yourselves. You've forgotten who you were before you came into this place. They tricked you, drained your strength. They made you regret your actions." Dios laughs. "You're all numb. But not you, Florida." She stoops down, so she and Florida are face-to-face.

Florida feels anything but numb. She is live-wire electricity. She is molten rage. But she can't let Dios see.

A slow, deep breath. *Just drive.* Her hands on the wheel. The windows down. The breeze hitting her face hard as she takes the curve in the road as if it were part of her own body. Seventy-two hours.

"No matter where you go," Dios says, "know that I know the truth. You aren't a misguided little rich girl who was in the wrong place at the wrong time. Remember, Florida, I was sent to school with girls like that. So many girls like that. So many misguided rich girls. And what I did learn? To be only half of what I could be. My background was something I had to outrun in order to succeed. I couldn't be me, only them—these half-people. And I know something else. You are only half of what you are too. There's something inside you you've kept hidden from the world."

"You don't know a fucking thing, Dios."

"Oh, I do. I know everything. You know what else I learned in high school and in college paid for by people like your mother? I learned that they were giving me the tools to dismantle the system. They were giving me a behind-the-scenes tour of the control room. I learned what makes them tick. Violence and fear. Same as anyone else. And I learned how quickly they can turn. How quickly their charity turns to hatred." Dios's eyes glint with green poison. "My question to you, Florida, is, whose side are you on?"

"No one's," Florida says.

Dios wraps a hand around one of Florida's. "But I know what lives inside this fist. I know what you want to do."

Florida clenches her hand within Dios's. "You don't know shit. Just because you went to some fancy-ass schools doesn't mean you know the first thing about me."

"We don't have to talk about this now," Dios says, her voice slippery and slick. She lets go of Florida. "We'll have all the time in the world when those gates close behind us."

Florida stands so she's chest to chest with Dios. "You and I have nothing outside this place."

"Look how hot you burn," Dios whispers. "You can't stand it, can you? You can't stand that fire inside. Let it out."

"No," Florida says.

"How bad do you want to hit me?" Dios backs up and pounds her chest, marking the target. "Look at her," she bellows for the whole room. "Look at Florida and her anger. Not so pretty now, is she? Not so quiet and docile."

"Fuck *off*, Dios," a woman calls from the far side of the room.

"Florida, are you scared? Worried because they are watching?" She makes a wide gesture with her arms at the rest of the room. "Scared they'll see what you can do?"

"I'm warning you. Shut up, Sandoval," the same woman repeats.

"I'll shut up when she shuts me up," Dios says. "Hit me, Florida," Dios cries. "Do it."

Florida presses her fists into her thighs.

Seventy-two hours.

"You don't want them to see, do you? You can't let them see." She turns her face to the side, as if she now wants Florida to take a shot at her nose. Then she lowers her voice. "Just like you didn't want Tina to see. Just like you couldn't stand her knowing, even though you were the one who told her."

Florida is red-hot, white-hot. She is burning from the inside out.

"Go on, do it," one of the women calls.

"Yeah, go on," Dios mocks. "Do it."

"Do it for what she did to Tina," the woman at the far end calls.

Dios whirls around. "You don't know shit about Tina," she says.

"Everyone knows," the woman says. "Everyone knows what you did."

Dios strides from Florida's table and approaches the speaker and her companion. "I doubt that." She glares from woman to woman. Then looks back over at Florida. "I really doubt that. Don't you, Florida?"

Dios jumps up on their table and stomps hard, rattling the

metal. A guard comes to the rail on the tier. Dios stomps again. "We are all Cassandra and we've been telling you who and what we are. But no one fucking listens."

"Get down, Sandoval," the guard calls.

Dios jumps down and is back at Florida's side.

"You exist inside my knowledge. The real you exists inside me." She flicks her fingers, the pantomime strike of a match. "I know you handed Carter those matches. Told him to burn that motherfucker down. Tina told me." She lights an imaginary cigarette and exhales hot air in Florida's face. "But you already knew that."

Seventy-two hours.

Florida unclenches her fists. She breathes deep. She puts out the flames before they consume her. As she's storming for the exit, she hears Dios's voice at full volume.

"Let me ask you something, Florida. Who is the fire and who is the match?"

Florida doesn't stop.

"Florida, answer. Who is the fire . . ."

Before Dios can finish the question, Florida is gone.

Forty-eight hours. Time moves at an inconsistent pace. Some hours race away in flights of distracted fantasy and others seem stuck on repeat, as if time itself wanted to imprint a harsh and indelible reminder of the last thirty months—a final slow-drip salvo. The paperwork is a new distraction, the first tangible promise of freedom tempered by a list of rules and restrictions that will persist outside these walls. Then a slide into the overly familiar stagnancy—each measured breath moving nowhere, counting the uptick as the thermometer climbs in brutal increments.

Florida feels eyes on her everywhere—looks passed back and

forth when she enters or leaves a room, when she searches for shade in the yard. A glance game of keep-away, the rest of the population trading messages around her, letting one another know and letting her know that they know she got lucky.

The yard is full despite the heat and the sickness. Florida finds a slice of shadow along the fence. The glance game is strong out here, some covert messaging that Florida wants nothing to do with. Too many women, too much time spent on grudges and gripes, a shifting landscape of allegiances and a minefield of rules.

This is just a moment. This is just a place. These are just things, benches, jumpsuits, grudges. Outside there will be the comfortable freedom of her old life. The possibility of escape and escape within escape—of coming and going as she pleases. Of going fast or slow. Of changing lanes. Of swerving and cutting corners. Of pressing her luck just a little. *Just drive.*

There's a stretch of road on the 105 as it passes the airport where the freeway slopes down, slowing into a traffic light, before emptying into Dockweiler Beach. When no one was on the road, Florida would accelerate on the descent, letting the Jag pick up speed as it raced to the light. She'd test her limits, knowing that if the light wasn't green, she might not be able to brake in time. The two times the light was red, she blasted through the intersection in a breathless terror that transformed to elation as she ran the following light too, only stopping at the coast when she ran out of road.

With her back to the fence, she can see the whole yard, women clustered in groups of two and four, standing silent as if the heat has robbed them of speech.

The sun is hellfire. The women trample their shadows. You could cook an egg on the picnic tables easy. Sear a steak too. Which makes it odd so many people are standing around, just baking in the full-force sun.

Florida wipes her forehead. She shades her eyes against the black spots that cloud her vision on the brightest days—the trails and contrails and nebulae that blind her even when she blinks.

The gate opens and Dios enters, her orange jumpsuit crisp and pressed, her black hair sleek and straightened, hanging loose like she's ironed that too. Her fiery eyebrows freshly painted. She looks as if she's emerged from a different ecosystem. She pauses and casts a quick glance around, getting the lay of the land. Normally there's a shift in the room when Dios arrives, a collective registry of trouble on the come-up. But no one moves or recoils. The women in the yard simply look at her impassively, a herd of doe-eyed animals minding their own.

Dios checks the groups one by one, searching for her spot. Then she begins to cross the yard, a giantess on the move, heading for an unshaded, empty picnic table. You don't even have to squint to see the heat rippling off the metal, rising in sheets and distorting the yard.

She's singing one of her narcocorridos: "Cuando se enojan son fieras / Esas caritas hermosas."

The silence in the yard is formidable, broken only by the dry dust scattering from Dios's feet.

Dios is halfway to the picnic table when four women spring from their posts. They are on her before she has time to react. Florida watches a fist connect with Dios's cheekbone, sees her skin crack, freeing a spray of blood. Another punch splits her lip. Her jaw is knocked from side to side with a fierce one-two. Her skin ripples, trying to catch up.

Dios shakes off the blows and takes a half step back. She spits blood and wipes her mouth. Her cheek is a red smear, her lip mottled purple and crimson. She spits again; this time a tooth hits the sand. Blood spatters onto her forehead. She looks wildly at the women who surround her, taking their measure, egging them on with the quick flick of her eyes and jerk of her chin. Dios licks the blood from her lips, grits her teeth, and balls her fists, pounding them once into her thighs. But she doesn't raise her hands.

The women surrounding her pause, sharing a quick look. There's a pin drop for Dios's counter. When it doesn't come, the women are on her again.

Dios's loose hair makes an easy target. Florida watches one of the attackers grab a fistful of the slicked strands and yank hard. Dios's neck jerks back. Her chin juts up. Her feet come off the ground, kicking up a cloud of dust.

She falls hard. Her head hits the dirt and bounces. Her hair is showered in dust. More dust rises as two of the women fall to their knees. The assailants surround her, landing kicks and punches, knocking Dios this way and that, indenting her flanks with their shoes, pounding her stomach.

Time slows. The beating continues in a suspended moment, when the rules of prison have been erased. The air around the women is thick with blood, sweat, and dust.

Dios is a rag doll, letting each punch and kick land. She doesn't raise her hands to fight back or defend herself. She doesn't shrink from the blows. If her attackers are dismayed by the ease of their target, they don't relent.

One of the women kicks Dios's cheek, making her face flip so she's facing Florida. Her lips are two swollen leeches. One of her eyebrows is smeared with blood and dirt. Her left eye is a rotten plum, oozing and purple. But—and Florida can't exactly swear to this—there's a look in the other eye, the one that has so far escaped the beatdown—of satisfaction. And then someone punches that eye shut.

When the whistle sounds from the guard tower, it's as if it has broken through from another story. The yard is all noise—women cheering from the sidelines, guards bellowing, the cough and sputter of one of the women still pounding Dios, a choking cough from Dios herself. Her shirt is torn. A breast hangs loose.

Three COs race toward the fight. Florida is so surprised by their appearance that she forgets to wonder why they haven't come earlier.

Before the officers reach them, the women retreat from Dios, as if they are cool with what comes next. They don't bother to fight their fate, falling into line as they are led off to their punishment. A couple of women on the sidelines applaud as they go.

Florida recognizes two of the officers, but the third is new. A fresh recruit with a long face, a buzz cut you could balance a book on, a wispy moustache, and blue-tinted glasses. He's paunchy and his movements seem already labored although he's fresh on the scene. It's clear he's new to the job by the way he's staring at Dios's bloody face, as if he didn't know women did such things to one another. Then his eyes trail down to her exposed breast. He squats and makes a show of covering her. But the whole yard can see his hands take their time with Dios's breast, fondling it like he's checking a bruised fruit before sloppily and slowly shoving it back in her shirt with a final tweak.

Dios spits. The rookie rises and pushes his glasses up on his nose. He takes his walkie-talkie from his belt. "Medic," he says into the static.

Dios's head lolls back. A strange quiet hangs in the yard, the aftermath of violence, the lull after a car crash. The only sound is the buzzing of the electric fence.

The flies come quick. They circle Dios's face like a halo. Florida takes a step from the fence to survey the damage.

It looks as if her face has been turned inside out. But she's in there, all right. Her lips are moving.

Florida steps closer. Dios is singing, her voice hoarse and choked.

When they become angry they are beasts,
Those beautiful faces.

She takes a rattled breath that whistles through her missing tooth. She swallows and fixes her less-battered eye on Florida.

One more dinner. That's it. Her last meal inside. Then she can use her teeth again instead of slurping the baby-soft food. Use a real knife too.

"They take you early," Kace is telling her. "It's a final power play, waking you up like it's your fault you gotta go. Last girl I celled with who got out, they took her before dawn. Shook her ass out of bed because they still could. Got me up too for good measure. They'll show you who's in charge up until the gate closes at your back. Their house, their rules."

"Until it's not my house anymore," Florida says.

"So enjoy this last chow."

There are still twenty minutes until feeding time. Florida sits on Kace's bunk, while Kace is up top, staring through the small, scratched window. "That's messed up how badly you wanted this view of nothing. You can't see shit." She flattens her nose against the thick, murky plastic.

"It's yours now."

"At least you had the tree." Kace bangs her head on the window. "Fuck me, that I missed that show yesterday," she says.

Kace is looking toward the yard, her forehead smashed against the glass, as if she's trying to see what she missed the day before. "They got her good, right? Painted her face all types of colors?"

"Made her spit a tooth," Florida says.

"A tooth," Kace says, savoring it. "A tooth. That's where the infection gets in."

"Molar," Florida says, although she has no idea.

Kace shakes her head slow. "Must have been something to watch Dios get beat down. I would have loved that. I would have loved to see her limp and lame after all these years of boasting how hard she is. All these years of trying to convince us she's a killer when all she did to land herself in here was fuck with a rich white kid with deep pockets." Kace's eyes rove wild across the cell. "Anyway, must have been some fight. Some fucking fight."

"It wasn't fair, though."

"What's not fair about that fight?"

Florida lies back, staring at the bottom of her own bunk, breathing in Kace's old-clothes smell. "You can't take a person down when she can't fight back. They knew."

"Now that would have been some shit. Being ad-segged when your release rolled around. Bet they'd leave your ass in there. Might even forget your ass in there."

"You see? Not fair," Florida says.

Kace turns around and itches the cobra that climbs her neck to her scalp. "Who are you to judge fair?"

Florida is confused by her desire to take a last look at everything, as if she needs to burn this place any deeper into her brain. But you can't help taking notice of each last—the walk down the line to dinner, a final tray, the ultimate slop of the food hitting your plate, the final check for a safe seat.

Soon there will be more—a final count, a last lights-out, a last sleep.

Kace stayed back, eating food from the commissary in the cell. So Florida takes her last meal alone.

The room is less than half-full. Mel-Mel is hunched over a table, the bandage on her cheek flapping as she chews. A few old-timers cluster in the back by the door, which is propped open, claiming the spot for a sliver of increased ventilation.

Florida slides her tray onto the end of Mel-Mel's table, not joining the gentle giant, but not ignoring her either. Mel-Mel is eating with her cellie, Tracy, a small, brittle woman with a manic patter that puts Kace's chitchat to shame.

Tonight neither of them are speaking, just working through their meals as if they are simply one more thing to survive. Suddenly Mel-Mel's head jerks up from her plate and her eyes lock on the door. Tracy swivels her spindly neck, displaying a lattice of veins and sinew. Florida follows their gaze and sees Dios making her way down to the chow line.

Her gait is stiff but balanced. She keeps a hand at her side, stabilizing whatever damage has been done to her ribs. Each step brings the hurt, but she is battling not to let it show. Her bruised eye has closed completely. Her lips are cartoonishly large. One cheek is swollen and shiny, with a deep gash sealed with Steri-Strips.

There's a hitch in her movement as she takes a tray, a wave of pain that slows her. But Dios pushes through it. She lets the kitchen staff slop her up. She lifts her tray and, with a stiff, painful turn, begins to search for a seat.

Florida feels as if she's watching a tightrope walker, both

hoping that Dios makes it to a table without incident but also thrilling to the possibility of disaster.

The whole cafeteria is on pause as Dios shuffles toward an empty seat. It's hard to read the expression on her distorted face—a grimace or a grin. But she's walking proud. No doubt of that. She pauses before lowering her tray and then herself into a seat at a vacant table.

All eyes are on Dios as she lifts a forkful of food to her lips, working it between those purple sausages, and then chewing slowly, slowly around the pain.

Dios—always the center of attention. Even now when she's been defeated.

Then, all at once, the women rise, everyone except Florida getting to their feet and filing out, turning their backs on their tormentor, leaving unfinished meals and trays behind, violating rules, risking punishment, all to send a message.

Florida finishes her food, her last meal already forgotten. Then she pushes back from the table, her gaze never leaving Dios's.

Now who's the victim? Florida wonders.

Because look at her. Look at her struggling to eat. Look at her lifting her fork gingerly like the very air around her is barbed. Look at her still pretending she's above it all, that she knows you and everyone else in here better than they know themselves. Look at her pretending for no one. Because no one is left to care. Look at her wincing as she swallows, trying to make one lasting impression of her superiority. Look at her, because after tonight, you won't have to look at her again.

Florida stands and heads for the exit, glancing over her shoulder at the solitary figure—a color wheel of purples, blacks, and blues.

"You never answered my question," Dios says.

But it doesn't matter. It's too late.

The cafeteria door swings shut.

And that's it.

Another in the list of lasts.

KACE

They might have walked out the door. But that's only part of the story.

Let me rewind and tell you how this all began.

It started on the hottest day of 2019 in early October. When a cough was a fucking cough and not a death sentence and murder rap rolled into one.

It started with the sun so high and fierce the sky was a white blister—the reflection off any metal surface searing your eyeballs.

It started with women collapsing in the suffocating indoor heat.

Then women collapsing in the outdoor furnace.

Then the lights fading from yellow to brown.

The heat lightning tap-tap-tapping in the distance.

The never-ending buzz of the high wire fence in the yard got louder, then went erratic, like radio static. Louder and louder until it fizzled out.

It started with the yard going silent. When we all realized that, it was as if we'd taken off tight shoes. Really fucking quiet. Scary fucking quiet without that buzzing we'd all stopped noticing after one night in this place.

Then the airhorn and sirens overrode the brownout, driving us inside, everyone cursing as we moved from one heat to another, worse—the fucking huddled mass of our own bodies suffocating us.

We were almost back in our cells, the lights in the prison flickering, fighting the power grid, clinging to life.

We were almost locked away, many of us where we were supposed to be.

But before our doors locked into place, the brownout went black.

The prison went dark.

The only light came through our small, smudged, scratched windows. You could hardly call it light at all.

I glanced outside my window. The fence was on fire. Blue electric sparks shooting into the sky. The backup generators not coming on.

We sat on our bunks. We roamed the tiers where red emergency lighting shone a demonic glow. We could not be contained—our doors frozen where they were when the power died. The COs dressed in riot gear. They marched us back into our places. But they could not keep us there.

Next door, in Dios and Tina's cell, Tina started to scream.

"Shut up, shut up, shut up," I said, banging my fist against the wall.

Florida put her hand on my back. "Ssshh, Kacey-Kace."

"Shut that bitch up," I told her.

There were too many of us. Too few of them. Night fell. The heat rose. We cooked in our cells, the stink and sweat of us filling the air. The dark was thick, a thing you could comb your fingers through.

There was an hour of uneasy calm—of whispers and waiting—then the realization that the prison was ours crashed like a tidal wave.

It was blacker than black. A hundred voices at once. The absence of radio and TV. The storm of boot strikes on the tiers. The banging of metal. The rattling of bars and bed frames. It was one scream. And another.

It was Tina screaming and screaming. And me screaming back.

It was the whole prison speaking in tongues.

It was the taste of blood in the air.

It was Dios going from cell to cell, her finger on the prison's rising pulse, the whole while singing her damn narcocorridos, singing us down into death and destruction.

There was a beatdown happening at the far end.

Prisoner on prisoner. CO on prisoner. It was who-the-fuck-knows. All the voices in my head, rising. My own victim and the rest of those dropped by my fellow inmates. It was everyone and everything all at once.

A siren somewhere.

A call for a medic. And another.

One by one we started to unravel and unleash.

Tina, Florida's old cellie and Dios's current one, ran down the line, screaming full bore. Tearing off her clothes. Calling us murderers.

"Make that bitch pay," I told Florida.

"Easy, Kace," she said.

Plots hatched all around. Schemes. Scores to be settled. It was trouble on the come-up.

Women getting it on in the dark with no one watching. Groans of pain and pleasure. The smell of sweat and sex and blood.

Women taking back what was rightfully theirs. Taking what they wanted and would never get otherwise.

A gut punch in the dark. A kick in the ribs. Crying. Sobbing.

My own manic laughter. And Florida backing away at the sound.

It was me, afraid of the fucking dark and all the voices. Dios's lips suddenly pressed to my ear—*You can kill a lady but can't handle the dark?*—before she vanished back into the chaos.

And then I was out of my cell, running and running. Running blind around the prison, getting bumped and bruised. Banging into railings, fellow inmates, COs who strong-armed me back to my cell so I could leave again.

Eight hours and no one slept. We were all wired by possibility, jacked by threat. We were cooked and cracked.

Throughout the night I heard Tina's voice down the line. Banshee scream. Curses and accusations. I heard her confessing to crimes she didn't commit.

Shut her the fuck up.

Put that bitch in her place.

Everyone else suddenly on my tip—wanting her to quiet down.

Rumors of death, brutality, and rape. Rumors of more electrical fires. Of electrocutions. Rumors of the never-ending dark.

Dios's eyes glittering in the light of a flashlight, watching a CO thwack a woman with his baton. Dios stepping aside to make room as the woman was carried away.

I covered my ears, but there were too many voices inside my head and out. I stared out the window, willing the sun to come up.

Florida was gone. One minute she was up on her bunk, the next she'd vanished. My goody-two-shoes cellie off to join the madness, proving that crazy was contagious.

They took over the commissary.

They took over the communal room.

They smashed the TV.

Someone had a hand-crank radio. Too many women crammed into her cell, trying to tune in to news of the blackout and the riot.

It was fucking hot. Hotter than hot. So little air that I could feel the oxygen in my brain being wrung out.

Tina again. Her voice always above the storm. "They're leaving us to die. They're leaving us because we are all killers and we might as well kill one another."

Shut up.

Speak for yourself.

I didn't kill no one.

Didn't kill a motherfucker.

"Shut up." Florida's voice on the line. "Shut the fuck up, Tina. Go back to your cell."

More guards arrived.

More riot gear.

More sirens.

Women made a stand in the commissary. They raided the supplies. They stole and ate and staked their claim.

Dios—watching two women pound a third in the red glow of the emergency lighting, smiling as the blood flew.

Gunshots. The electric sting of a taser. So much shouting and crying.

There was a beating on the tier below. A body being driven into the metal walkway. A crack of bone. A woman was screaming for a while and then she stopped. For a moment there was silence. And then chaos again.

A new light outside—not the sun or electricity, but sirens. The prison surrounded.

Tina screaming, screaming. No words this time, just sound.

Shut the fuck up. That was me again. *Shut the fuck up. Shut the fuck up.* I would straight-up kill her myself, if she didn't stop adding to the madness.

A new rumor—more guards, maybe even the National Guard. And quick, get the fuck back to your cells or this riot is going to become a war.

More running.

A searchlight streaming into the prison—its roving eye probing the dark.

Another beating nearby. I felt each punch as if it were landing on my own body. I could feel my breath being knocked free.

Tina went quiet. Fucking finally.

I was back out on the line—walking cell to cell, taking my time before the coming lockdown. Because when they got us in, they'd keep us in for a month.

The women clustered around the radio scattered.

The commissary emptied.

The searchlight caught blood smeared along my tier, black streaks of blood. A whole fucking trail. Drag marks.

The light vanished.

In the dark I followed the blood. I had to.

You see, there's this thing with me. I told you earlier. I'm a library of voices. Each victim of those inside these walls comes and lives in my head. I honor the dead. Your dead, her dead—it doesn't fucking matter. I do the thing you forget to do, that you overlook. I care when you forget because I have no choice.

I passed Dios and Tina's cell.

I passed my cell, passed Florida chewing her nails in our doorway, looking at me with some kind of fucked-up panic the riot painted on her face.

I passed Dios, standing with her back pressed to a wall between cells.

The searchlight crossed over—hitting the line back behind me, passing Florida, passing Dios, and landing on Tina.

In the quick white flicker I saw her, crumpled and stomped. Her face plum purple. Her eyes fixed. Her mouth frozen, final. So fucked she was beyond fucked-up. Beyond-recognition beaten. Beyond everything.

I covered my mouth and turned back.

Dios blocked my path, her arms crossed, her green eyes figuring a way to shine in the dark. "You don't even fucking know," she said. "You don't even know what you don't know."

So now you see how it started. And by the time you read this, they're probably gone. Turned loose into the big, wide world. Roaming free—their will their own. And that should be enough. But you know this isn't where their story ends. You know their road isn't a five-lane highway to all the happiness they missed in here. Those two couldn't take the easy way if it was marked with a big red fucking X.

Marta said they never come back, but bitch doesn't know what she's talking about. She's straight-up incorrect.

We bring them here with us. And when we leave, we leave them. They are the magnet calling us back. Our dead, I mean. We bring them inside and we forget them when we go.

These women with their early releases, they may be gone, but they're still around, at least in part.

They left their demons here—their dead, who haunted them night after night.

Maybe you saw Dios and Florida and a few others up and

walk out the gate. Maybe you cheered for that shit. Maybe your heart got all fucking big because they had a second chance fast-tracked to them on a silver platter. Problem is, now I'm stuck here with those angry hippies white-girl Florida barbecued in the desert. I'm here with my second cellie's boyfriend she dropped with his own gun.

And I'm here with Tina. Dios's Tina.

Like I needed Tina on top of the rest.

But they all demand to be heard.

So I listen.

Dios is half right. Don't imagine you're going to be reborn and rehabbed on the outside. Not going to happen. But also . . . don't imagine you're better than what you did. Don't make Dios's mistake. Don't get all big and proud. High and mighty. Don't imagine your calling to this life is greater than the rest of us—the living or the dead.

It will get Dios in the end.

Marta told me. And that I believe.

I know you all think I'm crazy listening to Marta. You'd find me even crazier if I repeated the words of everyone I'm stuck here with. Dead husbands, lovers, kids, girlfriends, rivals. The accidental collateral of your accidents.

So I keep on keeping on with Marta, drowning those other people out.

So go ahead, ladies, leave me here to fucking stew in a soup of words. Walk out the door and don't look back.

Let me tell you, there's more to the ghosts than ghosting. More than haunting. That's what you all don't get. Never did.

SING HER DOWN

Kill someone and she becomes part of you. How could it be otherwise? Take her life and where do you put it? You think you discard it like a weapon or an inconvenient piece of evidence? That's some foolish bullshit.

Dios will be back. I already told Tina.

They never come back? Fuck that, Marta. They never leave.

FLORIDA

Outside the gates and nothing changes. The same desert. The same heat. The same scorching shimmer and the same stretch of nothing going nowhere. If it weren't for the sound of metal rattling into place behind her, there's not much difference between standing here or in the yard.

Florida is dressed in state-issued civilian clothes. Her socks and underwear feel like sandpaper. Her jeans are stiff and too heavy for this heat. Her shirt looks prison pressed. Her state-issued boots are a half size too big. She has a small bag with the clothes she came in with and basic toiletries. Her old jeans are way too big, her T-shirt stupid-cropped and useless. She has a debit card in her pocket that has her gate money plus the remainder from her commissary. Her parole officer's phone number is printed on a piece of paper. But she doesn't have a cell phone to call him. She couldn't furnish the name of anyone who would be able to transport her to the designated motel for her two-week quarantine, so she waits for a ride from Wheels of Hope.

"Florence Baum?" The shotgun window of an early-model

Prius rolls down. The driver is a middle-aged woman. It's hard to tell much behind her scratched sunglasses and surgical mask. "I'm Maureen. You can get in back, please."

Going out the way she came in—in the back, driven by a stranger to a destination not of her choosing.

Maureen hands Florida a mask, then douses her hands in sanitizer that smells like cinnamon potpourri. "Welcome back. It's a big day." Her voice sounds tight. "A fresh start," she adds. The car begins to roll away from the gates.

"So I've been told."

Florida hates the quiet roll of hybrid vehicles—how they sneak up on you in do-gooder silence. Barely feels like driving at all.

"Life is full of setbacks," Maureen says. "But we overcome."

"Is that so?" Florida glances back, one quick look over her shoulder just to make sure she's really on the move.

It's bleak out—a bleached landscape of not much. Derelict strip malls, empty shopping centers, parking lots and parking lots and parking lots with no cars.

This isn't the city. It's a sub-sub-suburb—a no-man's-land. In fact, it's hard to imagine it with people. "Nice place," she says.

"Do you want to hear the radio?"

"I want the quiet."

"You'll do fine at the motel for two weeks then," Maureen says. "If you need help with housing after that, hold on to our brochure—if you need assistance reintegrating."

"To what?"

"To society. To the workforce. We provide those services—job training, résumés. Housing."

They pass a shuttered swap meet, a dust bowl trapped behind a sagging cyclone fence, some lost items lingering in the dirt.

"How does it work?" Florida asks. "Is there room service?"

"We only do the driving," Maureen says. "The DOC feeds you."

Pawnshops and rubble and the remains of half-built houses. Shuttered restaurants and cocktail lounges and movie theaters with letters falling from their marquees. They get on the 10 heading in the wrong direction as far as Florida is concerned—not toward the coast, where she imagined she'd go, but deeper into the desert state that has claimed her. Deeper into the hard-baked land punctuated by the same big-box stores and restaurant chains that punctuate everything. After a while a subtle city skyline, muted by the sun and dust, rises in the distance like a ghost civilization.

The freeway is empty. The shopping centers and service stations and retail clusters and fast-food joints are empty too—arches dark, flashing neon at a standstill, current offers expired.

Florida stares at the sky and at the exit signs for places she doesn't want to visit, at overpasses where banners assure her that WE WILL GET THROUGH THIS TOGETHER.

After thirty minutes, they pull off onto an access road that takes them into a city that strikes Florida as a *Tetris* game of subdivisions, unpeopled Southwestern-styled strip malls, and small business parks with dry water features.

Maureen heads north on a wide avenue where a slew of off-brand chain motels face off for the scant clientele.

The motel is called Sleep Away—the sign shows a drowsy crescent moon dozing off on a fluffy pillow. It's a motor court, which Maureen explains is preferable because of its lack of communal spaces. A study in distance and isolation.

The swimming pool has been drained. There's a padlock on the pool's gate. The lounge chairs are in a disorderly stack on the verge of toppling.

Maureen parks in front of the office but keeps the engine running. "This is where I leave you."

Florida gathers her few possessions.

"Good luck," Maureen says.

Florida enters the small office. A young woman with dyed black hair and so many piercings her face looks stapled together glances up from behind a plexiglass barrier. She's got a surgical mask around her chin. "You have a reservation?" As if she can hardly believe it herself.

"If that's what you call it," Florida says.

"Oh, right." The woman can't be more than twenty. A weighty silver barbell through her bottom lip hangs heavy, giving her a bored expression. "Name?"

"Fl—Florence Baum."

"Florence. That's a nice name."

"It is," Florida says. It's her name once again. And yet dressed as she is, standing where she is, feeling like she does, she is still Florida—a dirty ex-con in a dirty ex-con costume.

The girl points to a rack of keys on the wall. "You're number twelve. You can use the phone for local calls. They're supposed to drop your food off."

"Do they?"

"None of you-all has complained even if they don't."

"All of who?" Florida asks.

"You know," the young woman says.

How many steps away from becoming one of the you-all is this kid? A drug deal? A kited check? A skim from the register behind her?

"Oh." The woman looks up, a dull light piercing her eyes. "You're not supposed to leave your room."

"What about in case of an emergency?"

"I don't know anything about emergencies."

The room is exactly as you'd imagine and not a whole hell of a lot more. Florida knows she should be relieved by the sight of a queen-sized bed and four pillows all to herself. She should thrill to a private shower. But the whole place feels stale, the rug and mirrors imprinted with the ghosts of previous guests.

As instructed, Florida picks up the phone and dials the number for her parole officer. She taps in her ID number and is transferred. She answers his questions.

"So that's it?" she asks.

"Until next week."

"And then what?"

"Then you call me the week after that and let me know where you've established residence."

"I just keep calling?"

"Until it's safe enough to check in face-to-face."

"What about an out-of-state transfer?"

"Nothing doing."

"What about permission to travel out of state?"

"You're not supposed to leave that room and you want me to sign off on travel?"

"How about eventually?"

"How about I get to know you a little better before I start granting favors."

Florida sheds her clothes. The shower is properly hot, a heat so intense and unfamiliar that it makes her flinch. She dumps the entire mini bottle of conditioner in her hair and leaves it in until the water runs cold. She shivers in the chilly, canned air as she wraps herself in a towel.

She winds her hair on top of her head and looks in the bathroom mirror, taking her time with the semi-familiar face that stares back. The years have worn on her. She's tanned but you can still see the pallor of a poor diet. The sun has cooked and creased her skin, creating rivulets from her eyes and cracking something like smile lines into her cheeks. The prison's industrial soap has been anything but gentle. The rough towels finished the job, leaving a chapped, shiny patina. Her arms are a mess. She's added scars to her unfortunate tattoos—real stories next to the phony and now faded ones written in Celtic and Japanese. She's also added a tattoo—a Roman numeral cuffing her wrist, marking the number of days in her sentence. Her hair is burned blond, a fried, colorless color.

The shadows now have the voices of children. She peeks through the curtain.

Three kids—two boys and a girl dressed in T-shirts announcing cheap, cheeky cheer: I Was Made for This, Up2NoGood, Sparkle Hard. Are they ten, twelve, fourteen? The kids are scaling the fence to the pool. One of them hoists a sun-bleached big-wheel to the others.

Soon their voices are drowned by the echo of the plastic bike clattering in the bowl of the empty pool.

Florida backs away from the window, lies down, and closes her eyes.

The kids rattle and roar.

The air conditioner ticks and heaves.

The sky that slips around the curtains turns from white to yellow to pink.

A boy's scream barrels out of the pool, followed by the sound of the tricycle crashing. A laugh follows the scream. The girl this time, Florida thinks. For a moment there is silence. Then another scream—this time from one of the rooms, someone yelling at the kids to be careful or she'll kill them herself.

Dinner is dropped off—steam-tray food that got steamier in transit. Florida eats slowly, splayed on her back on the bed.

And time passes as it always does.

There's nothing she can do to distract herself from the fact that this room isn't all that different from the motel she'd retreated to with Carter after the desert rats had ripped them off, after one had stuck his hand down her pants and tried to pick her up like a six-pack. Rolling and high, she'd listened—that's it, just listened—while Carter had ranted and rambled about how badly he'd been ripped off, never mentioning what that asshole had done to her.

If only she'd stayed put.

If only she'd let him rant.

But . . .

There's what happened and there's the official story of what happened. The official story—she listened, just listened—as Carter raged against the desert rats, plotting his revenge. Then, careless and high, she'd followed his lead, driving him back to the trailer, unaware of what he was about to do. Because under the influence of Carter's own MDMA—euphoric to the point of insensible—how could she have known, how could she have understood, how could she have meant anything that she may or may not have said?

Carter, the leader. Florida his unwitting accomplice. The pretty rich girl along for the ride.

The truth—she'd been itching to get back behind the wheel. She'd been itching to get out of that hotel room. She'd been itching from the inside out.

The drugs made her want to move, to drive, to drive fast.

She had kept the engine running as Carter got out of the Jag, a bottle filled with gasoline in one hand. She'd handed him the match and watched him touch it to the scrap of pillowcase dangling from the bottle's neck. She'd held her breath as he threw it through an open window.

Carter had raced back to the car.

Florida had revved the engine, but he restrained her with a hand on her wrist. Together they'd watched the trailer. Nothing had happened. Just a small wisp of smoke curling from the window where he'd hurled the makeshift bomb.

Florida put the car in gear but held her foot on the brake. Her entire body was vibrating. Lines and ripples swam across the window. She wanted to close her eyes. She wanted to pop them wide. She wanted to hit the gas and drive as fast and as far as she could.

Just wait, Carter had said.

Florida had wanted to do that too. She'd wanted to do everything at once—all at once. She'd wanted nothing to happen and the whole world to blow.

One minute. Two minutes. Three minutes.

And then an explosion, so brilliant and terrifying it was almost beautiful.

Florida had wanted to get out of the car and dance in its magnificence. She wanted to bend and swoop and sway in the warmth of those hot desert flames.

She wanted to join the man who was already dancing as he burst from the trailer, his arms raised above his head, the flames flying back behind him like wings, his hair a fiery halo. A goddamn phoenix was what he was. She wanted to join his wild bonfire song.

Drive. Drive. Just fucking drive. Carter's voice reached her from another world. And Florida hit the gas.

She drove by feel, barely able to see, barely aware of the road. She drove until she ran out of gas, out of road. She pulled the Jag off the freeway somewhere across the California line and parked in a lot behind a truck stop. Then she and Carter crashed hard, slept until sunrise.

Florida had woken first. Her brain was cotton-candy soft and her head hurt like hell.

Then came that moment she'd read about in books, seen in movies, when Florida had hoped that it had all been a dream—the explosion, the dancing man, his screams that she'd imagined were a song.

But the gas and smoke smell in the car had jolted her back to reality. She'd slipped away and called her mother, who called her lawyer, who said the only thing Florida could do was turn Carter in, turn against him. If she didn't, she'd be charged as a full accomplice.

Florida squints at her reflection in the mirror. Dios was right—and so what that she was? She *had* lied to everyone about what really happened that night. Everyone but Tina. And that had been a mistake, a sad attempt during her early days inside to appear harder than she felt. The first time she heard the truth about what she had done returning to her from her cellie's mouth, she'd slapped Tina across the face. You can't give shape to that sort of truth, or it takes hold, makes you something you're not.

But none of that matters now. The how and why of what she said and did over three years ago. When it comes down to it, sometimes you just want to watch the world burn.

At sunset Florida cracks the curtains to see the hallucinatory palette of pinks and purples in the west. But soon a darkness surges from the horizon, rising upward instead of falling from above. The world's color is gone and it seems a plague is descending.

Those kids have scrambled out of the pool, taking that noisy tricycle with them. Florida notices one of the boys has a broken arm and the girl's eye is now black-and-blue. They glance up at the swallowed sky. They see the lights go out, the beauty smothered by the dust.

The courtyard is empty. But nearly every room has its curtains wide to witness the storm as it surges forward. All that formerly garish color—the stuff of desert trips and motel prints—is devoured by this swarming, pulsing dark, a roiling violence consuming the sky.

A haboob. Florida knows the word from her mother, who spent months in Tunisia, Morocco, and Tangier—a wild sandstorm that marches across the desert, turning day into night.

The domestic haboob is just a dirty dust drop, gathering the worst of the worthless landscape and piling it at Florida's feet. Overnight, the dust worked its way through the windows in her room. The air has a gritty taste.

Well after dawn, the sky remains an unhealthy, dirty brown. The ground is streaked and swirled with dust. The cars in the courtyard are smeared and smudged.

At 10:00 a.m., Florida's food hasn't come. She takes a few tentative steps outside, her feet making tracks in the dirt. She is alone in the courtyard. The storm has brought a suffocating silence with the dust.

At noon they still haven't fed her.

Florida waits an hour, then ventures out again.

It's silent in the courtyard, the only sound the shush of her feet through the dust.

There's a different attendant on duty, a paunchy, middle-aged man. Florida stares at him through the glass door. He looks back and looks away. Florida bangs on the glass to get his attention.

From her side of the doorway, she pantomimes eating, then shakes her head.

The attendant waves her back. "Go away."

Florida pushes the door open.

"You are supposed to stay in your room. Those are the rules."

"They are supposed to feed us. They have to feed us."

"They will."

"When?"

"Go back to your room."

She crosses the threshold. "I want my food."

"They'll bring it."

The borders around things are dissolving. Florida's head begins to spin. She steadies herself in the doorway.

For almost three years life ran on a schedule: wake, chow, yard, chow, activities, chow, lights out.

There were rules, disciplinary actions, a give-and-take of crime and punishment. Every action with its equal and opposite reaction. Not fair necessarily, but reliable.

"When?" Florida crosses halfway to the desk. She looks around, searching for some indication that she hasn't been left to starve in a business park motel.

The man shakes his head—he doesn't know. Another break in the system.

"When?" Florida demands. "Tell me when."

"You can't wait here. You can't be here."

Florida takes another step. She's off-kilter. Her foot stumbles before finding the floor again. What happens if she closes in? What's preventing her from bridging the gap between herself and this man? What if she charges him?

The room sways.

What is stopping her?

She holds out her hands for balance.

What can he do?

The attendant lifts the phone and looks at the receiver meaningfully. "You need to go back." His fingers hover over the keypad. "Now."

There is someone he can call if Florida takes another step. There is an authority over her and over this moment.

The world settles and finds its hard edge.

At three o'clock no food has arrived. She calls the front desk hoping for a different attendant. She hangs up at the sound of the man's voice.

She eats ice from the ice machine and watches TV.

She peeks through the curtains. The only people outside are the three kids, one of whom has his arm in a cast.

Florida stations herself by the window waiting for the attendant to leave. At dusk she sees him crossing to a dusty hatchback. She phones the office and reaches a different man.

"I'm in room twelve," she says. "We've been waiting for food all day."

"We don't do room service."

"I'm a guest of the state and the state hasn't fed me."

"Order a pizza," the guy says.

"Who pays for that?"

"You do."

Florida has four hundred and change on her state-issued debit card. She's got twelve days left here and that money's going to evaporate if she starts paying for her own chow.

"They'll bring food tomorrow?" she asks.

"I haven't thought about tomorrow," the attendant says.

The pizza she orders tastes like cardboard, like the dust storm. It's the first non-institutional food she's had in years and it still tastes like prison.

The air is clear, but the dust and dirt linger. They've been pushed to the edges, ringing curbs, doorframes, sills, window screens. An uneven outline around the world outside the window.

No breakfast.

No lunch.

The sun, smothered behind a Martian haze, climbs and hovers over the empty pool.

Florida keeps the curtains wide, her eyes trained on the office for some sign the state will hold up their end of the bargain.

Noon ticks away.

She's doing her part. She's obeying. But she cannot pay for her imprisonment.

Just after noon the phone rings. Her parole officer finally returning her call. He sounds annoyed with her predicament. "Feel free to use some sense. Get yourself some food," he says. "There must be a convenience store nearby."

"But I'm not supposed to leave the room."

"You're not supposed to starve either."

"Isn't the state supposed to feed me?"

"Technically yes, but things don't always work out."

"They're keeping me here. They need to feed me."

"They let you out early. And you want more."

"I want reimbursement."

"I'll see what I can do," he says, hanging up almost before the words are out of his mouth.

———

Florida looks around the room for what she needs—key, debit card, surgical mask. What more does she have? She blinks in the sunshine.

The kids are riding their big-wheel in the pool, creating an intricate network of loop-de-loops in the grime. One of the plastic wheels is busted and the tricycle clatters down the pool's slope.

The boy with the broken arm stands on the pool deck watching the other boy and girl take turns. After a few more goes there won't any bike left to ride.

"Chickenshit," the boy in the pool yells at the injured kid. "Pussy."

He hurls the big-wheel up to the pool deck. The boy with the broken arm hesitates. He shoots a sidelong glance at the girl before standing up and dragging the bike away from her.

He sits back down. The plastic cracks under his weight.

"Pussy," the waiting kids chorus.

Florida can't look as the kid with the cast begins his descent. She hurries toward the motel driveway, her back to the plastic shatter.

The attendant who checked her in is smoking on the sidewalk. She glances up as Florida passes. "Enjoying your stay," she says. Her voice has a robotic ring to it.

Florida pauses a few feet from the cigarette nimbus. "Where can I get some food?"

"They stopped bringing it again?"

"Again?"

She tosses the butt. "Most restaurants are closed. You can check the Super K. It's a half mile that way." The woman gestures vaguely to the north. "There's also a Rite Aid up there. And delivery. The delivery guys complain you-all don't tip."

———

The simple act of walking is strange at first. Florida imagines it's a little like flying without a parachute, or the first plummet on a roller coaster. She feels untethered and out of control. The lack of restriction and the availability of space are so disorienting she feels drunk. She must look it too, rushing forward, then stopping to look over her shoulder, like they—whoever they are—might be on her in an instant.

The haze has dissipated but for once the sun doesn't bother Florida. There are few people out. Few cars. Few signs of life in this hollowed world.

The city is not designed for pedestrians. The blocks are preposterously long and the wait at the crosswalks feels endless. But soon Florida hits her stride. And soon the motel feels like a memory from a different lifetime. Outside her room—simply outside—she is shedding her recent past, leaving it on the sidewalk like someone else's skin.

She takes a deep breath of the hot air. She has her debit card. She can get clothes, some better toiletries. A pair of sunglasses.

Florida picks up her pace. Now that she's on the move, going back to her room feels unimaginable, waiting out the rest of her quarantine impossible.

Sweat breaks out on her back. Her state-issued jeans stick to her legs. She wants a drink of something besides the off-brand orange juice that the DOC dropped off or the cloudy hotel water.

She can see the Rite Aid up ahead. A few cars in the parking lot. Florida joins a line of people spaced evenly outside, waiting their turn. She knows she will be overwhelmed by choice when she enters, and she also knows nothing will be satisfying.

She emerges with a yellow tank top that reads Desert Nites, a pair of aviator shades, a store-brand face lotion with SPF, a large unsweetened iced tea, a bottled smoothie, a sack of miniature blueberry muffins, and a giant bag of tortilla chips. Behind the drugstore is a colonnade of mostly shuttered shops. Florida takes her purchases and sits in the shade of their overhang.

A group of people is gathered at the far end of the colonnade waiting for something outside a shuttered Vietnamese sandwich shop. From time to time one of them ducks out from the shade to check the street for whatever is supposed to be coming.

Florida pops a muffin in her mouth, chasing it with iced tea. She looks down the colonnade. The group of people in front of the sandwich shop shifts and shuffles. Some of them are carrying what look like large laundry bags wrapped with cords.

As if instructed by an unseen voice the small crowd reshapes itself into an orderly line at the exact moment a white bus pulls up. There's a small sign taped in the window in what Florida imagines is Vietnamese. Underneath that the destination is written in English, but from where she is sitting she can't quite make it out. She gets to her feet.

The passengers board quickly. As Florida draws closer, she can see that most of the bus company's identifying decals have been painted over or picked away. She can make out a few words in both languages. But this is clearly a ghost ship, operating against regulations.

The driver slams the luggage door shut.

"Phoenix? Ontario?" His eyes bore into her over his mask.

Florida stares at him.

"Los Angeles? Los Angeles?" His words are fast and clipped.

The driver jabs a finger toward another handwritten sign on the side window. *Phoenix, Ontario, El Monte, Los Angeles.*

"How much?" Florida asks.

"Twenty-five."

"You take credit?"

"Cash."

Florida wheels around wildly, searching for a bank.

"ATM," the driver says, pointing to the far end of the colonnade. "Three minutes and I go."

Twenty-five dollars to get out of state. By tonight she can be in Los Angeles. She spoke with her PO a few hours ago, so she has four days before she needs to check in again. That should give her enough time to figure out her next move. Grab her car. Drive back if need be.

Her heart is racing as she dips her debit card in the ATM. It's slow and the screen is scratched. The glare of the sun makes the letters fade and dance. Twice her request is denied.

She shades the screen and squints. She can hear the bus rumbling into action.

She pounds the machine. It's asking her an illegible yes-or-no question. Florida jams a button.

The ATM begins its slow-churning whir. Florida snatches the money and sprints back to the idling bus.

She holds up two twenties as if they are a passport.

"Get on," the driver says, shutting the door and forcing Florida up the steps.

He hands her the change.

"Sit."

Florida steadies herself as she surveys the scattering of masked passengers. Toward the back of the bus there's a cluster of empty seats.

She can hear a last desperate passenger hammering the bus's door for admission. She drops her bag on one seat and sits next to the window.

The driver puts the bus into gear and begins to pull away.

Only then does Florida glance down the aisle at the late arrival.

It's Dios, her green gaze glittering above the black bandana that shields her mouth and nose. One of her eyes is still swollen, but the other bores into Florida with delighted menace.

Florida leaves her seat and steps into the aisle.

"Sit, please. Both sit," the driver barks.

The bus leaves the parking lot and makes a right turn.

Dios lurches and comes to a halt at Florida's row. "So, you finally left that motel room. I got worried that you were going to starve to death."

Florida freezes. The bus bucks again, sending her toppling into her seat.

"Sit, now," the driver commands.

Dios sits in the row opposite Florida and pulls down her bandana.

Her bruises are turning from purple to yellow. A spiderweb of blood has exploded in one of her blackened eyes. Two stitches flutter by her mouth. She's covered the bust in her top lip with lipstick, but she can't mask the deformity.

Like Florida, she's wearing some of her state-issued clothes. But she's pegged and pinned them, giving herself a more tailored look. Her hair is loose and the curls bounce with the road.

"Let's roll," Dios says. She leans back in her seat. Soon the familiar lyrics of Macario Leyva rise above the bus's squeak and rumble.

Pero nunca se fijaron
En tan humilde señora.

Florida inches over to the window. The air-conditioning is on full tilt, expelling frigid air with a chemical scent. She presses her cheek against the freezing glass, trying to ignore the stinging chill.

The bus picks up speed. Soon it is throttling onto a ramp for the 10.

Florida closes her eyes, hoping—praying—the rhythm of the

road will lure her to sleep. Dios keeps singing, keeps repeating the phrase about Camelia La Tejana coming to Los Angeles to betray her lover.

Florida leans over the aisle. "What's your game, Dios?"

Dios stops singing, then angles herself toward Florida, her face inches from Florida's own. "Just following your lead."

"Masks on, please," the driver crackles over the PA system.

"Why?"

"Because, after Tina, you actually think I'd let you out of my sight? Oh, Florida, I know you. Skip parole, get hauled back, then what? Another lie to get yourself out of trouble. Another shirking of the blame. You would have laid Tina at my feet to save yourself."

"Tina was months ago. Tina is over."

"No," Dios says. "I've told you before. None of this is over. It's only just begun."

The bus pulls off the freeway and rolls through another neighborhood of strip malls and prefab office parks. It wheezes to a stop in front of a Vietnamese supermarket. Florida slips into the row behind her to put some space between herself and Dios. She clamps her eyes shut, praying Tina's mutilated body doesn't take the seat next to her.

New passengers load, wary-eyed over their masks. They shuffle down the aisle, searching for vacant rows.

"Hurry, hurry," the driver barks. "Sit, sit."

Florida presses herself against the window. Seven hours until they reach Los Angeles. It will be dark. And who knows where the bus will drop her. And who knows how she will reach Hancock Park. And whether anyone will be home. And what she will do if they aren't. And how she'll get her car. And where the keys are.

And how she will shake Dios.

She presses hard into the window, letting the reverb of the engine sink into her ears.

The bus kicks into gear.

A final passenger is coming down the aisle—a boxy, ungainly man. Flattop and tinted glasses. A mask advertising the Diamondbacks covers his mouth.

A jolt of recognition hits Florida. She knows him. She knows she knows him.

The sensation vanishes as quick as it hit. Dios has made her jumpy. This whole fucking escape—this unplanned flight, Tina's name—makes her nerves light up when anyone looks her way.

The man takes the empty row in front of her, his head rising above the seatback.

There's no way. She doesn't know this guy.

She doesn't know anyone, anywhere, which is why she was shelved in that motel and then abandoned. She is utterly fucking alone.

Except for Dios now. Always Dios.

The bus is picking up speed as it hits the on-ramp for the seven-hour, straight-shot trip west.

She stares at the stranger's head, flattop bobbing slightly with the rhythm of the road. There's something organized—meticulous—about the way he sits, something institutional. Like he's army. Or police.

Or . . .

The driver slams the brakes. Florida glances out the window to see a small hatchback veering wildly away.

Or . . .

The driver curses the car loud enough that his words reach the back of the bus.

Or . . . she *does* know him. The man sitting in front of Florida is the rookie CO who broke up Dios's beatdown, the long-faced newbie who took his time with Dios's exposed breast.

Florida rises to her feet, then sits.

There is nowhere to go, no exit until she's crossed the state line, breaking the law.

Her heart beats in her fingertips. It beats in her throat.

She leans across the empty seat to check on Dios, who is staring at the CO as if she's willing him to look her way.

Florida knows the daggers of Dios's gaze too well. Soon enough the CO feels Dios's eyes on him.

"Do I know you?"

"I don't know," Dios says. "Do you?"

"Maybe," the guy says. Then he turns away.

Florida tries to force her shoulders to relax, her fingers to unclench.

"Do we all look the same to you?"

"Women?" the CO says. "You think women all look the same to me?"

"Did I say that?" Dios asks.

"It's hard to tell what you actually look like with that bandana. Maybe we've met. But I'm guessing we haven't. Although—"

"What?"

"Maybe I *do* know you." Over the headrest in front of her Florida sees the CO lean closer to Dios. "Give me a minute."

"You've got seven hours," Dios says.

"It's not coming to me," the CO says.

"Not yet," Dios says.

Florida closes her eyes. She wraps the shirt she bought at Rite Aid around her head to stop the sound of Dios's voice.

Still, it leaks in.

—*Come on. You really don't know me? Maybe we do all look*

alike to you. We look like your busted aunt, your crazy sister, your cousins from out of state.

Shut up, shut up, shut up, Florida chants silently.

—*We look like the girls at school who wouldn't give you the time of day, who spit, laughed, and teased your loser ass. The ones who lived large and crashed bad. Made you happy to see them fall, didn't it? Made you happy when they were put in their place by their fathers, boyfriends, husbands, and brothers. They scared you. They deserved what they got.*

Dios's words are hard, but her voice is all heat and sex, straight-up poison dripping in the CO's ear.

Florida peeks through the crack in the seat at the CO. She sees him nod his head slightly like he's got gears turning in there, like he's tuning in to Dios's frequency and tuning in to who she is.

"Shut up!" the exclamation slips out.

Dios whirls round and catches Florida's eye. "Are we bothering you?" she asks.

Florida looks away and shuts her eyes before the momentary connection between them takes dangerous shape.

"Maybe I'll move over there," the CO says. "Seeing as we seem to be bothering that lady."

Florida watches him slip across the aisle.

"You know, you are starting to look familiar," he says as he sits.

Florida's heart quicksteps against her rib cage.

They are driving through a sprawl of big-box stores and business parks. They pass under a maze of cloverleafs. Then the city flattens. The new construction falls back. A few forgotten outposts—derelict family restaurants and run-down motels—and then nothing, just desert and a ridgeline of distant mountains.

The canned air is giving Florida a headache. She's sweating hot and cold.

The space between service stations grows longer.

Florida drifts in and out of an uneasy sleep. Dios has been monologuing hard for hours.

"You're that bitch," the CO says.

"What bitch?"

"That bitch who got beat up."

"You mean the bitch whose breast you grabbed."

"I didn't grab shit."

"You probably told your boys all about it."

"What the fuck you doing on this bus?" the CO says.

"Traveling," Dios says.

"You have permission?"

"What about you?"

"I don't have to tell you shit," the CO says. "You're the one who needs to be telling me things."

"Not anymore," Dios says. "Just relax and enjoy the ride."

"I don't ride with the population." The CO rises out of his seat.

"Looks like you do now. Looks like you're slumming it with the rest of us. Looks like you're going somewhere you're not supposed to go. Probably not supposed to leave the state. Probably supposed to be safer at home or at work."

"None of your fucking business."

"Inside all you COs wanted was a little alone time with us prisoners and now you're running away. I guess you only want us when you can control us."

"Who says I'm not in control?"

"Stick around and find out," Dios says.

The CO takes his seat.

Florida tries to drink her smoothie, but she can barely swallow. She pulls the tank top tighter around her head. But Dios's words are on a hyperloop in her brain.

"You think we want it hard—that we need it hard—your beat-downs, your little personal punishments. And you like to give it. It restores the order we disrupted with our so-called crimes, right? But you know what? I've felt the fear on the far end of your club."

Florida checks the window just in time to see the bus pass the state line. She's in the shit now.

"Want to hear about the last time I rode a bus—I mean before the state bussed me out your way, put me in your hands?

"It was back in college, a place so small and fancy you've never heard of it. One night we drove from our campus way the hell out in the woods into Boston. There were five of us packed into some boy's brand-new Volvo. On the way back the driver got lost in a tangled section of town.

"You listening?

"This hood was called Roxbury and I'd never been there before. But I know it. You'd know it too. A neighborhood that looks like every other neighborhood until you squint at the details and see this is a place for Black or brown people. The little things. The minor derelictions and oversights. I don't have to tell you, do I? I know you know.

"Derelictions? Look it up.

"Anyway, there's three of us in the back besides the two in the front and we're rolling through this hood where the shadow activity is being played in the open. The other kids are starting to get jumpy, locking the doors and whatever. And now we're deep in some Boston labyrinth of all right turns and no way out.

"There's a smell in the car. I'd know it anywhere. I bet you would too. I've smelled it on myself alone on the subway at two a.m. I've smelled it on me alone with my older cousin on the couch when my mother was out. I've smelled it the first time the lights and sirens picked my crew up drinking stolen liquor in the park. I've smelled it coming from others who didn't want to see me coming.

"You've smelled it too in the yard before a fight, on the line when you got one of us alone, in the back of the bus bringing in the new girls.

"Fear.

"And just like those dumb college kids had planned it, just like they'd summoned their own nightmare with their twitching and nail-biting, the Volvo stops at a light and a couple of boys in black hoodies and baseball caps bang on the glass, pantomiming *I'm gonna blow your fucking brains out* with their fingers cocked like pistols.

"I almost laughed as the dumb-ass driver cracked his window, asking if he can help these kids—like if he played dumb the thugs will stop doing what they're doing—which was enough for them to get the door open, pull out the driver, and pound him on the pavement.

"Everyone in the car started screaming except me. I was placid as a fucking lake while the driver was getting pummeled into the asphalt. I kept my eyes on his eyes as each fist hit its mark, splitting his skin, darkening his pasty complexion. I watched the fear get pounded out of him. I kept my cool as the boy who messed up the driver slid behind the wheel, scattering the rest of the kids from the car. But I didn't fucking move. I caught his eyes in the rearview. I held his gaze as his partner took the shotgun seat.

"I let him see me. Not just see me but *see me*. Then I gave him his own goddamned smile back. Slowly I got out of the car before they tore out of there. When I watched them go, I felt the air swell inside me like I was a balloon and could goddamn float away.

"We took the bus back to campus.

"Like I said, I hate the bus. But sometimes you make do."

Florida's heard this story before. The pride Dios felt in the gulf that opened that night. The vision of herself she caught in that rearview. How she staked her claim as more than a scholarship kid along for a ride with her rich classmates. How she understood she was learning the tools to take them down. That is, until one of their mothers took *her* down—went to town on Dios after she had assaulted her son. Prosecuted the scholarship girl from Queens from the depths of her privately managed wealth. Like she was brushing lint off her sleeve.

Florida closes her eyes, squeezing them until she can hear the blood in her ears. Her heart flutters lamely, running low on panic.

Three hours.

They chase the sunset along the 10, barreling down the freeway toward the tiger-striped sky.

Two hours.

The surrounding landscape and landmarks grow familiar from weekend getaways, music festivals, and business trips with Carter.

The bus is buffeted as it passes the wind farms outside of Palm Springs. Florida watches the blades trying to slice the early moon out of the sky.

Up ahead she can see the dimmed lights of the Indian casino standing sentinel in the dark.

An hour and a half to go.

If she were driving, she'd be there by now. Because the bus has come to a section of the freeway that Florida knows from her early days taking the Jag as far from the city as she dared. And suddenly this road is her road, these curves and merges, these off-ramps and exit signs part of her story. She wouldn't need to think. She'd just keep an even pressure on the gas, a light hand on the wheel, as the car melded to road, the slightly unfamiliar surroundings blew past, becoming recognizable, then second nature.

The CO presses close to Dios, listening hard. Or maybe not listening at all. Maybe he's ignoring her words. Maybe he's drugged by them. Maybe he's asleep.

Night has come.

Dios rattles on.

The bus is slowing, its blinker on as it heads for an exit ramp. It rolls to a stop.

It's like I used to tell my cellie Florence—you don't know the half of us. You don't know half of the half. We've done things you can't even imagine. We've done things you've never even known.

Florence. Her name explodes.

There's a pause in the conversation. Then Florida watches Dios turn and wink.

The bus exhales a hydraulic sigh.

Florida is on her feet. She's in the aisle. She's rushing off the bus.

"Isn't that right, Florence? They don't know a goddamned thing about us, do they?"

Her name chasing her down the aisle. Her name driving her out and away. Her name loud enough for everyone to hear.

She doesn't turn back. She's down the stairs.

"Lady! Not Los Angeles. This . . . ," the driver calls through the open door. But Florida is moving too quickly to catch the rest of his words. Redlands, Upland, Chino—it doesn't matter as long as it's not on the bus with Dios.

She staggers away, wheeling toward the storefronts. She hits plate glass, her hands splayed on the window. Then she sinks down, collapsing in a doorway.

There are no awaiting passengers. The ghost bus glides away.

Florida leans back against the doorway. She's been sitting for hours but she's bone-tired—her muscles and joints cramped from tension. She takes stock of her surroundings. Another strip mall. Another shuttered space. She squints at the sign across the parking lot: WEST ONTARIO PLAZA.

Ontario. Close to LA but nowhere Florida wants to be. A satellite airport city. A drive-by city. Somewhere to get gas or coffee.

Now what? Florida doesn't want to blow her cash on a motel when she's less than an hour from Los Angeles. So, hitchhike? Walk? Camp out until morning? Find somewhere to make a phone call? Try to reach one of her derelict friends if she can recall one of their phone numbers—a long shot at best?

Despite her exhaustion, Florida rises to her feet.

It's unearthly quiet—a city without city sounds. Just the hush-hush of the trees and the random skitter of something blowing down the street.

The bus has dropped her on a four-lane thoroughfare. To the north, Florida can see the suggestion of the San Bernardino Mountains looming in the dark.

A squeal of rubber. A distant flash of brake lights sparks the night.

It's quiet again.

Another minute of walking west. Up ahead a service station glows garish in the dark.

Her footsteps now have an echo—a lonely, hollow reverb. Florida pauses. The echo continues, coming closer. Not an echo after all, but someone approaching from the opposite direction—

the silhouette backlit by the gas station's glare, a lone woman rising from the street.

Florida stutter-steps. But Dios—because of course it is Dios—doesn't falter, a towering demon stepping toward the light.

Florida's urge is to backtrack.

Dios will see that as weakness.

So they meet in the middle—facing off, Florida on the sidewalk, Dios in the street, the pale dome of her forehead incandescent. A second moon.

"I missed my stop," Dios says.

"This is your stop?" A momentary flush of relief hits Florida. "Ontario?"

"Is that where we are?"

"Fuck you, Dios. What are you doing here?"

"That CO was getting on my nerves. Anyway, I already told you that this is our story."

"And I told you it isn't."

Dios glances over her shoulder. "What are *you* doing here? What is Florida doing in Ontario?"

"Getting away from you."

"Yet here I am." Dios turns and starts back in the direction of the gas station. "Are you coming or what?"

Florida hesitates, letting Dios put more pavement between them.

The fluorescent lights burn Florida's eyes. The familiar snacks and drinks seem foreign.

Dios stands in front of the coolers, her bandana over her nose and mouth. She pulls the door wide and grabs two six-packs. She shows the clerk her out-of-state ID, mugging with her eyes over her face covering, like maybe it's me, maybe it isn't. She asks him to throw in an opener.

Outside they crack the beers.

Florida tucks her six-pack under her arm.

"Cheers," Dios says. "To the future. To the now. To the eternal present."

The beer is an echo of remembered sensation as it goes down. It is a thousand nights and a thousand stories that all started out the same way.

"Cheers," Florida says. She nearly polishes off the bottle before taking a breath. Her head is swimming. She'd been three years sober—never succumbed to contraband temptations inside. And now it hits her hard, like the come-up on ecstasy or the gut swirl of a couple of shots back-to-back.

"Easy, girl," Dios says.

Florida swigs to make Dios fade from view. She swigs again and the world spins faster.

"So here we are," Dios says.

"There's no *we*, and we are nowhere," Florida says.

Dios drapes an arm around Florida's shoulder. "You should have thought of that before you tried to close that circle with Tina."

"No."

"Before you needed me to clean up your mess."

"No."

"How hot were you burning the night of the riot? Did it feel the same as when you handed Carter those matches?"

"I don't have to listen to your shit, Dios."

"Or did it feel better because you weren't high? Because you knew what you were doing?"

Florida swigs her beer. "I don't have to—" Florida feels her free hand curl into a fist.

"Or did it feel better because you were in control? You weren't just calling the shots, you were making them. It was *your* foot kicking Tina in the ribs. It was *your* fist in her face. Was it a relief? A release?" Dios takes Florida by the chin and pivots her head so they are face-to-face. "It must have felt good, right? It must have felt good to let it out after all those years. That first punch must have felt like a dam breaking."

Florida's mind is slowing. Just a few sips of beer have made her thoughts sluggish and soft. But one thing is certain—it hadn't felt like a dam breaking. That first hit she landed on Tina—that first hit she'd landed on anyone—had felt urgent and immediate, as essential as breathing.

"You had to shut her up, didn't you? You had to close that circle."

Tina—raving up and down the tiers the night of the riot. Tina—calling the whole prison murderers. Tina—calling everyone out for their guilt. For their secrets. Tina, who knew the truth about Florida.

"So I fucking punched her, Dios. So what?"

"You punched, kicked, and beat her when she was down. You broke her and then you didn't stop. You couldn't stand it, could you, that she was going to tell us all about the real you? Funny thing—you didn't have to. She made you show us."

"I didn't kill her."

Dios wags Florida's chin side to side. "But you came so close. So very close. And that's where I came in. I finished what you started. I closed that circle for you. And now here we are."

"I keep telling you, there's no *we*." Florida tries to jerk free of Dios's grasp. But Dios tightens her fingers, pinching before letting go.

"But you're wrong. Without me, Tina might have survived, might have told everyone what you'd done. I saved you so you could be yourself."

"That's insane."

Dios hurls an empty bottle. The glass shatters like an explosion. "Is it? Or did you want her to regain consciousness, tell everyone who beat her and how bad? Because then, well, then, none of this." Dios spreads her arms wide to the dark street.

"I don't want *this*. I'm going home."

Dios tilts her head back and laughs. "Home. There is no home for you, *Florence*. Not anymore. Not after what you've done. You might return to your mother's house—but it's never going to be a home. Let me tell you something." She loops her arm through Florida's as they move in lockstep away from the service station.

"I tried going back to Queens when I dropped out of college. You know what I found? My old crew had broken up. They were mothers now. Wives. Fucking baby mamas and mistresses. Only three years after I left and they fell apart—abandoned, broke, and beat down. They let that shit happen. Because why? Because they were playing the part that had been written for them. One day we're all stealing from bodegas and the Rite Aid, the next they're letting their boyfriends and bosses run the show. Suddenly they're working for my former classmates at that fancy college. They were their nannies and cleaners. They were checkout clerks and tellers.

"They hung in parks and on stoops, bitching and moaning about their fucked-up lives. And still they froze me out, like *I* was the lowlife. Because who the hell was I? A kid who won the scholarship lottery, got silver-spooned up in the world. They acted like my rich New England stink made them gag.

"But they weren't paying attention. They were getting packed closer together and sidelined as hipsters arrived in our hood looking for the next cool thing—invaders who spread and sprawled like they owned the place. Didn't even look at my old crew. Looked through them, in fact. Looked through everyone.

"Sometimes one of these kids caught my eye. Sometimes one of them mistook me for part of their tribe."

Dios squeezes Florida's shoulder. "Are you listening? This is the good part. One night I was cutting through the small park where I used to break dawn with my girls. This white girl with hair that looks like it's been cut by nail scissors appears. She stops and looks up at a street sign like it's written in a foreign language. She's drunk or high. She's staggering and smiling at fuck-all.

"She sees me. At first she takes a step back. Then she relaxes, like there's something copacetic between us. And she's all, *Excuse me, um, do you know how to get to, um,* in her white-girl way. Then she holds up her phone. *Thirty-Seventh,* she says.

"*Avenue or street?* I ask her.

"*Avenue, maybe,* she says, her tone letting me know that where she comes from avenue numbers don't run so high. She looks at her phone again. *Oh, Thirty-Seventh Avenue and Eighty-First Street.*

"So I raise my hand to point the way, but then something knocks loose inside me. Instead of pointing, I punch. And then I fucking punch her again and again. I just full-on batter the woman's face. I broke her nose and split her lip like I was snapping a hot dog. Blackened both her eyes and delivered a couple of kicks in the ribs, then stomped her skull to make sure she wasn't going anywhere.

"Don't look at me like that, Florida.

"Two days later, my college roommate turns up in Queens. She's all on edge as we walk down Broadway. She tells me that a young woman got a terrible beatdown right around the corner. *This place isn't safe,* she said. Like because she comes from a safer place she can explain my own neighborhood to me.

"Like I don't know the violence of my own life.

"She told me I needed to get out, that I can't backslide into this world. That I'd come too far.

"She was fucking right and she didn't even know it. I had come too far.

"Florida—once the violence cracks open inside you, home is a place you leave behind. You burst from it, reborn. Fucking parthenogenized into your own life. Your home becomes a place that fits like a shrunk glove, an old shoe. You outgrow it like you outgrow the self who'd lived there. You become you and there's no turning back."

They are three beers in. They've been walking north. The pavement sways beneath Florida's feet. The mountains sway in the distance. The booze makes the world dip and bow.

Dios hurls another bottle.

The shattering glass sparks Florida's nerves.

"Easy, girl."

"Ghost town," Dios says—inside Florida's thoughts as always. She raises her voice to the darkness.

Pero nunca se fijaron
En tan humilde señora

"Shut up with that narco shit," Florida says. The songs remind her of jail—of being trapped inside with Dios's bullshit.

"Just listen."

"I've been listening for two years."

"*They never noticed such a humble lady.*"

"And that's you, the humble lady?" Florida laughs.

"They'll never see us coming," Dios says. "Never ever."

They pass a shuttered saloon in a strip mall whose parking lot is filled with overflowing dumpsters. Dios heads for the bar. It's locked, of course. A single light illuminates the dusty bottles. Dios rattles the door handle.

"Come on," Florida says. "Don't."

"Don't what? What do you think I'm doing?" Dios cracks a smile, splitting her already busted lip. She rattles the door even harder. It groans. Florida scurries back across the lot. She swigs a fresh beer.

"You're not breaking in there," Florida says. But it's too late. Dios has smashed the glass with a discarded paint can from one of the dumpsters.

There is no alarm, just the sound of Dios's shoes crunching over glass. "You coming?"

By the time Florida enters, Dios is uncorking a bottle.

Beneath the musty scent of disuse, the bar smells like bar—sweet, sticky, smoky. A smell Florida associates with bad sex and bad decisions.

Dios dives behind the counter, fumbling with switches. Lights flicker on and off. A motorized disco ball pivots overhead.

"Jesus, Dios," Florida says. "Kill the lights."

Dios slides her the bottle. "Drink," she says. "Drink and shut up. Or drink and enjoy yourself."

Florida takes the bottle.

"See," Dios says as the warm—what is it, whiskey?—hits Florida's lips. "They didn't rehabilitate you for shit. B-and-E and chasing beer with booze."

Florida blinks away the whiskey's burn. "This was all you."

"You and me."

They pass the bottle, drinking their legs to jelly.

Then the music comes on and they are dancing, spinning and staggering, slip-sliding on the broken glass and holding on to each other before they fall.

Florida stumbles over to the stereo and cuts the tunes. Dios chases her but aborts her mission as headlights slice the dark outside.

Together they cower beneath the bar, numb, dumb excitement drowning Florida's fear.

The headlights vanish. And it's just the two of them, squashed together on the rubber no-slip mat, a tangle of breath and booze.

Dios's viper face is inches from Florida's—a trickle of blood spidering down her busted lip. She yanks Florida to her feet.

Then they are outside on rubber legs.

Then Florida has fallen to the ground. *Just leave me.* Then—she's not sure after how long or what happened in between—Dios is standing over her again. The blood has dried on her chin.

"Eat." She holds out a bag of chips. Florida tears them open sideways, spilling them onto her lap. The salt, grease, and solid food make the world spin slower.

They have come a few blocks from the bar. They are sitting on a low overpass that looks down into a bracken-filled basin.

"Desert," she says, nodding at the scrub.

"This isn't the desert," Dios says.

"Desert," is all Florida can reply. Because it's too much to explain that the desert seems to have crawled west and met them here.

"Florida," Dios says, "listen to me." She squats down, her mouth inches from Florida's. Florida squints, trying to steady Dios's face, which is a kaleidoscope, spinning and fragmenting.

"The world is on pause," Dios says. She puts a hand on Florida's shoulder. "But we aren't. We are on the move."

"I'm sitting," Florida says. "Just let me sit."

"The world isn't paying attention to us. We can do what we want. This is our time." Dios's eyes glitter in the dark. She smiles broadly, releasing another trickle of blood from her lip. Florida squints. Her head rolls back against the chicken wire fence that's preventing her from tipping into the desert below.

Dios is beautiful. She is a goddess and a demon. She holds out her hands and pulls Florida to her feet.

"You and me—this is our moment. It's happening."

There's a trick in here somewhere but Florida can't find it.

The world is spinning. Florida's getting on board. It seems safer than being left behind, dizzy and alone.

Her hands are in Dios's. She is allowing Dios to spin her wildly.

"I don't understand," Florida says. "What are we going to do?"

"We've already started."

"Okay," Florida says. "Okay."

Dios lets go. Florida staggers backward and hits the pavement. She rolls over so she's staring at the sky, where the stars are smeared crossways. Then she sits up and watches headlights approaching the overpass. As a white pickup rolls to a stop, Florida closes her eyes again and lies back, blocking out the world.

Florida comes to in the cab of a pickup halfway closer to nowhere from the look of things. Dios is holding out a tiny white pill that Florida recognizes as trucker speed. She and Ronna used to buy it from out-of-town gas stations or when they went roadtripping with Renny.

Renny? Where did that name come from?

She closes her eyes and lets Dios place the tablet on her tongue.

The last fifteen minutes come back to her in flashes, like someone's rewinding an old VHS tape.

The pickup rolling to a stop.

A man leaning over and out the passenger window.

Dios asking for a ride to LA.

The man refusing. Something about a cesspool or a shithole. Something about slick billionaires and the dirty homeless. But he could take them *somewhere*.

Then Dios helping her up. Then Dios giving the man their real names. His name: Drew. Then Dios whispering into Florida's ear not to worry. *This is our game.* Then black.

And now black again as Florida lolls her head back and the truck rattles on.

The Mini Thin hits with a jolt, electrifying Florida just in time for her to feel the pickup buck over some railroad tracks. In the distance—a train whistle.

It's more country than suburb or small city now. Florida realizes they're heading toward the mountains.

"Just me and a few buddies out back. Let them camp on my spot. Free and all. Don't have any use for the exchange of currencies. At least right now. What I own I own free and clear. No bank. Nohow."

The pickup winds up a hill.

"World's heading that way. Infrastructure is a thing of the past. Banks are a tool of oppression. A trick. That's how they steal your money when the world collapses. They cut off the electricity. Lock your cash inside."

Up and twisting up until they grind to a halt on an uneven driveway.

The house is a cabin wrapped in peeling clapboards. Behind it is a small RV and a camper trailer with a curtain over the back window. Two men slide from these like shadows, spilling into the light of a campfire that shouldn't be burning in the brittle, thirsty land.

Florida's buzzing. The tablet has numbed the booze and she's more alert than drunk. She follows Drew and Dios to the fireside. She sits on a plastic crate watching the flame-licked faces across from her, everyone lashed by devil tongues. One of the men is tall—half his face mottled by a burn scar, skin like melted wax. He wears three enormous rings—dark stones cupped by claws and talons, the kind of jewelry Florida and Ronna bought for kicks on Venice Beach. The kind of jewelry Renny gave them.

That name again. Florida claps a hand to her forehead, trying to bury the memory as she stares at the man across the firepit.

He's missing teeth. He has an ankh painted or tattooed next to one eye. Half of his nails are blackened or polished black.

The other man is small, reddened, and bumpy—skin pickled and pocked by booze and the wind. He's shaking—he holds his hands toward the fire for warmth on the warm evening. His fingers glow. His nails are yellow. His hair is yellowing gray and pulled into a ponytail.

"I brought friends," Drew says.

Florida gets a good look at him too for the first time—tall, skinny, hollow-cheeked with a crease from eye to jaw on each side. Scraggly brown hair that brushes his shoulders. A face like a hawk.

"Sit," Drew says. "Gary and Bob." He points first at the pagan dude, then at the ruddy one.

Florida's heart is beating a two-step. She straddles a crate near the fire and picks up a stick, snap-snap-snapping it and tossing it to the flames.

"Ladies," Gary says. He has booze in a mason jar. It smells homemade—a tang of motor oil.

"You girls far from home?" Bob asks.

"We don't have a home," Dios replies.

"You girls lost?" Bob says.

"We aren't lost."

"Careful with that one," Gary says.

They pass the jar. It burns like hell but dampens the cheap speed.

Bob begins to drum on a crate with a stick, a quick-time rhythm out of sync with Florida's pulse.

"Where'd you find them, Drew?" Bob asks. "Where did these ladies come from?"

"What makes you think we can't speak?" Dios replies. She holds Bob's gaze.

Bob flicks his grizzled ponytail. "Your friend hasn't said a word."

"Tell them, Florida," Dios says, drilling a finger into Florida's side.

"It's none of their business," Florida says.

"Feisty," Bob says. "I like it."

"I wouldn't if I were you," Dios says. "She's a killer."

"I like it even more," Bob says.

The fire crackles and an owl drops a lonesome note. Drew pours water into a bag of freeze-dried stew and stirs it before offering it around. The smell of the desiccated beef and powdered herbs takes Florida back inside. She gags and gulps the pine-pitch air.

Bob is smoking schwag, his face redder, like the fire is inside him. His words tangle. *Back then I was a hairdresser for Pat Benatar. I did all the singers.*

I wrote a few letters to the president.

I got a reply. Once, just the once.

We had a shop on Hollywood Boulevard. Everyone had a shop on Hollywood.

We used to party at Guitar Center. We partied at the Viper Room. I did hair in the toilets between sets. I did hair on private jets. I've been to Moscow. I've been to Estonia.

The letter I got back had his signature. The signature of the president of the United States. Dirtbag traitor.

They love American rock in Eastern Europe.

They love it more than Americans do. They can explain it to us. They hear things we don't. American rock is full of code. It's encrypted messages to the communists. It's spy shit.

"Easy, Bob," Drew says. "You don't want to bore our company." He scoots over, closing in on Dios.

"Pass me that." Dios reaches for the jar. She swigs and offers it to Florida.

Bob's voice is a bass refrain—a story that stretches on, only now and then interrupted by a drag and exhale.

"So you two aren't going to tell us where you're from and how come you're wandering around after curfew?" Drew asks.

"What curfew?" Florida says.

"She speaks," Bob slurs.

"You don't know about the curfew?" Bob asks.

"We're from Arizona," Florida says.

"And they don't have news there?"

"We were in prison," Florida says.

For a moment the only sound is the snap-crack of the flames. Then the men roar as one, billows of laughter that knock them forward and back as if they are being buffeted by actual gusts of wind.

"What?" Florida says.

"What'd you do?" Drew asks.

"Lemme guess," Bob says. "Domestic violence. Beat up the old man."

"Forgery," Gary says. "It's always forgery."

"Forgery. Or fraud," Drew says. "One or the other. Got to be."

"My cousin did time for bad checks," Drew says.

"When I worked retail all the ladies skimmed," Gary says. He holds his hands out and the flames light up his cheap pagan jewelry.

"That's what you did, right?" Drew says. "Took a few bucks. Took a few more. Bought yourself some new clothes, some new makeup. Thought no one would notice." His eyes bounce from

Dios to Florida, his face a lopsided smirk, the smile of a superior drunk.

Dios wraps her hand around Florida's wrist and pulls her toward Drew. "Hit him," she says.

Florida's mouth opens and closes like a Venus flytrap, catching nothing.

Dios shakes her wrist and tightens her hold, her finger digging into Florida's fine bones. "Hit him."

"Now, now," Drew says. "That's not ladylike."

"And what does that mean?" Dios says.

"It means she's not going to hit me," Drew says.

Dios yanks Florida's arm. "What do you know?"

Florida's wrist is burning. She's unsteady on her feet.

Drew is staring up at her with his smug smile but there's worry in his eyes fed by the chill fury that's emanating from Dios. "Go on," Dios hisses.

Florida tries to jerk away.

"Do it."

"Stop," Florida says.

"*Stop*," Dios mimics.

"What do I know?" Drew says. "Seems like I know something."

Dios lets go of Florida, then feints toward Drew, her own fist raised. He flinches and falls off his crate. "You know jack-shit."

Florida's cheeks are blazing with shame and fury. She pushes past Dios so she is standing over Drew. Then she presses a foot to his chest. "Accessory to murder after the fact," she says. She presses harder. "That's what I did. Pled down from accomplice to murder."

Dios pivots, her eyes on Florida's, their green glimmer flecked with fire. "Well now," she says. "What do we have here?"

Florida removes her foot and stands tall. In these woods, in this dark, she is bold. "Pass me that jar," she says.

Drew takes his seat. His expression is frustrated yet hungry. Florida knows this look from the COs who kept them in line by summoning the women's worst behavior for their own pleasure. She knows it from the CO on the bus who looked at Dios with the same eyes. Make them misbehave so you can devour them later.

The fire gives a castanet sputter. Somewhere an owl lends its voice.

The mix of booze and speed makes Florida both loose and wired with an energy that needs to flow.

She breathes deep, drinking in the forest, a smell and taste so free and clear it scrapes her lungs raw.

"Look at her." Florida is barely aware of Gary's voice, his gross, gravelly admiration of her as she drops her head back, tilts her face toward the sky, and begins to sway.

She feels it all fall away. Carter. Her mother. The years inside. The smells and sounds of hundreds of women crammed together. The echo of their fears. The air—so tight and heavy.

Gary finds another stick. His rhythm on the crate accelerates, working against the drag and drone of his companion.

Florida whirls, feeling the warmth of the fire revolving against her body. Feeling the towering trees and the forest expand on all sides, the world receding until it's just her dancing alone with limitless space and endless time.

Now there is music coming from the pickup, songs from a tinny radio. The headlights are on, sharpening the focus on the party.

Bob is bowing and weaving on his crate, nodding off, his joint between his lips. Dios takes the joint just as Bob slumps to the ground, his face slack with chemicaled sleep.

Gary cups his hands over his mouth and starts a pagan wail. He takes off his shirt and steps up to the fire. One side of his chest is scarred from shoulder to waist—a half vest of rippled, ridged skin.

Dios slides her arms around Florida's waist. "We hold them in the palm of our hands," she whispers. "All we need to do is squeeze."

Gary howls and calls and guzzles his home brew and then staggers back toward his trailer, where he passes out on the steps.

Then it is Drew. Hungry Drew.

"Ladies," he says, "shall we dance?"

Florida pulls Dios to the far side of the fire.

Drew's eyes never leave hers. "Playing hard to get?"

She gulps from the mason jar and the scene swirls faster. The trees close in. The fire grows higher. All the space that was just there evaporates as Drew circles the flames, trying to catch them.

It's a game at first, this counterclockwise prowl.

Florida wobbles as she dashes around the firepit, keeping away from Drew. Dios steps to the sidelines.

"Are you going to let him catch you?"

"Come back, Dios," Florida says.

"Come back, Dios," Dios mimics, retreating behind the truck's headlights.

Florida circles fast. Drew circles faster. Then he reverses course and catches her in a sloppy bear hug, wrestling her to the ground. She falls hard. Her head knocks against something sharp. The pain is startling.

She feels the fire at her back, dirt and dried needles in her mouth.

Drew's hands are all over her, a frenzied clawing that gets under her clothes.

Florida is stunned by the fall. Drew's clumsy fingers probe. He tears her shirt. He tugs her pants.

The fire cracks, shooting sparks that shower them. Drew yelps and recoils, freeing Florida.

She rolls away and staggers to her feet.

"Show him." Dios's voice comes out of the dark. "Now is your chance to show him who you are."

Florida makes a fist. Drew is rolling at her feet.

"Hit him now."

Florida stares at the man on the ground brushing sparks from his hair and his shirt. She watches him blink, blinded by the smoke.

"Do it."

Drew is struggling to his feet.

"Now."

Before he can stand, Florida delivers a kick.

"Again."

Another and another.

Drew groans and doubles over.

"Show him."

Another kick and then she is down at his level. Her fists fly like they belong to someone else—a rat-a-tat hailstorm of blows. Dios's voice driving her on.

She's pinned Drew against the concrete of the firepit. Her fists and feet flying, alternating kicks and punches. Her fists bleeding. Her feet throbbing. Still she continues. She feels her knuckles split, the bones in her fingers bruise and swell.

She punches until her hands are numb and her breath gone.

Drew lies limp, his eyes closed, his head rolled toward the fire.

Florida falls back. She is empty. Dios comes to the fireside— pristine and glorious. She helps Florida to her feet.

Florida is slick with sweat and spattered with ash. She looks down at Drew, motionless and spark-showered.

Her knuckles ache. Her wrists too. Her head is heavy, her

stomach sour and churning. Florida looks at the blood on her hands and the blood on Drew's face. She retches, then wipes her mouth. She finds the mason jar and takes a swig.

Dios is already making tracks. Florida hears her boots striking the gravel. She takes a look at the bodies strewn and slumped around the campsite.

Bob mutters something.

Florida needs to hustle. She can't be around when they come to.

She stumbles over crates and bangs into the pickup. She finds the driveway but then veers off, unable to navigate in the dark, unable to steer herself straight.

"Florida!" Dios's voice again, but farther way. "Florence."

Florida takes a few steps down the road but then stops. In the woods she can hide. In the woods she can be free of Dios.

She waits.

"Florida!" Fainter now. "Get your ass down here."

When Dios's voice fades away, the only sound is the erratic thump of Florida's own heart. Then boot strikes returning in her direction.

Go. In the woods. Over rocks. Through brittlebush and tumbleweeds. Into the trunks of towering trees. Past more rocks. Over dried moss. Over fallen branches.

Go. Faster. Away from Dios. Away from that campsite and another person she'd beaten senseless.

Go. Dios's voice still in her ears, egging her on.

Go. Faster and faster until she trips over a tree trunk and is thrown headfirst into a small clearing.

The air smells of blood and pitch. Florida holds her breath, hoping for enough silence to hear if Dios is calling to her, chasing her, summoning her back. But the only sound is her own heart pounding in her chest and the forest settling back to stillness behind her.

The sun leaks through the low branches of the towering pines. Florida's throat is parched, her eyes crusted with dirt. She slept on the forest floor. Her hip aches. Her hands throb. In the trickling dawn she can see most of her nails are broken and her knuckles swollen.

She stands. She has to move and put this behind her—just another drunken revelry, a woodland rave, a fire-dance.

Florida has no idea how far she came in the dark last night before she fell to the ground and slept. It could be minutes or miles. Time was a funnel that made her spin and spat her out. She pats her pockets. She has her debit card. She's lost everything else.

Down. That's all she knows. Head down and one way or another she'll come to a road. She's in the woods but civilization can't be far, the suburban, exurban sprawl that snakes away from cities until all cities are one city.

The forest is bald in patches—rocks slicked with a carpet of dried pine needles. Florida slips, breaking her fall with her bruised hands. She slides.

There is the road—a twisted cut between the trees.

The descent is easier now on the pavement.

Her mind churns—a painful collision of thoughts and the aftermath of last night's booze, a hangover three years in the making that coats each decision in a penumbra of worry, confusion, and panic.

Down. Down.

Florida's feet are running away from her, leaving her mind behind. She turns and looks back. She's a long way down. The trees on top of the mountain are lost high above.

Her feet slap hard, sending shivers up her shins.

She is on level ground. Florida pauses to catch her breath. She must look wild—a feral creature clawing out of the woods. She rakes her fingers through her hair and tries to rub away the dirt on her cheeks.

Keep moving. Her body wants to stop.

Keep moving.

The ache is everywhere.

Keep moving.

Because if she does, she can get home. It won't take much. Just a little thinking. The city limit of Los Angeles must be forty-five minutes away, her mother's house a twenty-minute ride across town depending on traffic, which, by the look of this new world, won't be much.

Florida takes a deep breath and exhales slowly to quell the staccato panic of her hungover thoughts.

Like she planned before, she will take things in stages. She will work it through and when she is comfortable somewhere in Los Angeles, when she has her car, when she is showered and groomed, the events of last night and the past years buffed and scrubbed away. When she's free of Dios, she will be all right. The mountain will be a memory.

She crosses the border where desert meets mountain. There are houses now, even a few cars. A shopping plaza. A gas station. She buys water, coffee, and a pastry that's sweating in its plastic sheath.

As she's paying, a thought breaks through—no, not a thought, a sound.

"You okay, lady?"

"Did you hear that?"

The clerk looks in the direction of the door, as if the sound might be coming inside. "You mean the train?"

"There's a train?"

"You just heard it."

———

The station is a ghost town—a few mission-style structures shade an empty platform. The waiting room is deserted, the benches roped off with police tape, the vending machines disabled.

Florida uses her debit card to buy a ticket from a machine. She feels her money ticking away. A sign taped to the wall suggests trains are running on a limited basis.

The train is almost empty. Its few passengers have scattered themselves. There's one other rider in her car—a man hidden behind a newspaper.

The air is cold and canned and bracing.

Florida takes a seat out of sight of the other passenger.

The rhythm is a balm, a pat-pat that soothes her.

The door at her end of the car opens and a woman enters, swaying with the to-and-fro of the train. She swings herself into the seat across the aisle from Florida.

She is all grunt and snuffle as she settles herself. This woman is too close, too loud, too much breath and heat.

Florida begins to make her way to another car. The rider who had been reading the newspaper is gone. He's left the paper behind. Florida sits down across from his now-vacant seat, her back to her destination, and watches the Inland Empire slide away. The train is rolling faster now, barreling toward the terminus, whisking her home. Home. She's not afraid to say the word now that she's free from Dios.

The landscape is starting to look increasingly familiar. The outskirts of LA—places she's passed with Carter or stopped with friends on the way to somewhere else. Places where someone who knew someone lived. Places where someone she knew lived.

Home.

She can feel it for the first time—an unburdening and an unwinding. A homecoming.

Florida reaches over and lifts the *San Bernardino Sun* from the vacant seat. Her eyes skim the pages, taking in the dispatches from a world on hold. Data and graphs and numbers and warnings. She is about to toss the paper when her eye catches something below the fold.

FEMALE SUSPECT OR SUSPECTS SOUGHT IN MURDER OF CORRECTIONS OFFICER

There is a stupid moment when Florida imagines that if she stops reading, the story will vanish or be a different story altogether. Her eyes continue before her mind can stop them.

> The body of corrections officer Oscar Reyes was discovered on board a Ho Fong bus that was operating illegally between Phoenix and Los Angeles on Tuesday. The cause of death was a knife wound to the carotid artery.

It sounds so clinical, so impossibly distant.

Florida's eyes fly up the page to the headline. *Female Suspect or Suspects . . .*

The train is starting to slow. Soon it is swallowed by the shadows of Union Station.

Then it stops with a screech.

KACE

Let me tell you a little about Tina. Now, I don't know much. But I know that lady had the sort of drug problem that made it so she could kill a bitch and not remember. Her blackout highs were so high that what happened in them might as well not have happened, as far as she was concerned.

Except it did.

Except Tina stone-cold killed a lady.

How do you apologize for something you don't remember? How do you make that shit right when, for all you care, it's another person who did that crime? How do you apologize for not being you?

You can't. You can't go back into that particular moment because for you it didn't exist. It's enough to make a lady crazy.

Own it. That's what Marta said day one she popped up inside my head. Own it that you up and killed me.

First time I heard her voice—let me tell you.

But *True, that,* I told her. *I sure as fuck did.* Didn't plan to. Thought I saw her creeping out of my house. Thought I saw her going with my man behind my back. Stabbed her before I could think twice. But I did what I done. Didn't really mean to until I did. I wouldn't do it again if given the chance, not to Marta. Not to anybody. Told them all and everything in our group sessions. Told them again and again. I'm not sure I learned from my mistakes. I just made them.

Dios called this weakness. I heard her bang on about it for years. She said I was selling myself short, because how many women out there have the strength to lay another human out? As if it was something to be proud of. Some fucked-up feminist nonsense, if you ask me.

Like there's no space for regret and power in the same body. Like these two things can't cohabitate.

But then the bitch skedaddled without even copping to dropping Tina.

Embrace your crimes, my ass. That's what I should have told her. I should have told her a lot of things.

Marta had a sense about Tina. I guess ghosts know when they got company coming.

Tina's ready to go, she told me the night of the riot, as Tina was raving up and down the tiers. Told me Tina was already halfway gone. Told me she smelled like dirty clothes. Like rotting fruit. Like sawdust. Marta talked about it so hard and long that I could smell it too. I still can.

She's ready to leave. She's packing up. She's done with this place.

Only place Tina's going is the psych ward, I told Marta.

Like me, Tina'd heat-of-the-moment up and killed some lady. Unlike me, she always claimed she didn't remember, what with the meth, booze, and whatever-the-fuck else she was running on.

A blur, she said.

A whirlwind.

A blank space.

Not in my right mind. Not in any mind at all.

Tina didn't notice the dead lady until the next morning, when she saw her splayed on the rug in her own damn living room.

Beat her with a fucking brick. The only way she was sure she had actually done it were the abrasions on her hands, the brick dust on her fingers, and the blood spatter on her arms.

Her best guess—she came back from the club wild-eyed and spinning and thought this lady was robbing the place. First offense and it's murder. Not so much as a speeding ticket before. Not even a parking ticket.

That's not what I mean, Marta had raged at me the night of the blackout. *Tina's gone.*

She's just losing her mind, I assured Marta. *We're all losing it in here with the lights out.*

She's gone, gone.

An hour later, Tina was. That beaten, bloody mass. Some fucked-up woman-on-woman shit. No one stepped up. No one squealed. Not even me.

And Dios, quiet as a church mouse on the subject. I guess there are some things too dark to admit, even for her.

Took Tina a few days to speak up after Dios left.

Marta was waiting for it. Marta was unhappy. Marta wants me all to herself. Marta says I owe that to her. Marta didn't want to give me space to hear Tina out.

I told Marta she didn't have a choice. I hear what I hear.

Tina wanted to tell me her story just like the rest of the dead do. It was the same story she was telling that night she got killed. A story about Florida. Funny, you can live with someone for a year and not know the first thing. But first I had a few questions of my own.

The moment I heard her voice, I asked, *Tina, what's it like being on the other side? You used to tell me I was crazy talking to all your dead and now look at you.*

The dead don't answer. Not directly. That much I know. Still, I asked. Because Tina was the first voice I knew personal from when she was alive.

Tina, I said, *does being dead—getting killed—make you regret what you've done?*

All these women are fucking liars, Tina said. *All of them. You, me, the rest.*

It was the same shit she was spewing the night of the riot.

That talk got you killed, I told her.

I was already dead inside. They just finished the job.

Sometimes you got to wonder if there's still beauty in this world or if you've become hardened beyond beauty. If things just are— neither one way nor the other.

Because I'm looking out the window in Florida's old bunk and all I see is a dry, dead world.

The sky just the sky. The ground just dirt. The clouds, when they come, a dirty smudge on it all.

The fuck did she see in that tree? The fuck did she imagine?

Funny thing—I used to think she deserved the view because she knew more than me, had less guilt than me, was somehow better than me. I imagined she breathed different air, belonged to a different world.

I thought she had the power to turn that desert and barbed wire and fucking nothing on top of nothing into a picture post-card, a beach sunset, a vacationland. I believed she could perform that magic. You would have too, the way she went on about it. All because of a single tree that wandered over from who knows where and toughed it out in her sight line.

But now I know—she's not some rich girl caught up in the world's currents, but a riptide dead set on dragging people under.

Too fucking careless with the gifts she was given.

Like the view from the top bunk. Assumed it could save her from herself. But it was just another lie. And it dragged her under.

Sometimes in here it feels like all you have to yourself is the thing that brought you inside. The thing that belongs to you proper—the weight you carry. That's it. There's no other you. And you have to reshape that thing into something you can live with, mold it and sculpt it until it fits tight to your body but doesn't over-whelm you. You have to find your way into it, like a tight sweater, pushing and pushing until you break free and can breathe again.

Girls like Dios and Florida, they don't get that shit. All they know is the shame or the glory. They don't get the everyday, the constant drag and drone of the past.

They don't know that at the end of the day, the everyday is all there is.

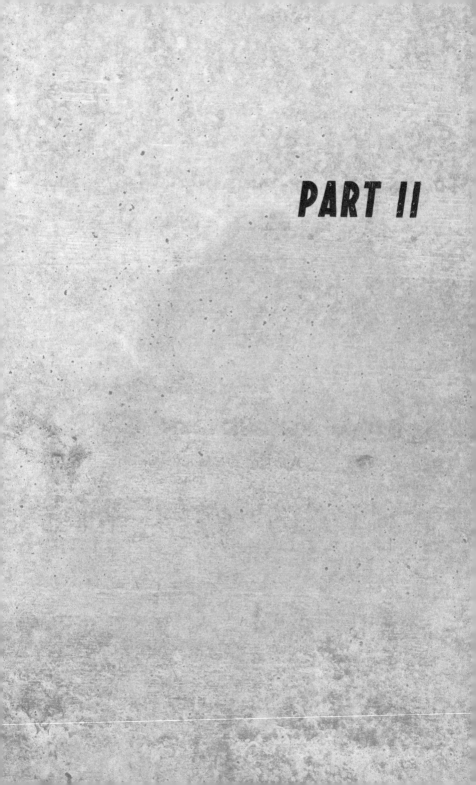

PART II

LOBOS

Tell me a story. Tell me your story.

Bathed in blood. Smears and smudges on the seats and windows. Splatter. A solo battle waged against a violent death. A violent battle lost.

The bus smells of iron. Even through her mask, the smell is unavoidable.

Lobos has ordered the engine to be kept on. The bus's AC helps with the smell.

She kneels on a seat, examining the body from over the seat back, keeping her distance from the blood smear.

He's young. Mid-twenties, maybe. Something about him signals army or police. But now his eyes are fixed terror wide. Mouth frozen in rictus.

Died with one palm over his throat as if it might stanch the flow, one hand reaching down the aisle, summoning help that never came.

———

It's dark. After curfew. The city is holding its breath.

A city of plywood and fear. The bus's rumble is a roar in the stagnant silence.

Lobos scans her audience. It's a tough crowd getting tougher as time ticks on.

You're not going to get much out of people who aren't supposed to be doing what they're doing, going where they're going, riding on a bus that wasn't supposed to be carrying them at all.

We've been told to stay home. And yet these folks are on the move, crossing state lines, incubating for hours with strangers.

Half of them may be illegal.

The other half don't speak English or don't want to speak it. Or are in the process of forgetting as you question them. Words slipping into silence. Witnesses unwitnessed. Everything unnoticed, unseen.

We can go now?

You will let us go now?

You let us go?

The driver—he knows nothing. Nothing about his bosses. Nothing about three passengers who disappeared before Lobos made the scene. Nothing about his permits or lack thereof. Nothing about any of the passengers he wasn't supposed to be driving on a bus that wasn't supposed to be running. Nothing about the people who got off at the stops before this Chinatown terminus. All cash. No passenger manifests. No trace.

I keep my eyes on the road. That's the job.

In the two hours since she's been untangling this mess, Detective Lobos has learned three important things.

Two women got on in Chandler, Arizona—but not together.

Two women disembarked early in Ontario—but not together. One halted the bus just before it rejoined the freeway because she missed her stop, which wasn't her stop to begin with.

If anyone heard this guy get his throat slit, they thought he was coughing and wanted no part of it.

A whole nation scared of the dying now more than ever.

Here's what else she's learned. The twelve sets of eyes staring at her over their masks want to go home. They want to fan out across this city.

They stare at her. Scared they're going to get sick just by standing here. And who knows, maybe they will. But they were the ones who boarded an illegal bus full of strangers captained by a driver with an expired license. Danger is relative. So is risk.

Eighteen-dollar fare. You get what you pay for, Lobos supposes, dead guy notwithstanding. So they can damn well stand here in the middle of Chinatown as evening runs to night and answer her questions.

None of you saw the women who exited the bus?

None of you noticed a man dying on board?

Heard coughing. Didn't want to get sick.

None of you noticed the blood?

Food spill. Food spills. Food spills on bus.

Lobos scans the eyes, trying to figure out who is speaking

Sticky. The bus always sticky.

Lobos can't argue with that. She rattles the Tic Tacs in her pocket. She pulls down her mask, tips the canister in. The eyes watching her widen in horror.

Good thing she gave up gum before this shit show. The tension in her jaw was keeping her up at night. One tension among dozens of other tensions that drove her to seek the night shift whenever possible. Any excuse not to chase sleep but to let it come like a hammer midmorning.

Spend your days solving puzzles—untangling knots and weaving threads until a smooth tapestry appears—and you miss the story unfolding in your own house. You miss the moment your husband's quiet isolation turns into quiet rage turns into full-throated anger.

Lobos crunches the candies.

The gum she could control. She swapped it for these small mints. They're easier behind the mask anyway. The ear loops would have given her blisters after a single day of relentless chewing.

Tick. Tick.

Lobos shakes the small container hard. Its size reminds her of the Zippo lighter she stole in high school. She flicks the latch open and closed like she can spark a flame.

Ticky. Ticky. A rattlesnake in her pocket. One by one her eyes land on the twelve passengers staring back at her.

The translator is scribble-scrawling details in his notebook. Names. Addresses. When she releases these people they will be ghosts brought in on a ghost ship to a ghost town.

One more question. The same one she's asked ten times. Lobos goes down the line one by one. "Women? You sure they were women who were talking to the victim? You sure it was two *women* who exited the bus early?"

Twelve sets of eyes, all sure.

The victim had been sitting in the back near two women. They had heard him talking to one of them.

"Let them go."

The translator addresses the crowd. They scatter.

"But not the driver. He'll come to the station. We need a full statement."

On board the bus the techs are doing their work. The body has been photographed and is now wrapped and ready.

A bus full of blood and no one noticed until the last stop. That, Lobos unfortunately understands.

"They can tow the bus now?"

Lobos is startled by her partner's voice. She's often startled by the very existence of her partner. She's not particular about whom she works with, which means her pairings are usually short-lived and inconsequential—an old guy on his way out, new guy on his way up. She's a way station.

"To the impound?" Easton adds, mistaking Lobos's silence for confusion.

He's like that, always explaining before she has time to answer. Never imagining she understood on the first go-round. He's a jovial blond—South Bay born and bred and, except for the badge, interchangeable with any number of sun-kissed surfers on the boardwalks and piers. As far as Lobos can tell, he's neither here nor there, which means he isn't going anywhere fast but simply treading water until retirement. A good old boy without having to grow old—a fount of conventional attitudes and conventional wisdom.

"Fine," Lobos says. "Take it."

Easton signals to a tow crew that's hovering on Alpine.

"You believe them?" Easton says. "You believe a couple of women did that?"

Lobos cracks her mints. "That's what they said."

"And you believe it?"

"Why shouldn't I?"

"It's just—" Easton breaks off. "It's just real violent, that's all." If he only knew.

"And you'd have to be strong, you know. To do that."

"Give it a name, Easton."

"To slit a man's throat."

Lobos puts her hand to her own throat. Close her eyes and she can still feel the imprint of her husband's hand in the same place. "You'd be surprised what weak people can do."

Twenty minutes on foot from Chinatown to Central PD. The uniforms take the driver in the squad car. An ambulance takes the body to the ME. Lobos walks. Easton tags along.

"It's just that I don't see that a lot. You don't see that a lot. Women cutting people. It's not exactly standard."

"Murder isn't standard."

"I'm just saying, it's usually a crime of passion with women. Some kind of passion. Statistically. Women kill people they know. They kill their kids."

"Who says she didn't know him?"

"They kill at home."

He's right, of course—*statistically*.

"Home is complicated these days." DV complaints down because there's nowhere to escape the violence.

"I'm just wondering if those wits saw what they think they saw."

Lobos rattles her mints. "And I'm wondering what kind of woman would do something like that."

"That too," Easton says. "What kind of woman *could* do something like that?"

Lobos eyes him. "You're saying a woman couldn't do that."

"I'm not saying anything."

"Come on," Lobos says. "You don't think a woman could."

"We'll see," Easton says. "Bet?" He holds out his hand.

"You want to bet against twelve wits?"

"Just making it interesting."

Lobos pivots so she's face-to-face with her partner. "You don't think the job is interesting?"

"How about lively, then?"

"Yeah," Lobos says. "This beat sure as shit isn't lively." She offers her hand and they shake.

Three hours into curfew now. Nothing to be done about those with nowhere to go. The air is wound tight. A tinderbox. A powder keg. A pressure cooker. Pull a pin, light a match, and this city is going to blow.

The illegal fireworks lighting up the sky for the last three weeks don't help.

The National Guard makes it worse. They transform Los Angeles into a war zone awaiting a war. Here they are rolling past Union Station.

Here they are parked around city hall. Here they are lounging on their tanks and trucks, soldiers at ease, which is somehow scarier than when they are on guard, as if they are prepared to shoot to kill without thinking too hard about it.

Beyond city hall there's no sign of the guard. Lobos and Easton pass Little Tokyo—restaurants dark—then cross the nebulous border of Skid Row, where the streets are less worthy of protection. More like Skid City. A favela-style sprawl of tents bursting from the original epicenter and now lining every freeway, on-ramp, underpass, riverbank, park, side street. Pushing way past downtown, crosstown, westward, and north into the formerly untouchable areas of genteel Los Angeles. The movable city on the doorsteps of those who built walls, gates, and gatehouses to keep it out. It's crawling down from the Mulholland Dam and away from the various reservoirs. Creeping in from the beaches.

Shrouding the city with another city—a skeleton city that can shift, mutate, and migrate, be torn down, scattered, and rebuilt with deep and invisible roots.

Now every lot, corner, and walkway harbors the tents that are no longer just tents but block-long shanties, elaborate structures of tarps and chairs, cookstoves, grills, repurposed office furniture, plywood boards, wiring jacked from lampposts and car batteries. Cars turned into micro-apartments: kitchen, storage locker, bedroom all-in-one. Cars that haven't moved in years, that are burdened until their axles break. Cars that are sinking into the street until they become part of it. Cars that are burned and then abandoned.

That's a new sight. Abandoned camps. Abandoned cars. Abandoned shelters and tents. Even the unhoused moving on, creating their own ruins.

This is a sick city getting sicker. The street is its own local pandemic within the global one.

Homicides. Overdoses. Death by exposure. Heat stroke.

Since she transferred to Central a year ago, Lobos has been called to all of these, witnessed every manner of death outdoors. So she gets how someone can die—can be killed—in plain sight or on a bus and no one marks it.

The straight world is now like the undomiciled one—too concerned with its own survival to note a neighbor in distress.

She and Easton turn from Alameda up Fourth and are forced into the street in order to skirt a patch of sidewalk someone has cordoned off by tying two tarps to an office chair lashed to a tree.

"Fucking mess," Easton says, skipping over a puddle of something oozing from somewhere.

As they pass, Lobos glances through a gap in the tarps to check the camp. The streetlight shows her a mattress, bike, some books, bedding, a battery-operated lantern. Her lingering is a habit she can't break—a futile hope that if she solves the present puzzle she will understand the larger picture of how a tough cop like her became an unwitting victim.

Lobos runs on secrets and puzzles. She runs on the small lies people tell that reveal larger truths. It's household objects, their arrangement, their dust, disuse, or high polish that unveils something their owners want to hide—the background noise, the timestamps, the light in the sky that tells a different story than the social media caption.

This game is harder here downtown.

The usual markers are gone, lost or stolen, erased by the grime, the hard living, the mental and physical dereliction. But they are still there, and each person out here has a story that brought him to this point.

Lobos wants to know them.

"Let's go," Easton says.

There's something about this tent that grabs her. It takes Lobos a second to dial it in. The place is clean—or cleaner than average. She takes a step closer.

"Lobos."

A charred scent lingers in the air. She remembers it now— last week whoever camped here had his spot torched. Lobos was called to the blaze. She saw the body. And now there's someone new. Somebody with fresh gear.

"You making yourself at home?"

It's a long shot—keeping an eye out for one man in this un-domiciled sprawl, in the unnameable city. One man among those hidden in plain sight. But Lobos can't help herself.

Lose your wife. Lose your savings. Lose your home. Lose your friends. Lose your way. Lose your mind. You have to wind up someplace. Her hunch is that her ex-husband is here or somewhere like it. She's a detective. It's her nature to keep looking although instinct tells her not to.

Puzzles. Logic problems. So much boils down to a process of elimination. When you lose the last thread tethering you to the straight world, the streets beckon.

Lobos rolls more mints across her tongue, pulls out her phone, and turns on the flashlight.

"Lobos, what the fuck? We have a stabbing victim at the morgue and a bus driver waiting back at Central."

It's the books that demand a closer look. Lobos can't quite make out their titles from the street, so she takes another step. Her face is now a foot from the space between the tarps. Eckhart Tolle and a DIY business book.

Her heart quicksteps. Her mind starts calculating—balancing evidence and probability. But before she can come to a conclusion, a man springs from the tent.

Lobos barely has a moment to react or to grab her badge before he's on her, shoving her from the entrance and back into the street. Lobos is a flyweight—a hundred pounds soaking wet—and reels back at the man's touch, falling into the street, where she has enough time to reach for her badge and gun.

The guy, riled and raging, doesn't see or doesn't care that she's packing. He keeps coming. Lobos has time, if she wants, to fire a warning or worse.

She has time.

But her mind is blank and then a blur. And instead of living in this moment, she's tunneling into the past, where the dozens of moments she failed to act occur to her simultaneously—the dozens of times she took her rage and packed it away so tightly it rendered her immobile.

Lobos has time.

The man in front of her is not who she's looking for. He's a complete stranger—grizzled with a blistered, ruddy face.

She has time. Her rage hammers her chest but she doesn't move.

Lobos has time and then she doesn't. But before the man grabs her, Easton pounces, pulling the guy away from her, tossing him back toward his tent.

Lobos scrambles to her feet. She holsters her gun. She brushes grit from her suit pants.

The rage hits harder now, transforming into shame. Her cheeks burn. Her heart stampedes in place.

Easton stands between her and her attacker. "Are we cool?" Easton asks the man.

"Bitch was peeping in my tent."

"This *bitch* is LAPD."

"She didn't announce as such."

"I asked," Easton repeats, "are we cool? Or do we have to continue this?"

"You can't just go peeping in people's property," the man says. "I don't break into your home. I don't peep in your motherfucking windows."

Lobos chokes back an apology before it escapes.

"Watch your language," Easton growls.

"Easton, let's go."

"This man assaulted you."

"Let's go. We've got work to do."

"Lobos—"

"Like you said, we have people waiting on us." She needs to be out of there, as far as possible from another failure.

"Fuck it," Easton says, stepping away from the man. "It's your lucky day. Isn't it?"

That's a funny thing to say to someone sleeping on the street, Lobos thinks. "Let's go," she says again.

They continue up Fourth.

"That motherfucker," Easton said. "All these motherfuckers. And what were you doing poking your head in there?"

"Nothing," Lobos said.

"You looking for someone?"

"Not really," she lies.

She checks the sky. She can see the blinking lights of the choppers on standby—one over city hall, one making a wide arc across downtown.

The city is still.

The city is hiding.

The city is primed to explode.

A pink-and-blue blossom of fireworks erupts to the east.

The station is quiet. It's quiet on top of quiet with officers and plainclothes dispatched to quell the mobs that flash and flare in response to out-of-town violence.

Lobos gets why a group of twelve strangers refuses to find cops guilty. Over and again. It's the same reason she sticks with her job despite its imperfections. A misguided devotion to a sense of authority. An inability to see the worst when the worst is staring you down. The world is crumbling. We try to hold on. Or we wind up pitching a tent on a spot where someone else was living until he got burned.

She passes the desk sergeant.

"They're waiting." He nods toward the interior of the station. "Translator complained you're taking your time."

"Tell him to go."

"You tell him."

———

The translator and the driver are in an interrogation room at opposite ends of the table. Easton melts away to chase down other information. He knows that if Lobos doesn't question the man firsthand, she'll have too many questions for him down the line. He cedes the honors. Lobos dismisses the translator, then pulls out a notebook and her phone.

"Tell me the route again."

"Chandler, Phoenix, Ontario, Los Angeles."

"And these women got on in Chandler. Together?"

"No. One needed money. She went to the ATM. I already told you. Then she got on. The other was late. Almost missed the bus."

"Did they know each other?"

"I don't know."

Lobos scribbles, then clicks over to her phone and starts to retrace the 10 back east. LA—Ontario—

"And the victim?"

"Gets on in Phoenix."

Ontario—Phoenix.

"And he sat with them?"

"No. Yes. Later. They didn't sit together. He sat with one. Near the back. I'm not sure. I just drive. Hard to see from the front."

"The women bought tickets to Ontario?"

"Los Angeles. I told you. But one gets off there. Then the other follows. Says she missed her stop. Made me pull over."

"And you do that? That's regulation?"

The driver's eyes darken. He draws back. "I let her out."

"Why?"

"She wanted to get out."

"What did she say? Did she seem agitated? Angry? Did you see blood?"

"Black pants. Just like the other one. Black men's pants. Maybe there was blood. I don't know."

"They were dressed alike?"

"Same pants. Same shirts. Blue, like for working."

"You sure?"

"I think so."

"What else?"

The driver looks at Lobos as if he has no idea what she's asking.

"Same pants," he repeats. "Those women. Same shirt too. I think."

"Like a uniform?"

"Same clothes," the driver says.

Lobos picks up her phone and zooms in on Chandler, Arizona—a blue dot on a gray-and-yellow grid. "What's it like?"

"What?"

"Chandler?"

"I just drive the bus."

"Who gets on in Chandler?"

"Passengers."

"And you're sure they were women."

"Women. I'm sure."

"Did you hear anything from the back after they got off?"

"Coughing. Lots of coughing. Everyone gets nervous. I think, maybe that's why the women get off. So much coughing."

The same information she's gleaned on-site. Except for the clothes.

There's a tap on the window. Easton holds up a notepad. Lobos moves to the door. "ME says our dead guy's a CO out of Perryville."

Lobos's brain splinters. She knocks back some Tic Tacs, swirls them side to side. She turns to face the driver.

"Do you pick up a lot of prisoners?"

"I just drive the bus."

"Do you clean the bus?"

"I just drive the bus."

"Does someone clean the bus?"

"Supposed to," the driver says. "To sanitize. Because of the virus."

"Do they?"

"Sometimes."

Lobos sits at her desk. The first part of this could be easy. She closes her eyes. She visualizes the bus.

Surfaces. The news is dominated by a fear of surfaces that contaminate, transmit, incubate. There's a collective paranoia about every shared space—the forensic record of fingers and other smudges as virus vectors.

The bus is a petri dish of surfaces—armrests and windows, tray tables and their latches. What the world fears will tell the story Lobos needs to know.

It could go two ways. If the bus is sanitized between routes, properly wiped down to remove germs and evidence, the only prints will be those of the last passengers. If it's not, Lobos is looking at dozens of people passing through—many of whom will be guilty of something.

Decades in this job and the science of crime still fails to grab her. She digs the personal stuff. The human shortcomings and error. The truth baked into the lie. The puzzle of emotion, motivation, and history.

She calls the lab. The seats are a fucking Jackson Pollock of prints. The blood doesn't help. They tell her to cool her heels for a bit. Read: three hours minimum. Four more like it.

Ten p.m.

Feet on her desk. Squad room quiet. Like she likes it.

The radio blips. A mob downtown. A mob going up Fourth Street.

Lobos is relatively new to this station. And she's back in homicide after a seven-year vacation in vice. She doesn't give out much to her fellow cops. They can look her up if they like, though there's not much to tell. A trail that will die out. Lobos is her maiden name. That's new again too.

Some of them know her from her old beat. They know her by her former name. Her old dye job. They also know better than to mention it.

They assume she's reverting to her roots—her heritage. It's a convenient cover.

Lobos's tailbone aches from where she hit the street, tossed by the man in the tent. The things she lets slide, the petty harassments and everyday aggression. It becomes routine. Easy to see this as your fault.

She wonders how Easton will frame the story.

Fifteen minutes later the call comes in that the mob has dispersed. The real action is out west in Santa Monica. A riot on the 3rd Street Promenade.

Don't be tricked by movies and television—more than half of Lobos's work takes place at her desk, phone calls and web searches, a jigsaw of information that will slowly start to show a larger picture.

The women's prison outside Phoenix confirms a CO named Reyes who matches the victim. The local station sends someone to notify. Soon that person will return with details about why Reyes was on the bus and whether he was flying solo.

She cups her hand over the phone and signals to Easton.

"CO at a women's prison," she says. "A women's prison. Pay up."

"We never settled on terms."

"You're gonna stiff me, Easton?"

"I wouldn't dream of it." He rolls over in his desk chair, hands her a five.

"Cheap bastard," Lobos says.

"You want to be right or rich?" Easton says.

"Right and you know it."

Easton looks at her computer screen, where Lobos has called up the Arizona DOC website. "Makes sense they're prisoners."

"How's that?"

"I'm just saying, they're already predisposed to violence. Conditioned for it too."

"Conditioned *by* it, maybe."

"Your average woman couldn't do what was done on that bus."

"I hope your average man couldn't either."

"You know what I mean."

Lobos stares at her screen, so close she can hear it buzz. "Not really," she says.

She hopes the blue glare hides the angry flush on her cheeks. She had nearly apologized to the man who'd knocked her down.

Easton slinks off to kill time at his own desk. She doesn't need him loitering, reminding her of her recent misstep.

Bad enough she has to live with the shame of having taken out a restraining order against her own husband. She knows how it looks, and worse, how it feels. How can she keep the peace on the streets when she couldn't in her own home?

———

Lobos reaches the warden at home and he doesn't sound happy about it. Dead is dead, he tells her, and can't this wait until morning? He doesn't have much of anything to say about Reyes. New guy. Nothing to report.

Lobos tiptoes around the question of whether he was known to use excessive force on the prisoners.

"Just because they're women doesn't mean they're a walk in the park," the warden says.

"I understand," Lobos replies. "What about Chandler?"

"Who's that?"

"The city. Do you know if Reyes has connections there?"

"I hardly knew him. He just started a month ago. Hadn't even cashed his first paycheck." There's a pause on the warden's end of the line. "We contract to Chandler. We use motels there to quarantine early releases."

Women kill people they know. Even Easton knew that.

It's coming together. Less exciting than you'd think.

"What was he doing on that bus?"

"Hell, if I know," the warden says. "Rules are no traveling during this time. Probably thought he'd sneak away for the long weekend, fly under the radar."

She clicks over to COMPSTAT. They are at the start of a crime wave. She can sense it. The police are stretched thin. The police are looking elsewhere. Dealers are hurting, as in any legit business. More layoffs, less cash flow. Turf wars are brewing. Tents on the streets are swelling.

Cars linger undriven and are stolen.

People have been cooped up for more than two months. Now it's turning warm. They're blowing off steam. They're broke and angry. They're opening fire on one another for no good reason. The results are mapped on Lobos's screen in hundreds of color-coded bubbles that denote assault, robbery, vehicular theft.

She empties the last mints into her mouth and closes her eyes.

She picks up the phone and calls the lab. "I'm not rushing you," she says before the tech can voice his irritation. "I'm just saying let me know right away if any prints match women with prison records."

Whoever killed Reyes isn't worried about being captured.

She isn't worried about getting away with it.

Something nags at Lobos. This woman—these women—there's a chance they even want to be caught. The crime is too flagrant. The exit from the bus too visible. If her hunch is right that she's on the hunt for two ex-cons, they must have known—no, they surely would have known—that there's no way to outrun this.

She stares at the blue light from her screen. Her eyes glaze as she tries to arrange the puzzle pieces in her head. But instead of the crime scene, her brain is flooded with another picture—the sky falling back as she was pushed to the street. The furious, ruddy face of her attacker. The barely stifled apology that she swallowed just in time. She pounds her desk to banish the memory.

Lobos stares at an overhead shot of the prison—a collection of squat gray squares in the shape of a skewed cross encased in a pentagonal yard. An old-school child's vision of a space station, but dropped into a bleak desert.

Lady-killers.

Femmes fatales.

Black widows.

Thelma & Louises.

Bitches with problems.

Lobos can hear it already. All the cute or sarcastic names the perps will be given to soften their crimes—to make a sport or light of what they did, to make men able to consider that women can kill.

"Two fucking lady-killers, huh?" Easton swings into the chair next to Lobos's desk.

"Lady-killers kill women. Technically," Lobos says. "Or rather they do it emotionally."

"How's that?"

"Lady-killers are men. Not women who kill. Your usage is incorrect."

"I'm just saying," Easton says. "*Lady . . . killers.*" He drags out the space between the words, as if the misunderstanding was all on Lobos.

Seven years in vice and you see a lot of battered women, beaten women, dead and dying women. You see angry women, scared and scarred women, tortured and trafficked women. You see women enslaved by women, pimped by women, turned out by women in their own families. You see women coerced by their boyfriends, pimps, and husbands into committing heinous and horrible crimes.

Why is it so hard to believe two women are guilty of killing the man on the bus?

Lobos side-eyes Easton.

"What?" he asks.

"It's staring you right in the face and you still can't believe that two women did this."

"I can believe a lot of things. But it doesn't mean I want to."

Lobos shakes her head and turns away from her partner. How is it that this polite frat boy is so deep in her own thoughts?

"You okay?" Easton asks.

"Fine," Lobos mutters.

This whole thing sits uncomfortable, like putting a shoe on the wrong foot or having a sock slip way down in your boot. Women can't be violent because that will justify violence against them. Women need other women to remain mild, docile, nurturing in order to save themselves from the wrath of men.

Lobos empties more mints into her mouth. She cracks several between her back teeth trying to think past her own prejudices.

She would have been within her rights to retaliate against the man who assaulted her. Easton would have backed her up. He might have commended her, seen her in a bold new light. Called her ballsy. Now there's a word.

"Well, anyway," Easton continues. "The prison is putting together a list of all the women they sent to Chandler for quarantine. And a list of motels."

Lobos checks the clock. Prison bureaucracy is fast asleep now. "We'll get the prints from the lab first. Maybe in two hours. Maybe less."

"I'll hound them," Easton says.

"Be my guest." Lobos takes a fresh canister of Tic Tacs from her top drawer and pushes back from her desk. "I'm going for a think."

Skid Row is dead quiet. Darker than dark. Stiller than still on the near-blackout streets.

The choppers over city hall and downtown have fallen back. The towers in the financial district a mile to the west are looming, lightless silhouettes over the ghost town.

Down here, though, there are people, actual ghosts strewn and sleeping. The quiet streets thrum with their collective living, their sleep sounds, their rumbles and coughs.

Lobos always marvels at the deference given to the night hours, how the chaotic daytime streets yield to the need for sleep after dark. There's action, of course, black-market trades carried out in the open. There's crime too, rapes and murders after dark. Homeless-on-homeless crime mostly.

But still the sleepers sleep, not necessarily safe and secure, but down for the count.

She turns off Sixth and heads down a side street, passing Seventh, leaving the precinct, the missions, and other services behind, and plunging into the darker recesses of Skid Row, where the laws of the nighttime are more fluid.

A streetlight on Bay Street is flickering, catching a heavily graffitied wall in its intermittent glow. Lobos pauses as she passes. There are murals all over Skid Row and the adjacent Arts District. But this one is different—so detailed it almost seems to be animated. It shows the current protests—the streets filled with people, their backs to the viewer, their fists raised, their banners flying. Maybe it's the on-off glimmer of the streetlight, but Lobos could swear the mural is moving, that the banners are flapping, the protesters' fists punching skyward. Then the streetlight loses its battle, leaving the wall in darkness.

Lobos keeps on, her eyes peeled, always looking, always searching.

Where do you go when there is nowhere else? To whom do you turn to when there is no one?

Her boot strikes echo.

People move about the streets, shifting through the dark, shadows within shadows.

Lobos knows some of them stay wired all night to protect their camps, then shoot up to sleep off the day. She knows that a great number of the undomiciled suffer a kind of day-for-night confusion that exacerbates or is exacerbated by cross-addictions and mental illnesses. She knows how quick the world falls away, turns hostile, and turns you even more so.

When she figured out what was happening in her own home, it

was too late. Nearly a decade of late nights—all nights—in fealty to his monitors, swapping daylight for their artificial glare, had chipped away at her husband's brain. Each click took him deeper down a hole until he began to drown in misinformation. Until he started to believe the mistakes he'd made, the jobs he'd lost, the money and opportunities squandered hadn't been his fault but the fault of a larger worldwide conspiracy to undermine men just like him.

Lobos let these complaints slide in favor of the increasingly infrequent ordinary evenings when they managed a meal together, maybe a movie on television.

He was supposed to be trading and investing their money. Lobos didn't ask questions.

By the time she learned that he'd grown mistrustful of the banks, it was too late. He'd grown suspicious of society altogether—social security, the Federal Reserve, geology, geography, and science. He'd begun to mistrust Lobos herself. He mistrusted her job, her civic employment. *People like you oppress people like me*, he told her.

Lobos laughed it off. If she had a dollar for everyone who bagged on cops. Easy pickings. A cop joke at every dinner party.

But then he lost half their savings.

Then he lost all his friends.

And when she questioned him—finally—he lost his mind. Rising, unkempt and unslept from his office chair, his eyes glazed, his lip curled, a snarl emanating from his throat, roaring *how dare you question me*. And before she knew it, before her years of training and experience kicked in, he threw her against the wall, pinning her, his hand over her throat.

It ended quickly. He backed away, she hit the floor, not a cop but a victim.

The excuses Lobos made—late nights, stress, isolation. The

lies she told herself—as long as no one knew what happened, perhaps there was a chance it hadn't. She gave him space, granted him the grace to apologize. And when he didn't, she willed herself to forget the incident.

But his anger grew, fueled by her acceptance. His rage intensified, revealing itself in short, sharp insults hurled as she walked past—thrown objects, pens, coffee cups, investment manuals.

Lobos turned prisoner in her own home—tiptoeing past the office on her way to work. Holding her breath when she heard him on the stairs at night, praying he wasn't returning to the bedroom.

An officer of the law but she couldn't protect herself at home. Her work suffered. She overreacted. She threatened people who had done little. She lashed out and accused. She lost sympathy for the abused and terrified. She reviled their weakness.

And then, after badgering a prostitute instead of her trafficker, Lobos snapped out of it. She moved to a hotel and served her husband with a restraining order.

That man on the bus—the terrified rictus of his features, the desperate clutch of his hands. Lobos would have liked to have seen her husband in that position.

So here she is—scouring the streets, looking for him based on a tip that he'd been spotted downtown.

Here comes a man, stagger-stepping down the sidewalk, doing the junkie shuffle, the shake-walk. There he goes, crossing in the middle of the street in the dark, not looking for cars as he stops to argue with someone invisible. Listen to him as he notices Lobos. Listen to him unload a jumbled tumble of curses and vitriol.

Fuckyoucuntwhatyoulookingatwithyoufuckingbitchfacefuckingfuckyoucuntstaringyoujustgetthefuckawayfrommeworldisfullofbitcheslikeyounomatchformeicancutabitchlikeyouicankill-

youwithmybarehandsicankillyoujustbylookingatyoumysuper-powerskillingbitcheslikeyouseeyoubleeddrinkyourblooddirty-fuckingbitch.

Listen to him hating on her for nothing. Listen to him roar. Curses and condemnations. Rage upon rage upon rage. An unceasing fountain of anger.

Now he's approaching her as she flashes her badge. Now he stops and jerks. Now he's quiet, like someone pulled the plug. Now he's down, falling like a collapsed marionette.

Lobos is stunned. She approaches the man. She toes away some trash with her shoe and steps closer.

She shines her flashlight over his body. He's breathing—a ragged up-down, spittle on his cracked lips.

She nudges him with her shoe. He groans. He's not overdosing. He's not in any immediate medical danger save lying in the street.

She nudges him again, as if she can roll him back onto the sidewalk. He doesn't budge.

Lobos checks the block to see if she's alone.

This guy. This guy who insulted her. This guy whose untethered rage at the world emptied onto her—why should he get a pass? Why do they all get a pass: her husband, the man in the tent earlier, the good old boys at work? Why are they all worthy of her hands-off goodwill?

Her body vibrates with rage. She reaches for her mints but leaves them in her pocket. She won't allow herself any distraction from her anger. No, let it flow, let it fuel, let it swell.

Lobos's mind flashes to the scene on the bus. Now she sees the crime differently. Here on the dark street, away from the duties of the job, the facts of the story hurriedly jotted in blue lines and dashes onto her notebook, it begins to look like a release.

Her breath quickens. It's part of the job, she tells herself, putting yourself in the perp's shoes. What was it like to wield that knife? What was it like to hold that power?

She holds on to the rage. Lets it churn.

Lobos glances at the ground, at the toe of her shoe and the man prostrate before her. Her foot twitches, like it's thinking its own thoughts.

Kick him.

The rage is swirling.

Kick him.

It would be nothing, trivial, worthy payback.

Kick him.

She feels the tension in her calf as the muscles and tendons coil.

Who would notice? Who would care? Who would know? A secret. A source of strength, a single declaration of power.

Kick him. Just once. Or as many times as she needs.

She jumps at the sound of her phone ringing and vibrating against her leg. She jumps as if someone has reached out in the dark street and touched her.

Her heart races as if she's been caught.

She fumbles with the phone, dropping it on the street as she starts to answer.

"Lobos?"

Her name called out, echoing, reverberating in the night.

"Lobos?" Easton's voice.

She retrieves the phone, brushes it off, and puts it to her ear. "What's up?"

"Everything all right?"

"Yeah . . . yeah. I was just . . . I'm heading back."

"No need. We're on hold 'til morning. Everyone's shut up shop."

"Even the lab?"

"No answer for the last hour."

"Okay then," she says.

"You sure you're okay?"

"I'm fine."

Easton lingers before disconnecting.

"I'm fine," Lobos repeats, and ends the call.

She pockets her phone and looks down at the man at her feet. He groans and heaves in his narcotic doze.

She pulls on a pair of plastic gloves, grabs the man under the shoulders, wrestling him away from passing cars, and hoists him onto the sidewalk.

Then Lobos steps back and screams. A chest-emptying bellow that pours out into the street, bouncing off the shuttered, abandoned warehouses, rushing over the sleepers, tangling with the trash around gutters and tree trunks, until it settles into silence.

There is no reply. No callback from the night. No concern or care.

She knows one thing for certain: the murder on the bus was not a crime of desperate revenge or self-defense. It was a stance, a stand, a demonstration of power by someone who wants to be seen.

Time to go home.

Lobos lives downtown in a loft on San Pedro. She got it cheap when the developer of her building was struggling to convince buyers that the Little Tokyo lofts were indeed in Little Tokyo and not smack in the middle of Skid Row.

She knows these buildings shouldn't be converted into so-called luxury living because it will only make the desperation outside worse—each neighborhood refinement driving those who rely on Skid Row's social services further afield, scattering them from the place where they are welcomed, reducing their permissible footprint and paving over their domain with a shiny ignorance.

Each slick new conversion means more residents with less tolerance for the undomiciled and more local landlords who will get greedy and jack their rents, forcing out the few businesses that cater to the homeless or offer them assistance.

She tells herself that being part of the community allows her to understand it better. But what she really understands is that the chaos is unceasing, the smell overwhelming, the press of bodies all consuming. She's glad she's on an upper floor—she has that sanctuary at least.

Lobos crosses through the heart of Skid Row, past the brutalist, windowless station where she works, past SROs and a few stalled constructions that promise low-income housing, past flophouse hotels, past tents, past the tentless, past the missions and those left outside who didn't snag a bed for the night, past temporarily shuttered businesses, past permanently closed ones, past signs telling her WE WILL GET THROUGH THIS—TOGETHER.

Together—a word for the rest of the city, those sealed away, safer at home with their stockpiles and projects and childcare headaches.

Even at night, even in the unusually thick silence, the city still quivers with tension begging for release. Lobos feels eyes watching her from tents, from sleeping bags, behind tarps, and on top of flattened boxes.

She's jumpy, startled by the usual noises—the scurrying, muttering, coughing—that soundtrack of nighttime streets.

She rattles her Tic Tacs, tips the canister into her mouth, distracting herself from the loose wires sparking her nerves. Lobos picks up her pace, ashamed of her fear. Another blight on her character, another weakness.

She drives a fist into her thigh. He did this, her husband. He unnerved her and unsettled her. When she finds him . . . Lobos doesn't permit herself to complete the thought, afraid of everything she wouldn't do.

And when she finds him . . .

One block to home. She crosses Fifth. A few shapes are passing in the dark, shadows under the shadows of streetlamps.

She passes the Downtown Women's Center. Up ahead is her building.

Lobos pulls out her keys, then one glance over her shoulder— a final safety check.

There he is, across the street, under the sick, yellow flicker of another faltering streetlight. Stalking her.

San Pedro is wide, but well under the mandated one hundred yards that her husband must keep away from her.

"Hey," she calls.

He doesn't move.

She has planned for this. Two years of stored outrage. Two years of visualizing her retribution. And the moment is here.

"Hey."

But she doesn't cross the street. She doesn't raise her fist. She doesn't look for something to throw or something with which to strike him. All that rage and the only thing she does is reach for her phone to call in this infraction.

But her phone is already buzzing—a call and a text message arriving simultaneously.

The message appears on the screen. A name. A rap sheet. A photograph.

Florence Baum.

Blond, pretty, a vacant stare. Not who she was expecting at all. Lobos squints at the screen, double-checking.

When she looks up, her husband is gone.

FLORIDA

Florida—Florence—whoever she is, stands on the platform in Union Station as the train waits before making its return trip. Somewhere a thought is begging for attention, insisting that she board and hurry back east, back to Ontario, then to Phoenix, and finally back to the motel in Chandler.

But . . .

Has time already run out?

Inside there was nothing but time on top of time. Here time is race-roaring away on a fast track of bad decisions.

If time has indeed run out there will be another back.

Back inside.

Too soon the loose circle the cops have already drawn around Dios's crime will become a net that ensnares Florida. Too soon, or already. There's time. And then there isn't.

Three years sober and now a night of drugstore speed, bottom-shelf liquor, and moonshine has crippled Florida's thinking, replaced logic with panic and planning with pain.

She is neither Florida nor Florence. Her head throbs. Her

thoughts are not her own. She's floating somewhere inside her own body, which allows her to ignore the nagging in her mind, relegate it to paranoia and irritation, make it the thinking of some other person who's bugging her. Another self inside herself. A stranger.

Shut up.

Florida glances at the steps that lead to the terminal where a transit cop is patrolling the platform.

Home. She has to get home, get her car, then choices will open up.

She can get back to Arizona quickly, without the threat of exposure on the train or on a bus. She can install herself in the motel as if she'd never left at all.

In the car she can go anywhere.

The car means freedom. The car means options. The car also means equity.

The city is muffled and muzzled. A marine layer blankets the sky with a heavy, uniform gray.

The only signs of life are a few pedestrians scurrying away like they've been caught out in an apocalyptic aftermath.

Florida knows downtown from loft parties, after-parties, and illegal warehouse parties. She knows it from late nights and pricey apartments of friends who'd figured their lives out better than she had. She knows it from tasting menus, artisanal bakeries, bespoke cocktails, and dealers who stay up late.

She knows it from Carter's friends, connections, suppliers, and debt collectors. She knows it from those months with Renny and Ronna.

She doesn't know it on foot or in daylight.

She cuts south toward the numbered streets to get her bearings.

There are tents everywhere. Skid Row exploding out of downtown into the Historic Core—its metropolitan charm now charmless in abandonment.

Tents everywhere. On the sidewalks, in doorways, on the medians, in and around the few pocket parks. She jags south, then crosses the 110 at Sixth Street. She pauses on the overpass, looking first south then north on the nearly empty freeway. Tents everywhere. Clustered under the 110's bridges. Lining the embankments. Hidden in the overgrowth of scrubby plants, camouflaged by soot-stained flowers.

Florida has never felt more conspicuous as the only person on the move in a stagnant city. And she is the last person who should be out at all.

She's a driver, not a walker. She prefers the city to speed by outside the car window at a remove, an indistinct blur that she can control with her acceleration.

She prefers the freeways to the streets.

She prefers the city when it's least like a city at all, when it's four lanes, on-ramps, and overpasses. When it's a sprawl of lights below the 134 or a fortress of smog and high-rises as the 101 hits the 5.

But here she is, in the trenches of metropolitan Los Angeles, powered only by her footsteps.

MacArthur Park is overrun with tents—nearly every square foot of grass made into a campsite. The lake is invisible behind a fortress of ripstop nylon.

Florida takes Wilshire through the park and walks down the middle of the street. Koreatown is shuttered.

There are tents on the slim median that divides Wilshire—a

fingernail of land transformed into a place to live. There are tents in front of the deco doorways of the old Bullocks. There are tents in front of the Korean consulate, the Filipino consulate, the Peruvian consulate. There are tents blanketing the steps of Robert F. Kennedy Park, where the Ambassador Hotel once stood. There are tents in front of the Oasis Church, St. Basil's Catholic Church, and the Wilshire Boulevard Temple.

At Serrano, Florida turns north. Her feet ache. She's dizzy and dehydrated. Her stomach is hunger-hollow.

Serrano is lined with evenly spaced shanties, each a seven-by-seven-foot square with a peaked roof. The only difference between them is their materials. One all plywood, another cardboard and mattresses, a third plywood and metal sheeting. A pre-apocalyptic subdivision, a no-income housing development.

Florida finds a convenience store and buys water, a sandwich, hand sanitizer, and breath mints. The shopkeeper doesn't meet her gaze, as if eye contact too is contagious. Outside she takes off her grimy surgical mask and dabs her face with the water, then drinks the rest. She devours the sandwich—her first meal since pizza at the motel.

Sixth Street's Korean strip malls are stripped bare of life. Stripped of the most basic civic exchanges. Their signs are dimmed. Their windows dark.

This is the city people from the future will find when they come to excavate.

A modern Pompeii. The city frozen in its final rictus of activities before time stood still. On the plywood that covers half of the businesses is the sheet music of a forgotten culture.

Concert posters. Tour dates for an April and May that didn't happen.

Comedy festivals.

Album releases.

Plays, musicals, summer series. Lineups and coming-soons, all a eulogy for a world gone ghost.

Florida crosses Western.

Here is a shuttered bar wrapping the corner—a megalith lounge that used to peddle late-adapted craft cocktails to a hip Korean crowd. Now its windows are boarded over.

Florida pauses. There's graffiti on the wooden panels but not like anything she's seen before—not the braggartly boasts or the gang tags she's passed on her journey west.

The mural starts on the windows on Western and flows around Sixth. It's a painting of tents just like the ones on the street. But unlike those Florida's walked past, the painted ones aren't dirty or tattered. They are vibrant, dynamic, lively. On the mural, the tents look as if they belong to the city, as if they are the city. As if a tent city is a true city in its own right. The tents swarm up the hill to the Hollywood sign. They run past the PCH to the Pacific. They tackle Sunset and devour the La Brea Tar Pits.

It's strange but Florida swears the painted tents are rippling as she passes, like there's a hidden breeze that blows for them alone. She walks the length of the mural twice. Each time it seems to move. If there's a secret on these boards, it's lost on Florida.

She takes a last look at the mural, wondering if this movement is a trick of the light or her addled mind.

Past Western the businesses recede. There are more apartment buildings, a few dog walkers who cross on the diagonal when they see another pedestrian.

There's more green. Less trash. More craftsman homes. More tree canopy.

And then Koreatown is behind her.

And then she's in her own neighborhood.

Florida is exhausted, bone-soul tired. Her feet are rubbed raw in her institutional boots. Her throat is parched again. Her brain is treading water. At least she recognizes her surroundings. At least they anchor her in a world that's spinning away.

Here's the big slate-blue craftsman Cary Grant supposedly owned. Here's the Tudor mansion where the mayor lives. Here's the 1920 Italianate house of the girl Florence dragged to a concert in Inglewood who never spoke to her again.

Here's that famous director's house—the one who made all those TV shows Florence never heard of. There's that aged rock star's house, the guy with drug-related brain damage. There's the house of the female TV mogul. There's the house that people whispered belonged to a Saudi warlord.

There's Ronna's house. Ronna's old house—her parents left after their daughter's death from an *overdose*, and not an allergic reaction, as they claimed. There's the elevated back garden where they had the engagement party. There's the gazebo where they had the bridal shower. There's the pool house where Ronna's father slipped his hand in Florence's shirt. There's the two-story garage where he put a hand down her pants. There's the backhouse where the rest of it happened. Here's the new garden out front, pricey plantings, towering cypress shrubbery and full-growth olive trees so you can no longer see in without craning and spying.

Florida stops. Behind those shrubs she and Ronna planned different futures. They were so bad, bold, and beautiful that they believed they were harnessing the world's dangers and turning them into strengths. They were invincible, adolescent Amazons moving too quickly for life to slow them down. They were outrunning the scars left by boys and men and strangers. They imagined that nothing stuck, nothing mattered, nothing would leave its mark.

How badly was Florence cut? How deeply? Was it a thousand cuts or just one that opened up the gash where Florida began to crawl out? When had she begun to change? When was she unreachable—irretrievable?

Was it before Ronna?

Was it before Renny?

Was it always?

All those hands, those years of hands groping, probing, grabbing, had they eventually ripped her open and pulled her new self out? Or had she done that herself?

And Ronna? She'd tried to plaster over the damage with a husband, a color-coordinated wedding, a forced reentry into the tasteful world she'd scorned.

At least Florida's alive.

In Ronna's old driveway are a kid's bike and a scooter.

Florida moves on.

A block from home she pauses to count backward. Time is proving unreliable. When did she leave Arizona? When was she last in her motel room? When had she last tried calling home?

How many messages had she left for her mother?

Will her mother be home? Will she open the door? Or will she keep Florida at arm's length as always, as if distance and time are all the help Florida ever needed?

Her mother knew. She knew about Ronna's dad. She knew about Florence's father's friend, who'd taken Florence and Ronna to Mexico. She knew about the men from the bars and clubs, the ones who wined and dined Florence when she was too young to drive but drove anyway. And her mother decided that none of it mattered. Maybe she thought her money made Florence invincible. Maybe she thought Florence was tough enough to withstand. Chances were, she didn't think at all.

Or maybe she knew Florence was already Florida and there was nothing she could do about it.

Her mother's house is a massive Tudor on a giant corner

lot—a gaudy spread with a tennis house, a pool house, and a guesthouse, as well as a six-car garage that, taken together, looks like a Hollywood delusion of a quaint English village. A whole mess of Ye Olde and New Age. But it's home and Florida loves and hates it in equal measure.

The house has been in Florida's family for two generations. Her grandparents believed in showing off, not hiding out. There's no gate. No security deterrent. Her mother has continued the tradition, claiming hers is a house for all and she has no reason to hide from the world. Inside a red flashing light tells a different story.

Florida wonders if the private security force residents of the neighborhood use is still on standby—and if so whether the password to summon them or to call them off is the same. She cups her hands over her eyes and stares into the window to the left of the door.

The house is the house—tidy, serene, lonely, and sprawling. So many rooms and outbuildings that if she could access one, she would be able to hide out undetected. She knocks and hears the echo of her fist travel down the hall, then vanish.

She knocks again.

A door. A window. A crack. Some way to access the interior. Florida looks up. Her old room is on the second story in a narrow wing that stretches north, overlooking the pool. There in the closet, just forty or so feet from where she is standing, is the box where she stashed what she needs to restart her life—her old phone, a debit card, and her car keys.

Florida knocks again.

There are landscaped pathways that lead around back to the garden with the pool and tennis courts and several outbuildings. Florida tries the door to the tennis house, the guesthouse, the pool house. All locked.

But the handles rattle with age. With a little effort she could work them loose.

She holds off on the garage, suddenly unwilling to know what has happened to her car. If it's not there, this is a different game, a different story. No freedom. No equity. Nothing.

She glances over her shoulder at the pool. It's skimmed and clean. The flaps on the cabanas are pulled back. The deck chairs are in their places. The cushions are out. The towels rolled in their racks.

She takes two towels from one of the cabanas, then kneels by the pool and dunks her head, opening her eyes and letting the chlorine sting. She scrubs her face and runs her fingers through her hair.

Florida stares from the edge of the pool into the house. What has she missed since she's been gone? More of the same cocktail parties where her mother hoped her grown daughter wouldn't make a scene? Cocktail parties where she was dressed up and trotted out for the aging bachelors? Cocktail parties where she felt the stony gaze of her mother's married friends? Cocktail parties where she was expected to be good and bad, prim and wild, anything and everything?

The sun is overhead. She can see clear through the conservatory. The light shifts. A shadow falls across the window on the far side.

Florida squints as a shape darkens the panes.

The light shifts again.

A woman is looking back the other way.

Florida's breath snags. She freezes, staring back despite herself. Then she ducks out of sight, hitting the pool deck hard.

She holds her breath. Her heart races in her ears. One minute. Then another.

If the woman saw her, she hasn't come running.

Florida crawls round the pool toward the house. She rises up just enough to be able to look through the window.

The woman is still on the far side. She's got her hands cupped around her eyes. Her nose is pressed to the glass of the first window in the conservatory, fogging it. Florida watches the pattern her breath leaves on the pane—a suck and blow of hot air. She's squinting, frowning, like there's something she can't quite figure out.

The woman moves to another window. Florida ducks and crawls, mirroring the stranger. Then she peeks over the sill to peep the spy before the spy peeps her.

The woman is short. She's wearing a blazer and holding something in her hand that catches the light.

She moves on to the next window. Florida moves with her.

Florida watches her tap the glass. Watches her mouth the word "Hello?" She watches the woman squint into the conservatory.

Hello.

There are two more windows before the house ends. And then Florida and the woman will be face-to-face.

Hello.

In, out—a blossom of breath appearing and disappearing on the windows as the woman probes the empty conservatory.

Hello.

The woman knocks on the windowpane and holds up a flashing object to the glass as if she still expects a response from an empty house.

It's a badge. But Florida already knew that.

Hello?

She can feel the woman through the wall. She can feel the intake of her breath against the glass and the reverb of her voice.

Florida is trapped. The only way out is around front. Her only chance is to hide in the garden.

Hello.

She hears footsteps round the end of the house. She lies flat, pressing herself into the wall, waiting for a chance to dash for safety behind the pool house or the guesthouse. The footsteps stop.

Florida crawls to one of the cabanas. Then she slinks behind the pool house.

She closes her eyes.

Dios. Dios did this to her—made her into someone hunted in her own home.

She waits. Ten minutes and no one comes into the pool area. She slips back to the front of the house. She sneaks through the fussy English shrubs, tearing her clothing. She skirts the driveway. When the street is in view, she bursts out of the foliage. Her feet hit the pavement. Each step sounds like thunder as she barrels away.

When she is halfway down the next block, she looks back.

A woman is standing in front of her house. One hand is on her hip, the other shading her eyes as she watches Florida go.

Here is a moment. A decision. A choice between possible equilibrium and near-certain catastrophe.

Here is a moment that Florida will be able to look back on, turn over in her hand until it's worn and shiny like a sea-smoothed rock.

Here is a moment that feels featherlight but over time or perhaps in a minute will have the heft of a millstone.

Here it is. One more second charged with possibility before you make your choice—one more second to imagine there are different outcomes before you toss this moment back or embrace it, grasp it forever and yoke it to you. One more second to choose.

Florida feels the woman's—the cop's—eyes on her.

She should go to her.

She should be Florence.

She should explain and confess her minor transgression to escape the consequences of Dios's major one.

Instead she runs.

South. Through Hancock Park. Past Wilshire. Into the no-man's-land of tidy houses and less tidy streets that leads from her neighborhood to the Mid-City enclaves—Oxford Square, Country Club Park, Dockyard down to the southwestern outskirts of Koreatown.

Florida crosses Crenshaw.

The streets are root-torn, trash-strewn. They ring hollow with the slap-bang of her solitary footfalls.

Sirens wail. Florida stops, trying to figure where the sound is coming from. The sound is closer now—churning, spinning the air with noise, pressure, and panic. No time to waste.

South. Farther south. And then she hits a wall—a literal wall blocking the embankment that leads down to the gully of the 10 freeway.

The sirens are behind her—their noise amplified in the silent city.

There's an overpass crossing the freeway, one of the few pedestrian bridges in Los Angeles—a narrow, caged walkway overgrown with morning glory and pipe vine. It's locked—barred by a gate that's chained and chained again.

Florida looks north and south. There are crossings on either side. But the siren is screaming behind her and there's no time. She scrambles up over the wall and down into a concrete trench—a dump of cans and containers, matted pieces of clothing, shoes, busted strollers, and furniture parts.

She picks herself up. There's a chicken wire gate, double thick, and a broken section of wall. She hoists herself over this and hits the embankment—a blanket of grit and grimed flora.

The embankment runs downhill to the freeway. The growth is dense in places, sparse in others.

Florida inches down the hillside and crouches behind a blue-flowering bush.

She waits for her heart to slow.

She waits for the sirens to fade.

It does. They do. Then it's just her, the ragged intake of her breath, and the whir of an occasional car.

The freeway is nearly empty. Each car seems like an unlawful trespasser—a nefarious alien invader. Florida imagines anyone on the move must be up to no good.

Her entire life in Los Angeles, and this is a wholly new outlook, this hillside by the freeway. It's a raw, vulnerable vantage that makes her aware of her pedestrian handicap.

In her Jag, she'd owned this section of the 10, dismissed it with the pressure of her toe on the accelerator. She'd weaved and merged—easy driving, a straight shot to or from the beach. Such a simple stretch of freeway she could drive it with her eyes closed. In fact, she had, allowing herself the moment of blackness when she was both in control and control could be snatched away.

She'd been on foot on the 10 too. Breakdowns and accidents and escapes from strangers' cars with Ronna. She'd felt the rushing roar and suck of passing traffic. She'd heard it squeal and screech a few feet from where she walked. But she'd never been on the embankment before.

Florida stares between the branches of the bush that shields her from view, across the eight-lane gulf of freeway. The opposite embankment is denser than where she sits—a full covering of rich green vines interrupted by a waterfall of trash dumped from the top of the slope. Car seats, playpens, a mattress, part of a chair, part of another chair, a shopping cart, two strollers, and several garbage bags that spew their guts.

Florida leans back and stretches her legs. She glances west and for the first time notices a pop-up canopy a few feet away, the sort you'd find at a farmer's market or tailgate. The black tarp advertises an energy drink rumored to get kids high.

Beneath the canopy she can see a camp—cookstove, sleeping bag, a tangle of plastic bags and bundles. Above it there's another tent camouflaged by the bracken.

Florida stands, taking in the hints of a community clustered in the ragged bushes—the clothing she now sees is hung to dry on the wall. The bedding draped in a spindly tree. Buckets for water and washing. A cooler and a storage container.

Her eyes move to the freeway, where someone is running, cutting across the sparse traffic from the eastbound lanes and over the divider to the westbound. He's waving his arms and bellowing a war cry. What's he holding? A stick? A crowbar? A jagged piece of metal?

He's locked in on Florida, gesturing wildly as he fords the freeway, making two cars swerve and slow. Then he's on the embankment.

She is a trespasser, an intruder, a threat.

And now she's running again.

This time down the embankment on the diagonal, away from the man who is heading straight for her. Over the bracken and vines, her foot caught on a root, a branch tearing her shirt.

The man is behind her now, still waving his piece of metal, still shouting his incoherent threats.

She's on the freeway, running, her pace mocked by the few passing cars. A couple honk. One offers a ride.

The man on the embankment is no longer yelling. He's defended his turf, leaving Florida to find her own—a patch of her hometown where she can rest and regroup, a small square of Los Angeles to call home for even a few hours.

Her legs ache. Her shins feel splintered and her feet blistered. Florida doubles over, hands on knees, her breath a ragged harmonica gasp.

And then there are sirens. They spur her westward until—

Until she can't go on. Her legs are on fire. Her feet numb.

Florida sits on the guardrail. She knows the exit well—the accident investigation site pull-off just before La Brea—a short service road that curves off the freeway.

She's too exposed, just cooling her heels along the 10. But the AIS will provide shelter and protection in the form of a wall that shades it from the passing traffic. A few more steps, and that is all.

There are no cars in the investigation site. The wall blocks the scant freeway noise. Behind Florida is a dense tangle of trees. Beyond that the city streets of a residential neighborhood, too close to the 10 to be desirable.

Five minutes and Florida's heart rate slows.

She breathes deeply, drinking in the quiet of this alcove off the freeway, the faint rustle of the trees, and the deep, unlikely silence.

And something else—the tang of human excrement. Fresh and specific. Her eyes cut to the side and find a bucket, next to it a torn towel on a branch.

She stands and looks behind her. A few ornaments—ribbons, old holiday decorations, two torn Chinese lanterns, and bits of mirror are hanging from a bush. Deeper into the trees prayer flags dangle from the branches, marking a definite perimeter.

The wind picks up, bringing with it the tinkle of bells and chimes. Florida's skin prickles.

Before she can move on, a man steps from the trees. He's white—with a dark patina of sun and dirt—pushing past middle age. His hair is an uneven, woolly cap of gray and black. A beard has patched his sunken cheeks, sparing the shadowed crevices that crater deep into his skull.

He's dressed in dark, loose-fitting pants that might once have been another color and a shirt that might not have always been a shirt but perhaps a dress or even a blanket. He looks like a scarecrow from some distant farmland.

Florida freezes, trapped and terrified.

"Welcome."

"I'm not—"

"But you are here."

The smell from the bucket is overpowering, but Florida fights hard not to show her disgust. She glances up at the sky, where the sun is the color of shale.

"You're tired." He scratches his beard. "Thirsty, I bet. You shouldn't be running wild along the freeway. The dust and exhaust will dry you out. There's water if you want."

Florida casts her eyes around the camp.

"You don't think it's clean, do you? Well, it's clean. You don't have a smoke on you? You don't have nothing, do you?"

"Nothing."

"Well look at that. You have nothing and I have something and you're hesitating to take it. At least move away from where you're standing. You can't like the smell much. Shame is the one thing I can't afford out here, but I do my best to keep everything tidy. You know what's the first thing they do when they take you to the hospital? They check your feet. Foot health—that's a sign. If you've got rot or fungus they send you home—doesn't matter if you've been shot. Doesn't matter if your intestines are poking out, you're having a heart attack. If you've got the black feet, you best turn right around."

Florida looks down at her boots, afraid of the blistered, raw state of her toes and heels.

"My sense is that you're a long ways from that sort of trouble yet, but I'm also saying that it could be coming. Change is what happens when you're killing time, just putting one day on top of the next. Day one through thirty out here feel like the world's revolving at a fraction of its speed. After that time is like nothing at all."

"I know about time," Florida says.

"Maybe you do and maybe you don't. They say it's stood still these days. But you're moving."

Florida has stepped away from the railing, closer to the trees where the prayer flags whip-snap in the light wind.

"I know better than to ask where you're going."

"Sounds as if you're asking," Florida says.

The man is holding out a dented water bottle. It's in Florida's hand before she can double-think it. The water is warm, but she swigs it in one go.

"You want more?"

She shakes her head, but the man hands her another bottle anyway.

"Drink."

Florida lifts the bottle to her lips. A siren rises, its brutal wail flattening the tinkle of the ornaments and paper flags. She sputters and drops the bottle, spilling water on her boots. She looks side to side—a route, an escape, a next move.

"You think that's for you," the man says.

Florida turns on her heels.

The man's hand is on her wrist—a second skin of hard ridges and scars. "You think that's for you."

She tries to jerk free.

"It's not for you. The sirens are not for you. They're for the sick. They're for the dying and the dead. The sirens are a lamentation. You'll see."

"Ambulances?"

"Fire trucks. Private transports. Anyone who will bear the bodies away to die alone."

"I'm sorry about the water."

"I'm sorry about the dying, but there's nothing we can do about these things. The water has spilled. The dying are nearly dead. The world spins slow and time seems to stop for some. Let me show you something." He ducks back into the trees. "Once I was a gardener up in the hills. I learned about plants from my grandmother in Michigan, who could make the gray earth blossom. I came here and worked some fancy estates—hedgerows, English kitchen gardens. Flowers and landscaping that cost more than any apartment I'd ever lived in. But it's a mean city here, a mean city in a mean world. The fires came. They came hard. I'm not saying I don't know who started them. I'm not saying that at all. They took the whole house. Guesthouse, gardens, and all. They took the people too."

He's carrying a box that he places on the ground. He lifts the lid and reaches inside, retrieving an object that he cradles in his hands. Florida takes it. A skull, small and perfect, somehow preserved or shellacked.

"This is a cat I saved from the fire. The only thing to get out alive. This is just a story. A story within my story. I'm not saying anything by it. I traded the body a few years back. A neighbor wanted it to make a lamp. This I'm not trading. I'm just keeping. A reminder of life. A reminder that those sirens aren't for you."

The man takes the skull back from Florida and nestles it in the box. "We need reminders," he says. "We need reminders of this world come and gone and what might remain when we ourselves are no longer." Florida follows the path of the man's hands as he tucks away his prize. "It's my barter box. My collection box. Alms and alma. You understand? The lamp man gave me a fishing rod and a birdcage for the bones. I traded the fishing rod to a guy who fishes in MacArthur Park. He gave me a carp the size of your arm. I tanned the fish skin and made a wallet. I kept the birdcage but traded the wallet."

Something in the box glints in the dim light.

"You never know what people want. Out here these are not things, these are currency." The man looks Florida up and down. "What have you got?"

Florida pats her pockets, feeling the smooth rectangle of her debit card. "Nothing worth anything." Only currency.

"For the wallet I got a set of walkie-talkies. For those I got a flare gun." The man reaches back into his box. "As I said, alms, alma, and arms. For the flare gun I got this." He pulls out an old .44.

Florida doesn't flinch. Maybe there was an older version of herself—a version of Florence—who might have recoiled as the man held the gun aloft.

"You live outside long enough there's no telling what crosses your path. You sure you don't have anything to trade? This one sits on me like a deadweight. A deadweight of death."

"I have nothing for you," Florida says, holding out her empty hands.

"Nothing begets nothing," the man says. "You've used one?"

"At my dad's in New Mexico. Out in the mountains and at nothing in particular," Florida says. She can hear the bullet crack against the distant mesas. She remembers the gun's weight, her father's phony cowboy hoot and holler as she recoiled from the recoil. Was it in her all along? Was it in her then? Is it here now?

"One day I'll trade it. Something better will come along," the man says. "But for now I hold on to it, not for protection. For protection I have these." He glances at the chimes, dream catchers, and prayer flags swinging from the trees. "I keep it for the same reason I keep my kitty. We are but passing through. Sometimes the world acts upon us, sometimes we act upon it. Either way, the same things remain behind." He takes his box and ducks back inside his camp and emerges with a milk crate and a folding chair missing some of its fabric. "You're welcome to sit a while. They aren't looking for you here."

Close your eyes and there's a chance you are camping.

Close your eyes and the intermittent roar of a car over the limit on the 10 is a fierce wind through a valley.

Close your eyes and the trash blurs, blends, is remade as undiscovered flora.

Close your eyes and for a moment be at peace.

The world is elsewhere.

The world is on pause.

It has stopped hunting and hurting you.

Close your eyes and you hear chickens—you are in the country, on a farm, far away.

But the chickens are there, pecking in the grit, sifting through the man-made grime—bottle tops, ring tops, plastic tabs, rubber rings—for grubs.

"They live over the wall," the man tells Florida. "They have a flock of about twelve with two roosters. Can't help it if they come to this side. Can't help it at all. Figure that makes them half mine. Figure I can help myself to their eggs. Figure from time to time I can do this as well."

He grabs one of the birds and, before Florida can say a word, snaps its neck.

"If only all death came with such swiftness and mercy."

You ate in prison. You ate food you could never have imagined eating—gray and tasteless. Shapeless, soggy, indeterminate. Your stomach growled despite itself.

You ate the steamy institutional takeout dropped at your

motel. You ate what you were given. You ate a cardboard pizza for a day and a half.

You eat this—a chicken killed and carved on the side of a freeway and cooked over a camp stove.

And then you sleep in a stand of trees, protected from the city and its sounds. You sleep with the sirens still searching in the dark, some perhaps for you and others mostly not. You sleep while fireworks light up the night, celebrating nothing.

You sleep while the helicopters take to the sky, patrolling from on high.

You sleep while the coyotes howl and hunt and the chickens flutter in their coop. While the eyes of the night animals pop from the dark like freeway headlights. And the world turns unfamiliar.

LOBOS

Easton rolls up as the woman vanishes, over the slight incline of Rimpau. The landscaped palms sway in the breeze. The sun stays sullen and out of sight.

"That's her?"

"That's somebody," Lobos says. She cracks a mint between her teeth, letting the splinters nick her tongue.

"Why'd you—"

Lobos silences him with a look. One promise she made herself when she transferred downtown, transferred back to homicide from vice: no more men casually laying blame.

How come you never reported your husband before?

How come you let it get so bad at home?

How come you couldn't handle the situation yourself?

How come your head's not in the game? How come you let your husband do that to you?

No more.

"What happened?" Easton asks instead.

"I was . . . I was looking for the wrong person."

"But . . . but wasn't that Florence Baum?" Easton trips over his words, stunned Lobos has admitted an error.

"I expected to find her mother. Not her. If that even was her."

"Like you said, it was someone."

"Someone who got away."

"Don't beat yourself up."

Lobos squares round so she and her partner are face-to-face. "Who says I'm doing that?"

"Easy now. I'm on your side."

"There aren't sides."

"Whatever you say, Lobos." Easton glances down the empty street. "Want to bet that we find her in the next forty-eight?" He holds out his hand.

"This isn't fantasy football."

"Live a little, partner," Easton says, forcing her into the hand-shake. "I'll give you the terms up front. Bottle of whiskey. I bet a woman like you knows her top-shelf booze."

"A woman like me?"

"It's a compliment. Take the bet or not?"

"Fine," Lobos says, withdrawing from her partner's grip.

They caravan back to the station, Easton speeding, Lobos white-knuckling it behind him in her borrowed cruiser. She hates driving, even in the vacant city. She knows better than to let her guard down despite the nonexistent traffic. This is when people turn their kids loose to play ball and ride bikes helter-skelter. This is when dog walkers cross on a zigzag, heedless of lights and cross-walks. This is when cyclists and runners reclaim the streets.

Back at the station they sit in a conference room, the photos from the crime scene in front of them. Lobos has pinned Florence Baum's mug shot to the wall.

"Remind me again, her crime?" Easton asks. "Besides being a pretty rich girl."

"Thought you boys liked pretty rich girls."

"Who said I don't?"

"Last I checked, being rich and pretty isn't a crime," Lobos says.

"It is if you waste it doing dumb stuff."

"You mean criminal stuff. Felony accessory to murder. Turned in her accomplice and pled down."

"Like I said, dumb."

"Seems more serious than dumb to me."

"But she didn't pull the trigger or whatever," Easton says.

"Easton, this woman most likely slit the throat of a man twice her size on a bus filled with other passengers. How come you can't wrap your head around the fact she might be violent?"

"Because look at her. Chances are, yeah, she did it. But until I know for sure, I'm gonna struggle to believe it. You have a problem with that?"

"I do if you're ignoring evidence."

"Chill, Lobos. I'm just giving it to you up front. I like my pretty girls pretty, not violent. Don't get bent out of shape."

Lobos dumps half a canister of Tic Tacs into her mouth so she can't respond. Always jumping down her partner's throat. Always expecting the worst. Always waiting for him to say the wrong thing. Because until Easton that's what always happened.

Lobos looks at the mug shot of Florence Baum. Party girl after long night. California blonde with racoon shadows under her eyes. "I wonder—" she says through a mouthful of mints.

She scatters Baum's case file in front of her. Her mind is on the crime scene photos. The strength and will it must have taken to slash a grown man's throat. The hatred.

She's trained to pretend she doesn't understand the hatred,

couldn't possibly identify with the lawless rage that comes across her desk. Desensitization is the norm. Understanding is off the table.

But she does. Years in vice gave Lobos an education in rage, hatred, retaliation, the emotional and physical scars that goad and spur someone to violence.

Good lord, a few hours in the breakroom with her fellow officers at her old precinct was enough to do it too. It was all she could do to keep her anger in check. How many times?

Occupational hazard—getting raped on the job.

Trick of the trade for a trade of tricks.

Hard to prove he didn't just take what he paid for.

On and on. Until Lobos slammed the coffee carafe down in anger, broke a glass.

Easy, Detective. Hos are criminals too. Don't forget. Don't let your heart bleed all over them.

They goaded her. They loved it when she snapped, even small things like sloshing coffee, tripping over a chair, dropping her cell. Any rise they got out of her was a win.

So Lobos tamped it down. Packed this rage on top of the other. Stored it away until it numbed her and she imagined that she'd stopped caring.

She sifts through the case file.

A fire. The man who was Baum's accomplice had been found guilty of two counts of first-degree murder as a result of arson. She'd been involved. To what degree was unclear. You never know the truth behind a plea.

Arson is a hands-off crime. It's a common juvenile crime—dumb kids not thinking about the deadly havoc a simple match might wreak. Spark a flame, end up with an explosion, even a pile of torched bodies, like nothing at all. Take down a hillside, a town, just like that. Take down half of the fucking California coast without getting your hands dirty. Without hardly lifting a finger.

A women's crime?

Lobos slams down her fist, driving the thought away. No such thing.

Easton jumps back. She hadn't noticed him looking over her shoulder. "Arson, huh?"

"You think she was in on it, don't you?"

"So do you," Easton says. "Because arson."

What if? What if people are better liars than we thought? What if cops like Lobos made as many mistakes as the public thought they did? What if Florence Baum was more than a party girl who got in too deep?

What if, even back then, throughout the high-priced defense and perfect plea deal, she had been a killer all along?

That happens. Lobos knows how quickly things can slip. How one minute you are staunch in your independence, your confidence, your certainty that you are operating aware of the danger around you but not compromised by it. And the next you are in that danger or, in Florence Baum's case, perhaps you *are* that danger.

When do you become the thing you've kept at bay?

When do you become the abused or the abuser?

When do you become someone frightened in your own home, rage-numbed and cowering?

When do you become the person for whom violence is easily within arm's reach?

Trace it back. Every incident is a stepping-stone to this recent incident. Violence is rarely spontaneous. It almost never occurs in a vacuum.

Accessory to second-degree murder after the fact.

What came before?

Speeding tickets. Lots of speeding tickets.

Driving underage and unlicensed.

A few DUIs and disturbing the peace violations.

Before that.

College friends. High school friends.

Reported as missing, possibly abducted.

Further.

Two counts of possession of an illegal substance.

Trace it back.

Cops called to a party at the house in Hancock Park.

It's in there somewhere. Find it. The moment that tipped the balance.

Everyone is a puzzle. The hardest thing to figure—what kind of puzzle you're looking at. A knot? A maze? A game of *Tetris*, with pieces angling to fall into place?

"Lobos?"

Of everyone she's ever worked with—or tried to work with—Easton is the most generous with her long pauses.

"Lobos, your phone."

She's back in the conference room. Back with Florence Baum's mug shot and the crime scene photos—her case file and prison records. Lobos glances at her phone. Two missed calls and three messages.

"Her prison record." She holds up the papers to Easton. "What did you make of it?"

"Your phone," Easton says with a meaningful look at the table, where Lobos's phone is buzzing again.

"Clean, right? Pretty damn clean for someone who does this."

She jabs a finger into a glossy from the bloody crime scene. "Too clean."

"Are you going to take that?"

Lobos glances at the screen. She doesn't recognize the number.

"The other woman," she says, knocking back a mouthful of mints. "What about the other woman?"

Her phone is still buzzing. She lifts it to her ear. "Lobos."

She'd expected official business—the lab with a hit on the other woman, a call from Perryville saying which other prisoner is MIA from the motel.

"Mrs. Lobos?"

"Detective Lobos."

"Yes, Mrs. Lobos. I have your cat."

Lobos tips a waterfall of mints into her mouth. "Who is this?"

"Mr. Franklin. Your cat, I have her."

Lobos's mind is nimble, flying from the immediacy of the present down a warren of past events or future eventualities. But right now, it refuses to leave this room—this present problem scattered in front of her on the conference table—and attend to whatever is summoning her over the phone.

"Mrs. Lobos, your cat, please. You will come home. You are coming? I cannot hold her."

It clicks. "Franklin. The super. My super. Mr. Franklin."

"I told you that."

Lobos is on her feet, gathering her stuff. Then she's out the door.

"Lobos? Everything okay?"

She turns, once more startled by her partner's presence.

"My cat got out."

Her mind—still tangled up in getting a foothold in Florence Baum's past—is lagging behind her feet. She's already on San Pedro before she pulls up short.

Her cat got out.

In her old life, in her old home with her husband and the fragile illusion of stability, the cat wandered frequently, disappearing for days at a time, out of sight and out of mind until she wasn't.

But the apartment—the only way out is through the front door, which Lobos closed.

The day is muffled.

Two more blocks until home.

Lobos has watched this same story unfold too many times to count—victims, family members hoping that the reality hardening in front of them will dissolve. Women claiming: *hedidntmeanit, hereallylovesme, hewontdoitagain.*

There must be a reason. The cat slipped out without her noticing. She left the door unlocked and ajar. Her cleaning person had come unexpected.

Mr. Franklin is standing in the entrance with a cantankerous cat in his arms. "He was outside. He tried to come back."

"She."

"You should be more careful. This neighborhood is no good for cats."

"Did you check the apartment?" Lobos asks.

"No answer. I called you."

The super didn't notice the scratch marks and dents on the lock.

The super didn't notice the rattle of the door handle.

The lock is hanging on by a few pins.

As she opens the door, Lobos is still hoping a different story awaits. Break-ins and property crime are peaking. The pandemic has driven people out of town, making their houses easy pickings for thieves.

Those homes are not apartments on the upper floors of a building in Skid Row.

And yet, Skid Row is simmering with a new tide of desperation. Services scaled back. Shelters taxed to the limit. There's no telling what risks people will take.

Lobos steps into her apartment. The feeling of violation is immediate.

The invasion is personal, not random.

And, of course, the last argument she'd had with her husband had been over the cat.

Her loft isn't ransacked as much as it is rearranged—small instances of minor disturbances that her eye is trained to detect. There are larger ones too. Her papers are shuffled and scattered. Her bedside table drawer is ajar, the pillows and covers indented and wrinkled. The photos and postcards have been removed from the fridge. The glass on her two framed commendations spidered and shattered.

Lobos strips the bed and jams the blankets in the closet.

She puts the broken frames in a drawer.

She texts her housekeeper and begs her to come as soon as she can.

She jumps at a tap at the door. She draws her gun. It's the super. "I'm just checking. You're going to call the police?"

Lobos pulls her badge. "I am the police."

She slams the door. Her cheeks are burning. She is the person to call. She is the person to ask for help.

For months—no, really, for years—her husband had retreated into his office, his only portal to the world, the blue glare of his monitors. Weeks passed without them exchanging a word. Lobos scurrying about the house as noiselessly as she could, worried

about disrupting the silence that she seemed to realize was her
only safety. And then there was the day she slowed as she passed
the office, checking on her husband—just a quick glance.

That was all it had taken to break the dam.

You never fucking talk to me anymore.

You belittle me.

You diminish me.

He'd burst from the office, the accusations flying fast.

*You've done this to me. You've reduced me to a coward in
my own home. You've terrified me. I tremble before you. You've
made me weak. You've made me scared.*

Everything he'd done to her emanating from his mouth as if
she'd been the aggressor.

*Even inside these doors you wield your badge like it gives you
power over me. I know what you're up to. "One wrong step, mis-
ter, and I'll have my friends from work sort you out." You are
a bully. My tormentor. You've brought me to my knees. You've
ruined me.*

If he'd only known that the last thing Lobos would ever do
was let anyone on the force know what went on in her own home.

You've made me nothing.

*You've enslaved me to this house while you work all sorts of
hours, never coming home, never paying attention to me. You've
left me with nothing except my computers. That's all you've left
me with.*

For a few days Lobos believed his accusations, because maybe
it was her fault. Maybe she did work too hard. Maybe after her
husband's accident, the one that led to his being fired, that led
to his social exile, that led to his fealty to his monitors and the
misinformation that dripped from them like poison, maybe it had
really been up to her to make it right. Maybe it had all been her

fault because she hadn't been able to deal with his spiraling depression and slow-burn rage. Maybe.

She had tried. She had cooked dinner. She had ordered takeout. She had bought flowers and suggested an evening out.

Don't pretend.

Don't go through the motions.

Don't act as if you love me when you hate me.

I know why you joined the force. It's been in you since you were little—your defect, your pathology. It's a scar from your childhood. You want to set the record straight. You want to bring men like me down. You're a cop out of vengeance, not responsibility. Right? Right? Am I right? I'm right.

You don't need to tell me.

I'm right and I know when I'm right.

Over and again. Every little thing weaponized against her. Her every move misread, translated into an attack. Everything she did recast by his hurt.

There's no arguing with someone stuck in his own mud, drowning in the quicksand of his own making.

Nothing good enough. Everything poisoned. Every book she read. Every phone call she made. Every movie she chose—a direct condemnation of him and their marriage. Every restaurant, every word out of her mouth—an empty vessel in which to pour his anger, his hate. Everything designed to demonstrate her contempt.

Except. Except for one thing. In the face of it all, in the face of his moods, his paranoia, his rising anger, she was still there. She wasn't leaving. She wasn't running away. She stayed and stayed. While his rage filled the house, while his accusations and insults reached a fever pitch. While he tore her down.

She stayed and it angered him. Even that choice turned against her as a demonstration of her disdain. She stayed until he turned violent. And then she slunk away, tail between her legs. Everything her fault, even when she knew it wasn't.

Lobos takes out her phone again. She knows the protocol—whom she must call to file a report about a B-and-E and a violated restraining order. She knows the stories too—women who failed to report their exes turning up. She knows what happens to these women, how they come across her desk as statistics or in crime scene photos.

She also knows what it feels like not just to lose control but to have control wrested from her. She knows what it's like to seem weak exactly where she must be strong. She knows that she appeared this way to Easton when she'd let the man in the tent knock her down.

She punches in a number. The lab tech picks up on the fourth ring.

"Who is the other woman from the bus?" Lobos barks.

"I was just going to call—"

"I don't care what you were about to do as long as you tell me who she is."

There's a long silence from the tech, long enough that Lobos wonders if she's going to have to enlist Easton to do damage control.

"Diana Diosmary Sandoval."

"*Diosmary*?"

"I think you heard me," the tech says.

FLORIDA

She wakes before dawn. She smells of her surroundings. She smells foreign to herself.

There's birdsong. A predawn chorus from tree to tree singing away the night. It's not just one song, it's many—different cadences and timbres, different pitches and rhythms. Rising and falling, calling and responding, louder, or so it seems, than any city noise.

The man is asleep in his tent under a web of dream catchers and bells.

She slips out slowly, making sure she doesn't hit the chimes or peal the bells. He let her rest undisturbed. There's a mercy there, Florida's sure.

Now in the predawn light—the purpling hour where the dark goes gray—she walks east toward the first slip of sunrise.

A name rises from her subconscious yet again.

Renny.

What happens to people like Renny? The aging drunk. The

long-toothed party boy. The burglar. The petty criminal. The sad gun for hire.

What happens when the bars close? The party ends?

What happens when you get old?

How old would Renny be now? Fifty? Fifty-five? He was older than them when he got tangled up with Ronna and Florence. Too old to be making time with sixteen-year-olds. Too old to do their bidding. Too old to care so much about their lives.

She and Ronna made a pact never to say Renny's name again even though he might say theirs.

Ronna was dead.

Florida was halfway gone.

Maybe Renny was the answer.

How old is she now? Just shy of Renny's age when they met. And although she and Ronna clung to him, they knew he was a dead end, someone who would eventually run his course as they raced on ahead to privileged pastures.

Look at her now, Renny to the max.

The sunrise is a slice of pink at the horizon past downtown. The pale light summons the long arms of the cranes that reach out over the city to grasp at nothing.

The light is fire on the mountains.

It will be swallowed and dampened by the marine layer hovering above the hills and penthouses.

This is the light's first and last gasp.

Summer in Los Angeles can be such a tease.

Back into downtown, to an area of the city that could be mistaken for any city in Central America with its storefronts and stalls, its quinceañera dresses and piñatas and ornate floral displays for the recently dead. The dresses are now bagged in huge Saran-wrapped bundles and the flowers are faded and forgotten.

There's one thing that stands out—a mural like the one of the tents rounding Western. This one showing the backs of protestors with raised fists clamoring for justice. Like the other mural, this one too seems to be in motion—the fists pumping the air, the placards, signs, and banners shaking.

Florida rubs her eyes.

She needs to sleep. She needs to eat. She needs the world to settle and solidify.

There's a small chance that Renny still lives above his family's old sweatshop between the Flower and Fashion Districts, where tents line the street—a city on top of a city.

Men like Renny like it easy, take the easy way out, the path of no resistance. He'll have stayed if he could.

No rules. No guidance. Nothing but a stupid sense of self-preservation. Living on fumes and running on empty is how Renny survives or survived. Hand to mouth. Foot in mouth. Day by day by day. And night by night.

So it's really no surprise to see his last name—Toth—scrawled on the doorbell. The bell clatters into the hollow echo of an empty warehouse.

Florida leans on the bell until her finger aches and then she slumps down. She'll wait here in this doorway. She'll wait. Renny will come. He'll be angry. But he'll help. He'll understand. Lost or worse. Ruined.

First the AIS and now this side street off Olympic. She never knew its name. But here she is, falling away, spinning into something like sleep as the sun struggles to brighten the streets. And

Florida, eyes heavy, heart and mind sluggish and sullen, struggles to see what the sun shows. So she sleeps.

This is a dream but also a memory distorted by two sleepless nights and the passage of time and by the time spent inside, where truth and reality got fragmented.

But still a memory and a dream—real and unreal, in lurid combination.

Florence and Ronna sixteen and flying free. Florence and Ronna just back from Mexico, where Florence's father's friend had taken them, where they learned what their youth and arrogance could do, how much power they had to enchant, entertain, and destroy a man more than three times their age.

They were too young to be blamed, so they must be blameless. That was what they were told.

They were also told not to talk about it.

They were told it was over. And that they were fine.

Leave all of that behind.

So. Florence and Ronna, high on their girl power, sneaking into Les Deux in Hollywood to drink vodka cranberries. Although it's not really sneaking when the club is going after girls just like them.

Florence and Ronna invited back the next day to the manager's office to interview for jobs they don't want. Florence and Ronna excited to see the club in daytime—the illicit after-after-after hours for the hardcore.

The girls lined up at the bar four deep waiting for their turn to interview.

Then after, Florence and Ronna downtown in Renny's apartment after he's learned they don't want the jobs he offered. They don't want anything from him except to feel older and more special and tougher than their classmates, that, and a fistful of drink tickets and a cut to the front of the line every time they show up.

Florence and Ronna and Renny flying on the PCH in Florence's Jag. Florence steering with her feet round a curve near Topanga. Renny grabbing the wheel. Florence driving too fast. Renny telling her to cool it. Ronna urging her on. Renny in thrall to them. Renny in the palms of their hands.

Swimming off someone's private beach in Malibu. The frigid Pacific no match for them.

Dinner at a restaurant even their parents would consider pricey, Florence and Ronna in the private room as Renny's guests—his calling cards at a party where the wines are older than they are.

Then the spring break weekend that turned into a week at Florence's house in Hancock Park, her mother away. Diving into the pool, which was bluer than blue that week. The sun somehow perfectly warm and never hot. Renny hanging with them as night rolled to day and then to night until Les Deux told him not to bother returning to work.

Renny fuming and furious.

Ronna and Florence making it up to him with their parents' credit cards, their parents' cars, their parents' booze and food. With long drives crammed into the Jag.

Ronna and Florence telling Renny their parents' secrets. And their own secrets.

Florence and Ronna competing, each one trying to seem older, wiser, more damaged and daring.

Ronna jumping in the pool fully clothed, drink in hand.

Florence jumping in the pool naked, smoking a cigarette.

Florence telling Ronna that Ronna's father likes to feel Florence up. Florence telling Ronna that her father likes to get Florence alone.

Ronna telling her that she is nothing special. Just another

stupid girl. One of her dad's stupid girls. She's one of many. Many, many, many.

Ronna crying and crying by the pool.

Florence backpedaling but it's too late. Florence hiding the fact that it's gone a little further than she has admitted to her best friend. That she maybe encouraged it. Because maybe she kinda liked having that power over her friend, being the one who her friend's dad liked.

Except she wasn't *the one*. She was one of many.

Then Ronna cold as a glacier.

And then Florence convincing Ronna that her dad betrayed them both. That he's an asshole. More than that. A perverted one. A cheater and a snake. A danger to them both.

And Ronna agreeing with Florence. And Renny agreeing with them both. Anything to keep the party going.

But there was a chill between the girls that didn't disappear the rest of that week.

Day into night. Night into day. Until the final weekend, when Renny slunk off to the loft above the sweatshop. And Ronna went home a few blocks away, where her parents hadn't missed her. And Florence driving and driving all night, afraid to be alone at home. Afraid of the empty house. Driving deep into the Inland Empire and then south toward the industrial Port of Long Beach. Driving until she came up with a plan to win them all back.

And then a week later, Ronna's dad assaulted in the street near his office. Deaf in one ear, traumatized, his brain permanently injured.

Ronna, who hadn't spoken to Florence since their weeklong party, called her and said one word: Renny. Florence already knew.

———

The memory hurts like a gut punch. A searing, pulsing pain that shocks Florida awake.

Here's where the dream ends and the beating begins.

Her assailant is too close for Florida to gauge the details, only that she's using some kind of stick to ram into Florida's stomach.

Bitchgetoutmyspot.

Bitchgetoutmyspot.

Bitchgetoutmyspot.

Inside, the beatings had a strange temperance and a quickness. A swift lesson that endured until the guards arrived to break up the fight. A lesson whose message was the painful meaning and not an eternal finality.

Bitchgetoutmymotherfuckingspot.

This woman will not stop until Florida moves or dies.

Florida tries to stand. But a blow from the stick clips her forehead, knocking her back. The pain is a bright explosion—a spark shower raining behind her eyelids. Blood trickles into her eyes.

Her assailant is a whirlwind, a dervish coming at her from all sides, driving into her flanks and back—the stick bouncing off Florida's vertebra with a crack like a fire-split log.

Florida curls into a ball, her hands cupped over her ears, her head tucked, part defensive, part battering ram. With one burst of strength, she plows forward, knocking the woman aside.

She's rolling down the filthy sidewalk, her bruised, battered insides on fire with each revolution. She bounces off the curb into the street and comes to a rest, her entire body a nimbus of hurt.

She lifts her head. Her attacker has settled herself in the doorway where Florida had waited for Renny. She's turning something over in her hand, holding it up to the light like a jewel. Florida's debit card courtesy of the Arizona DOC.

———

Like an animal, crouching, cowering, fetid, and feral, Florida slinks across the street, curls into a doorway, and watches.

The woman's skin is a color that Florida cannot identify. Weathered by the wind and sun. Tanned by years of dirt and smoke. Her skin is more animal hide than human. Her hair is the absence of color—a canvas for the ambient splatter of life outside.

But she is regal and poised. She carries herself with the confidence of a conqueror.

She has arranged four enormous plastic bags bound together with tape and twine at her feet. She places the debit card on top of one of them. A temptation and a challenge. The stick she beat Florida with lies to her side.

She takes out a stack of newspaper and spreads the pages wide, marking her turf. She begins to unpack her bags, unfurling a blanket, arranging knickknacks, turning her body into the focal point of a scavenged shrine.

Florida only has eyes for the debit card, its small hologram glinting faintly in the gray sky.

She feels her bruised abdomen, her battered flanks and hips. The bruises will blossom—the color of a storm along the horizon. Her eyelashes are sticky with blood. She wipes her forehead, feeling the rough, damp wound.

Her injuries can wait. For now she must watch her assailant. She watches the woman slip the debit card into a pocket. Florida knows where to search. She knows something else. She knows this woman will soon sleep. Because she's fumbling in her pockets, finding a syringe, prepping to inject herself to take the edge off whatever put the fire in her veins and drove her to beat Florida.

The sun is up now. Those who move through the city have begun their journey, making their slow revolutions on the streets.

Florida's bruised stomach pulses. Her hip bones ache. Her forehead throbs.

The streets will settle soon. The day will fade. Before dark, she will make her move, reclaim what is hers. That debit card—the only thing tethering her to the straight world.

For now she will wait. The day will pass. She's an expert at holding a vigil over each passing second until they are all gone.

KACE

The rumors are like wildfire. All that breath being passed from cell to cell. All those germs. A story in the wind.

Dios and Florida on the run.

Dios and Florida guilty of murder.

Dios and Florida killed an officer of the law.

Dios and Florida on a revenge spree.

Dios and fucking Florida—their names whispered between the coughing. Their names inside the coughing. Their names transmitting the disease up and down the rows.

Marta tells me not to say a thing. Not to get involved. Not to speak my piece. Like I need her advice.

I know better than to pass along intel I got from Tina's ghost. I know how that will sound.

And yet—Tina's story bears telling.

Tina was the keeper of Florida's truth and she paid the price.

Sometimes I hear them—those dead desert hippies Florida

torched. It took me a while to figure out who they were because Florida never owned up to that crime. They were angry, those dudes. They were unclaimed, at least by Florida. They wanted their due.

It was Tina who finally explained them to me. Tina who told me Florida had lit the match that ignited the bomb that lit those motherfuckers up. She'd been flying high, but she wanted revenge all the same.

You see, more revenge. A pattern. But Marta told me not to tell.

Also, you see, not like Tina's story at all. Florida straight-up remembered what she did and she stone-cold lied about it. That shit just isn't right.

Own it. That's the one law. The one command of inside. Own it and you can keep on. But Florida—she kept it at arm's length.

Except to Tina. She told Tina one night not long after she came inside. One night she was hungry for human connection, hoping to be as hard as the other women.

Problem was—Tina couldn't talk shit about her crime because she couldn't remember shit about her crime. Doesn't mean she pretended she didn't do it. Not like Florida.

And now, I've got the warden up in here asking questions about a CO named Reyes. New kid. Got killed on the outside.

I don't know shit about Reyes. Never even heard his name. And I don't fucking care what happened to him.

You know him, Marta says. *Think.*

I close my eyes, trying to picture a Reyes.

Like Tina, I come up blank.

———

But the warden won't let it drop. And I'm hearing him, but really I'm practicing meditating on my inner peace. I'm tripping on some soothing ocean vibes, feeling the sand between my toes and tasting the salt water. I'm pretending to drink the fresh air instead of this diseased shit that's fixing to kill me one way or the other. I'm doing the thing they told me, keeping my cool, hoping for a better world, a better me, even if I know there is only one me. And now this nonsense.

Not your fucking business, Marta says. *They made their own beds. All of them.*

Marta's got her hand on my throat when they start asking me about Dios and Florida. *Sandoval* and *Baum.*

They keep wanting to know if those two had something cooking.

They keep wanting to know if I knew their plans.

"I don't know shit," I say. "I don't know fuck-all."

"Because if they were planning something and you didn't tell us, that makes you an accessory," they tell me.

"Get the fuck out of my cell. Get the fuck away from me. You're going to kill me coming so close. You're going to kill me with your poisoned outside air."

I could straight-up murder that man with his questions, his outside-world problems. I could hammer his face into oblivion. I could . . . I could . . . I could.

They light such a fire under me, I worry I'm going to go up in smoke.

I'm rage hot in the hellscape of the yard.

My head is roaring with all the voices calling at once.

The women clear as I come, even slipping out of the shadows to make way for me.

The fuck is wrong with you, Marta says.

There will be no release. No reprieve. We are yoked to our fucking path eternal. Our path and our past.

There's no helping it.

There's no overcoming. There's no straight and narrow, only this motherfucking stranglehold that's got us tight.

Even those fancy-ass bitches and their goddamn tree.

All their big talk and what do you know? The only thing that matters is that we are given our time in this world, yet some of us choose to run in a single spot.

And that's sometimes the only thing there is to do.

LOBOS

Diana Diosmary Sandoval. Aggravated assault. Two-year sentence.

Smart. Educated (not the same thing). Former cellmate of Florence Baum.

No known Los Angeles connections as far as her mother or parole officer knew. Father not in the picture, now or ever.

No contact with her former employer.

No social media presence.

No trace.

There's something coded in the way the prison staff talks about Sandoval. The way they drop the words "smart" and "educated" like they have special meaning. As if prisoners are expected to be a certain way and Sandoval was not that.

"What do you mean, 'smart'?" Lobos asks the warden when he finally gets on the line.

"What do you mean, what do I mean? You've never heard the word?"

"Not the way you say it—like it's a crime."

"Maybe it is," the warden says.

Lobos stares at her phone after the warden has disconnected. *Smart*: like it's something to fear.

"Easton." Lobos summons her partner by shaking her mint canister. "What do you think when someone tells you a woman is smart?"

"That I don't want to date her."

"Why?"

"She's intimidating. She's work."

"What else?"

Easton rubs his round chin. "There's something wrong with her."

Lobos knocks back the mints and cracks a couple in her molars. "Would you say I'm smart?"

"Driven."

"That also sounds bad."

"Listen, I'm just telling you. And you are. And you've got issues."

"Like?"

"Like I don't know. But I know you do."

Issues. Problems. Ideas. Vague words men—her husband—use to drag her down. To make her question her thinking and to belittle her thoughts.

"I don't have *issues*," Lobos says.

"Well something's eating you," Easton replies. "Something's got you peeking in tents and scanning the streets. I got my eye on you."

His tone is almost playful.

"Mind your own business, Easton."

Easton's jaw tightens, then relaxes. "Jesus, Lobos, all I'm really saying is if you want my help, I'm here."

Where does the anger come from that rises from her toes to her fingertips, that makes her want to bang her keyboard, spit her mints, spill her coffee? Where does it hide the rest of the time?

"Lobos?"

Sometimes she can still feel that hand around her throat. And always, her own powerlessness to do anything about it. That's the worse hurt.

"The only help I need is with this." Lobos points at Diana Diosmary Sandoval's photo on her computer.

Black hair. Green eyes. High forehead. Part Latina if you look closely, but easy enough to miss.

"Pretty," Easton says. "Very. That's what I would have said instead of smart. You wouldn't think, would you, that she could kill a man the way she did?"

"Why not?" Lobos asks.

"It's just hard to imagine."

"Can you imagine someone else doing it?"

Easton takes the time to think. "You know, I really can't. Not until I have to."

Trace it back. But with Sandoval it's a dead end. No record before her assault charge. Lobos pulls the case file.

Defended herself against a colleague who was behaving aggressively, accidentally blinding him with a cell phone. Seems cut-and-dried—conventional. A woman fighting back and still serving time. Prosecuted to the fullest by a high-powered lawyer paid for by the vic's affluent mother. A story Lobos has heard time and again. The inciting incident spelled out for her on the page.

Follow it back until you bang your head on another dead end. Diana Diosmary Sandoval's record was clean until the moment two years ago when it wasn't.

Florence Baum is a different story. There are marks and smudges all over the place. Little transgressions. Larger stories in which she was often the defendant, not the accused.

Taken across the border as a minor.

The passenger in a drunk-driving accident where the driver was charged with possession.

There has to be something somewhere that shows how she got to today. Because there's always an incident that tips the balance, a point of no return, the final moment that makes you who you are.

A coffee cup thrown at your head.

Insults as you pass down the hall.

Your husband's hand around your throat.

Another instance of violence excused. And another—the one that turns you into a victim. It's there. For victims and criminals alike.

Ronna. Ronna Deventer. Her name linked to Florence's several times. Also brought across the border. Also charged with possession and let go. Another rich girl generating her own problems.

Deceased. Overdose six years ago.

Also with a childhood home in Hancock Park. *Deventer*. There's something there too. Jan Deventer. Lobos searches for the name. A newspaper article.

CLUB PROMOTER ARRESTED IN NEAR-FATAL ASSAULT OF HOLLYWOOD MEGA-AGENT JAN DEVENTER

And then buried on a back page: *Charges dropped when Renny Toth was alibied by a friend of Deventer's daughter, Florence Baum.*

You see. It's there. Something that didn't make it into Florence Baum's file, something either ignored, overlooked, or suppressed.

That fire, that accessory-after-the-fact charge, wasn't her first turn at the rodeo.

She's been at this for a while now.

At the sight of Lobos standing up and gathering her things, Easton bounds to her side. "You don't need to come."

"I'm coming."

Lobos gives him a look—*don't complain if this is a timewaster*.

But really, she wants to go alone. Renny Toth's address is on the far side of Skid Row at the edge of the Flower District, which gives her blocks to cover in her search for her husband. Find him before he finds her, before he can surprise her again. Find him, and then what?

Whatever it is, she doesn't need Easton along to see.

"I won't complain," he says.

"I didn't say anything," Lobos replies.

Where are you? Where are you among these tents and shanties, under these tarps and along these sidewalks? In front of these murals. That mural—the one that seems to be alive?

She's a master tracer: credit cards, bank accounts, phones. He's either lost them or given them up. Friends, relatives—she's checked and rechecked. Nothing.

He's not there.

Which leaves here or somewhere like here.

"Lobos?"

"What?"

"You haven't said a single word."

"Maybe I've got nothing to say."

"You could say where we are going."

Lobos checks the street sign. How far have they come from the station? Seven blocks at least. "Renny Toth," she says. "Seems like he was a nightclub manager who got tangled up with Florence Baum when she was a teenager."

"And?"

"I don't know the and."

She can't figure it. Not yet. But there's something there. Or maybe there isn't. Maybe this is just another excuse to pace the streets, her eyes bouncing from tent to tent, scanning, scouring, trying to figure which ones might be worth revisiting without Easton. Faces, some masked, others bare. Some hyped, some drugged, some just waiting out the day.

"Lobos?"

He can't be calling her out for another long silence already.

"You still not going to tell me who you're looking for?"

"I told you. Renny Toth."

"I mean in the tents," Easton says.

"I'm just looking." Lobos's eyes bounce along the dirty tarps. Faces. Weathered and worn. Defiant and proud. Lost and diminished.

Will her husband join their ranks? Will he become part of this world instead of an interloper? Will she cease to recognize him? When will he reach his point of no return?

"And you think this guy Toth knows where Baum is?"

"I don't know what he knows," Lobos says.

"Okay, okay," Easton says, holding up a hand. "You told me I didn't have to come."

"I'm just trying to paint a brighter picture of who we're after."

Lobos scans the street, tent after tent, face after face. Fewer faces here. Fewer tents. More space in between.

She knows this street, this block.

"Let's go."

"We are going," Easton replies.

Here is where she nearly kicked the man who'd fallen to the ground. He could be any one of the bodies sleeping off the day, strewn and scattered on the sidewalk.

"Let's go faster."

If only it were that simple to outdistance yourself.

They pass through the Flower District, where open stores are making only funeral wreaths. These blocks would normally be gridlocked with shoppers, cars, and small carts selling hot dogs and tacos to the vendors and their customers. Today the only people are those who sleep outside the empty storefronts.

They stand across from Renny Toth's building—a small, blue two-story warehouse between two flower wholesalers.

"Let's do this," Easton says, "whatever this is."

As they step into the street, Lobos's shoe snags on something she'd overlooked, a shape, a person huddled on the curb.

She stumbles but catches herself before she falls, now face-to-face with her human obstacle.

It's a young woman—younger than the average undomiciled—her dirty face smeared with dried blood, her eyes red.

She holds Lobos's gaze as if she's challenging her, daring her. And then she lowers her head and hides it in her folded arms.

Lobos hesitates, her hand on her phone, wondering if she should call this in. But why this one and not the hundreds of other people she passed on her way here? "Are you okay?"

A slight nod in response. Nothing more.

Easton is waiting across the street. Lobos hurries to join him.

A woman is blocking the doorway to Renny Toth's building. She lies surrounded by a mess of small objects strewn about like religious artifacts, her prostrate form so deep in narcotic slumber that she doesn't move as Lobos and Easton step over her. Easton finds the bell and lays into it.

But Lobos's mind is no longer here. She's in the squad room, back in front of Florence Baum's file.

Florence Baum.

She spins around. The woman who'd been sitting on the curb is gone.

"Easton!"

Lobos yanks his hand from the bell. She doesn't wait for him to follow as she charges back across the street. She dashes south, checks up and down the wide expanse of Olympic, then doubles back. She runs east. Makes a tour of the entire block, then backtracks, racing past Easton a second time. He grabs her arm as she passes, slows her to a halt.

"What the fuck?"

"It was her. That was Florence Baum sitting on the curb."

Lobos pounds a fist into her thigh. All that time looking for a different face has dulled her senses and taken her mind off the job. And who's fucking fault is that? Her husband still messing with her head, still making her dull and slow.

"Give yourself credit. I didn't mark her at all."

Lobos tips the remainder of her mints into her mouth, cracks them so hard she worries she's split a molar. "Let's go."

Once more they step over the woman in Renny Toth's doorway. Her trinkets and knickknacks are arranged in some sort of symbolic order. She's bedded down on an assortment of overstuffed plastic bags and newspaper.

Easton presses the bell. "No answer a few minutes ago."

"Try again."

"If he's not here, he's not here. All this ringing isn't going to change that, Lobos."

Lobos crouches, close to the woman's face. Her skin is a network of dirt and deep scars. A curtain of greasy gray hair covers her eyes. Lobos puts a hand on the woman's shoulder.

"LAPD, wake up."

"Dead to the world," Easton says.

"LAPD."

The woman's eyes flutter open—yellow whites and dilated irises. Then she nods off again.

"Wake up," Lobos says, lifting her to sitting.

Easton shuffles in place. "What do you think she's got for us?"

Lobos slaps the woman's cheeks lightly. "I said wake up or I'll order you to move on."

The woman opens her eyes, brushes her hair away. "I've got every right . . . you don't have any right."

Lobos flashes her badge. "I have every right and then some. What's your name?"

"Empress Amber."

"This your spot, Empress Amber?"

"You can call me Indira."

"Okay, Indira. You live here? You know the man who lives inside?"

"He calls me Goddess India."

"Goddess, you know him or not?" Easton says.

"He's not here. That's why I guard the place for him. He needs me. I'm his watchdog. I am all the eyes of the night. I am Durga. I am the all-seeing Argus."

"That's why you're sleeping?" Easton asks.

"They come in the night," India says. "They come with the moon. So I sleep with the sun."

"And where is Renny Toth?" Lobos says.

"He brings me food when he comes back. He comes when he knows I'm hungry."

"When's that?" Easton asks.

"Today. Tomorrow. I don't know the days."

Lobos stands. "How long has he been gone?"

"Two nights. There was the first night with the raccoon. Then there was the night with the intruder. You see why he needs me here. The raccoon I scared with my voice. He heard the power of my call and knew that this was not his place. The woman I took care of with my stick." She holds up a large wooden stick with a taped handle.

Lobos is down by the woman's side again. "What woman?"

"This is his house but this is my spot," India says. "I thought I could leave for a moment, but when I returned she was in my spot. She was asleep in my place. This is where I build a shrine to myself. This is where I make myself queen."

"I thought it was empress," Easton says.

Lobos shoots him a warning look. "Who was this woman?"

"The enemy. The one in my spot. But I defended my place. I fought for what's mine." She raises the stick, brandishing it like a weapon. Lobos places a hand on the wood, lowering it. "I beat her and took my place. But she'll be back."

"Why?" Lobos asks.

"I have something of hers."

"I'll take that." Lobos holds out her hand.

The woman fumbles in her pocket. "It's my prize, you know."

"We don't have time for any law-of-the-streets shit," Easton says. "Whatever you stole from this woman—"

"My prize," India says, and drops a bank card into Lobos's hand.

Lobos flips it over. JPay Progress Mastercard. "DOC issue,"

she says, holding it out to Easton. She presses her finger onto the plastic: *Florence Baum.*

"I won it," India says.

"Tell you what," Lobos replies, pulling out one of her business cards. "I'll give you one of mine. If she comes back, you can pass it along. Tell her I have her cash card."

India stares at the card. "Lobos," she says. "Are you the lone wolf?"

"Just a cop," Lobos replies.

Whose voice do you hear in your head? Who is speaking in your ear? Through whose eyes do you see?

Don't look.

Don't check.

Don't glance or even wonder. Keep your head in the game at hand, away from those tents. *Who is in there?*

On the way back to the station, Lobos trains her eyes ahead, her ears tuned to whatever Easton is saying about the probability of Florence Baum turning up at Central PD for her debit card. Slim to none is Easton's prediction.

"You never know."

"Never know what?" Easton asks. "I know criminals don't just present at the precinct. If they did, we'd be out of work. Anyway, you owe me."

"Owe?"

"Told you we'd find Baum within forty-eight."

"Jesus, Easton. For real?"

"Just sayin'. We found her."

"No fucking way. Not paying."

Ticky. Ticky. Ticky.

"You got a rattlesnake in there, Lobos?"

She holds out the mint canister and shakes it once hard. "Want one?"

"I couldn't deprive you."

"I'll pay you when we catch her."

Twice she's been face-to-face with Baum and twice she's let her slip. What are the odds in this sprawl of a city—a city perfect for anonymity and concealment—that Lobos would corner her quarry and let her slip?

Perhaps Easton would care to bet? *Slim to none.*

"You like a good bet, Easton."

"You know it."

"What's your racket?"

"The Super Bowl, sometimes March Madness. Football poker."

"The fuck is that?"

"An excuse to drink."

Lobos stops walking. "You want to wager on Baum turning up?"

"That's a sucker's bet."

"Take it or leave it." She holds out her hand. "Double the whiskey."

"You just want to get me drunk, don't you?"

"No, I want to win," Lobos says.

"A couple of days ago you thought we'd let her slip and now you think she's going to come calling. That's a fool's bet on your part."

"Let me worry about my part."

They shake.

How many more chances will she get with Baum?

Chances. Even her thinking isn't her own. Chances are out of her control. Opportunities are her own making.

"She'll come or we'll find her. You were right—in fewer than forty-eight hours we've sighted her twice."

"I'm not saying we won't get her. I'm saying she won't come to us," Easton says.

"We'll see."

Skid Row is sleeping, stirring, stumbling. Each tent a temptation for Lobos. Instead, she narrows her mind to the case at hand, trying to put blinders to her surroundings.

"Where would you go?"

"How's that?"

"If you had nowhere to go? Like Baum."

"Everyone has somewhere," Easton says.

"That's not true," Lobos says. "Look around."

"This is where they go. This is their home. They have their spots, either chosen or accidental. It's not all random down here. You know that."

"True," Lobos says.

"It's a decision. Along the freeway. Underneath an overpass. In a community or solo. On Skid Row or adjacent. There's a magnet for everyone, something that draws them to a place. Maybe you think you're going to be that magnet with that debit card but I'm guessing there's a stronger one somewhere else."

Lobos stops walking in the middle of Seventh and stares at her partner.

"What?" Easton asks.

He's right. These tents, they're beside the point. She is the magnet. Her husband will come for her. He already has.

"Lobos?"

She looks up and down the street at the clustered tents. It's people, not places who exert the pull.

No cars. No one passing through downtown on their way to

somewhere better. The only movement is in the air. The choppers circling and circling.

"But what about the other one—Sandoval?" Lobos says. "What's her magnet?"

"Beats me." Easton puts a hand on her back, trying to usher her out of the street. But his caution is unnecessary. Lobos could pitch a tent right here in the middle of Seventh and sleep soundly.

"Well, there's some reason she broke parole and got on that bus. Something pulling her toward Los Angeles."

"Lobos, get out of the street."

It's hitting her all at once. A cascade of thoughts too hard and fast to sort them from one another. "They're not together, Baum and Sandoval."

"Yeah, so? We know."

"Why?"

"Lovers' quarrel?"

"Come on, Easton. Think. They boarded the bus separately. They got off separately."

"Maybe they just want to make our job harder," Easton says. "Them deciding to split up. Two trails. Two chases. Double trouble."

"Unless . . ."

Lobos tips her mint canister into her mouth. She rattles the candies between her teeth. Then closes her eyes, her head tilted toward the gloomy sky.

"Are you gonna get out of the street or what?"

She waves Easton away, waves away the street, the sounds, and the accompanying smells. There is no street now. Instead, Lobos is in Chandler, waiting for the bus. Baum already on board. Sandoval coming after—a last-minute passenger before departure. Then Baum exiting first. A stop early. Forty miles from her destination.

Why would she jump parole, risk a trip to LA, but bail before her destination?

Why would Sandoval follow?

Unless . . . Here it is.

Sandoval is pursuing Baum. Baum is running from Sandoval. Baum gets on the bus first. Sandoval follows. Baum exits almost as soon as she can. Sandoval maintains her chase.

Baum is the magnet. Sandoval the magnetized.

Lobos opens her eyes. "Why would Baum run from Sandoval?"

"Scared."

"Right. Exactly. Scared." Lobos exhales. "We're looking for the wrong woman. We need Sandoval."

"You're the one who said she's got no anchor here."

"She's got Baum. She's chasing Baum."

The city vanishes as Lobos hurries to the station. Easton is a torrent of questions. How and where and why.

"Trace it back," Lobos says.

"What's that mean?"

"There's a moment, a point of connection, something in their shared history that leads them to the present. Some story of Sandoval and Baum. Something that links them and draws them together."

"And what is that, exactly?"

"Damnit. Shit." How long has her mind been out of the game, her eye off the ball? Two perps and she'd written one off because it was more convenient to do so. Easier to focus on Baum—her LA story, her good-girl-gone-wild tale, a woman who became exactly what she was not expected to be. A story that so perfectly suited her own.

"I fucked up."

"We're just figuring this thing out."

Just. Just now. Finally in this game instead of in her own head.

And whose fault is that? His—her husband's? Or hers?

Time to stop blaming him for her mistakes.

"Lobos, slow down."

She's hurrying. The streets blur. The tents slip past, a moving train of tattered, torn fabric passing in the other direction.

"Lobos."

If she keeps moving, she can accelerate past this place and back into the case, free from the distraction her husband has proved. These streets are their streets, not his streets, not a place to search for him.

She stops walking a block from the station and whirls around so she's facing Easton, her eyes level with his chest. "Listen, Easton. You're right. I was looking for someone in the tents."

"Was?"

"It doesn't matter who."

"You sure?"

"If I'm telling you, I'm sure. We have work to do."

It's like an apparition the way he is standing there. Right there on the steps of the station. Her workplace.

Lobos is two feet away before she notices.

In her mind—in the place between hope and despair—she imagines there's a chance that he might not actually be there at all. Like she could blink him away or shake him gone with a flick of her head. Make the world settle back into reality.

"Hello, Detective."

The tricks the mind can play—the fear it can conjure in three goddamn dimensions.

"I said, hello, *Detective Perry*."

No regard that she dropped his name. No regard for the restraining order. No regard for her place of work. Her *line* of work. Because she and Easton and the scores of other cops a few feet away can take him down, bust his ass, read him his rights, and lock him away.

"I said—" Lobos's husband reaches for her arm as she passes on the steps.

She jerks away before he can grab her.

"I said—"

"I think she heard you," Easton says. "Whoever the fuck you are."

"You don't know who I am? Essie, didn't you tell this man who I am?"

"Whoever the fuck you are, you back off these steps," Easton says. "Whoever—"

Lobos is already inside, the heavy station door blocking the rest of the exchange.

FLORIDA

How long must she run? How far? This time up Olympic, into the stopped heart of downtown. That's just for now. Later she will have to keep going, keep ahead of the woman on her tail.

Her footfalls echo on the quiet streets, her speed rustling their stillness. This is how it's been for the last twenty-four hours—to move she must expose herself in the dormant city. There is no end in sight, no goal, no purpose, no harbor or haven. Just more running, more hiding. More surviving.

It's funny when you think about it. Dios, who had always wanted Florida to become the predator, has made her prey.

She turns on Broadway and shelters under the marquee of a century-old theater reborn as a hip music venue before being shuttered.

About three hundred and fifty on her debit card. In the before times that would have been a fancy dress, a pair of cab-to-curb shoes, two nights in Las Vegas, one night in Malibu, a night of taxis and drinks and food and drugs. A spa treatment. A cut and color.

Now it is everything. Safety. Shelter. A bus ride back to Arizona. Because that is the only sane thing to do—to return on her own before she is returned and stripped of what few freedoms remain.

But first, that debit card.

Her sides ache. The bruise on her stomach has blossomed into an inkblot that covers her abdomen. The cut on her head beats a one-two rhythm.

She leans back against the ticket booth and stares at the street, where discarded masks and gloves swirl like tumbleweed.

The facades are boarded with plywood. The plywood is covered with graffiti.

Then, like an apparition from a different apocalypse, an army tank rolls by, its caterpillar tread grinding the asphalt, flattening the trash, and scattering dirt and dust. The soldiers clearly bored patrolling a city where nothing's doing.

But this is another signal not to rest. When the tank recedes to the north, Florida gets to her feet once more, plunging south.

This is what happens to other people, right? Battered, bruised, hunted, haunted, and hiding. This is not what happens to Florence Baum.

But now, digging through a dumpster at the northern edge of South Central for something sharp. And finding a scrap of sheet metal.

Those women inside, women like Dios, and rougher, tougher customers making shivs and blades out of everyday items. Every dustpan, hot pot, pencil a potential weapon. Every prisoner a target. That was someone else's violent lockup. Now it is Florida's outside.

Her hands probe the junk. She slices the meat of her palm.

What's one more injury? Her body, a bloody, bruised map of each mistake since she got on that bus.

A piece of metal. Some twine. A stick. Now she has the makings of a weapon.

Florida glances in the direction of downtown, where helicopters have taken to the sky, vultures circling the carrion city.

She begins to wrap the stick with the twine, giving herself something solid to grip. Then she threads the string through a hole in the sheet metal, lashing it into place. She finishes and swings her blade through the air, slashing at nothing. The metal whines and whips.

Now it is time to wait for the slow crawl of night. Time to slither and slink back toward the Flower District. Time to make a quick survey of Renny's block. Time to check for the short woman in the suit. Time to double-check that her assailant is still crashed out on the doorstep.

The sky is a wash of gray. The sun, never having shown itself, begins to set.

The streets are a slow stir, a pre-night crawl.

More choppers take to the air, anticipating a disturbance their presence is likely to summon.

Hunger has made Florida sharp, alert to the task at hand. The woman sleeps in her doorway at the center of her miscellany.

Florida touches her makeshift blade, wondering how it will feel when it slices skin, when it separates flesh from flesh, when it hits bone.

Is this what Dios thought about before she drove that fork into Mel-Mel's cheek, or was she more taken by the emotional thrill?

Will it be like sawing into an overcooked steak or slicing open a package? How fast will the blood come?

The woman on the doorstep stirs.

There is no more time to waste.

Florida crosses the street and pounces, her knee on the woman's back, her blade to her cheek.

"Give it back."

She feels the skin's momentary resistance. But then the woman's cheek opens like a peach releasing warm juice. The woman howls.

A warm trickle of blood wets Florida's finger. She stares at the crescent she's carved with her blade. How easy it was to rip that hide.

The woman puts her hand to her face. It's a shallow wound, but the blood comes fast.

"Murderess. Temptress of the dark and the devil." She fixes her yellowed stare on Florida, eyes wild with pain and drug-dulled. "Killer," she spits.

Florida lunges at her with the blade, but the woman curls up and backs deeper into the doorway, sheltering from the attack. Florida reaches for her arm, dragging her forward to accept her beating. "Coward." She slashes at the woman with the blade again, opening a gash on her forearm where blood streams out, mixing with the rivulets of dirt caked onto her skin.

"How dare you try to kill the queen. How dare you kill the empress. You brought the universe to its feet. You brought down the stars."

"Shut the fuck up," Florida says. "Just give me what's mine."

"There's nothing in this world that belongs to any one of us alone."

Florida drops to her knees, straddling the woman, her blade to the woman's throat. "I don't have time for that shit. Give me my card."

"What's mine is won in fairness. What's mine has been given," the woman croaks.

"No one gave you anything."

"The universe gave it to me."

"Fuck the universe."

Florida presses the blade into the woman's neck. She feels the skin's weak resistance once more. She feels the taut sinew and cord. She feels the inches, millimeters between life and death. The power makes her palms itch. "Give it to me."

"Thief," the woman says. She thrashes side to side. The blade cuts a streak across her neck, a lopsided smile. It's another superficial wound, but still Florida recoils at the blood that trickles toward her victim's clavicle.

"Thief," the woman repeats, getting to her knees, lunging for Florida like a wounded bear.

"What the fuck did I steal from you?"

The woman waves her hands wildly, blood spattering the air from her fresh wounds. "This. This. All of this. You stole my air."

"Give me the card or you'll have no use for any fucking air," Florida says.

"You tried to steal my spot. I earned what's mine."

"You're the one who stole from me. You're the one attacked me first."

The woman clutches her dirty hands over the slice in her throat. "You made a hole where my soul could slip out. Thief."

Florida places a boot on the woman's chest. "Give me the card or I'll take more than your soul."

"Our soul is all we have." She fixes her cloudy eyes on Florida. "Though you've squandered yours already."

The streets are stirring. Helicopters thwack and vanish. A man with a voice like sawdust starts an incantation.

"Give it to me." Florida presses her boot harder into the woman's breastbone, feeling the bones beneath her garments and flesh. "Give it."

"When you lose your soul, you lose your way. You are just a collection of actions, each one taking you closer to your death." She raises her arms. Florida kicks. The woman falls back, pinned to the ground by Florida's boot. "You think you've won. But I see the loss that's coming for you."

"Give me my fucking card."

The woman reaches into her garment. She works her hand down through the folds, fumbling. She pulls something free and hands it to Florida.

Florida takes the card and removes her boot. She flips it over. It's not her bank card. It's a business card that now is smeared with bloody fingerprints.

"I said give me *my* card."

"That is your *fucking* card," the woman says. "That's all the card you got left."

Florida grips her weapon and raises it over the prone figure beneath her. "This is a business card."

"I made a trade."

Florida runs her finger over the embossed seal and squints at the letters. *Detective E. Lobos, LAPD.* "What the fuck?"

"I made a trade with the devil," the woman says. "And the devil has your soul." She sits up. There's blood everywhere—down her neck, along her arms, dripping from cheek to jaw.

Florida looks at the wreckage in front of her, the bleeding woman, the strewn parcels and packages of her camp, the tumbled icons. "I don't give a fuck about the devil."

The woman laughs. "But she cares very much about you."

———

Florida holds the card in her hand as she makes her way up the street.

This woman—this Detective Lobos—is a shadow she can't shake.

She flips the card over and over again, trying to rub away the bloody prints from the woman she'd attacked. But now she must carry this reminder of her violence along with the name of the woman who holds her only chance of rescue.

"Watch it."

Head bowed over Detective Lobos's card, Florida rams into a man heading in the opposite direction.

"Watch the fuck where you're going. And put on a fucking mask."

The man is wearing a red bandana over his mouth and nose. His black hair is speckled with gray. The skin around his eyes has worn paper thin from nights that never end before sunrise. But it's unmistakably Renny.

"And get the fuck out of my way."

Florida doesn't move.

"The fuck is wrong with you people," Renny says, sidestepping her.

You people. And like that Florence Baum keeps going, leaving only Florida behind.

KACE

Some stories come like a broken dam, like a tidal surge, a stampede across the plains. Some stories can't be stopped. Who am I to try, to bend against a will stronger than my own?

The voices won't allow it.

I do it for them. And for you.

And now I'm doing it for Tina, who's been screaming and screaming, as loud as she did the night they brought her down. She's been screaming over Marta. Screaming over the screaming down the line.

I scream too so that soon she will be quiet.

You know when it started, Kace! You know! . . . In the dark . . . the blackout. I was telling you. Them. You are all goddamned murderers and liars and devils. That's all I was saying. That's the truth I was telling. You all are. You . . . you . . . you . . .

And you know it. You know. You know. It's nothing you don't know.

Unlike me, who can't remember.

Got told what I did. Feel like I'm doing time for someone else's crimes.

But in the dark, I knew it was time and I was telling you.

You, Kace. Florida. Dios.

Because you needed to hear it.

"Shut up, Kace. Shut the fuck up." Voices in the hall. Down the line. Everyone telling me to be quiet.

I've heard it before. I've heard all their voices telling me to be quiet.

Don't they fucking know that I carry this shit for them? I have to let the noise inside my head out. I have to make them hear. "So shut the fuck up," I holler. "Listen up. Listen to Tina."

"Shut up. Someone shut her up." Them shouting over the coughing. All the coughing. Shouting until they are swamped by coughing.

Now two COs are trying to stop me. Pinning me. Restraining me. Binding me so I can't thrash this way and that.

"Fuck Tina," the women down the line say.

And that's when I let the guards have it. That's when my limbs are everywhere all at once, my fingers becoming claws, knives. My feet battering rams.

That's when they jab me. That's when they haul me off to the psych ward.

But Tina. She's still talking—screaming.

I told Florida that she was one lucky-ass bitch. Told her. Told her. Told her. I told her she was able to fucking atone for what she did. Able to know what she did. And still she lied about it.

Liar.

Always a liar.

And I told her. Finally. Once and for all. At the end.

In the blackout, I couldn't see her anger. In her eyes. I couldn't see her come for me. I only felt it when she got me from behind, when she drove her fist into my stomach, knocking the wind out of me.

I told her that I always thought she was a liar. That I knew why she lied. That I knew she wanted to watch those desert rats burn. To light that match.

She punched me again. Hard and fast. Each breath felt like my lungs were splintering. I could feel the joy in her fists. I could. Believe me.

"I did. Did it. Did it." A prayer she repeated as she pounded me. "I did it. I did it."

Each kick driving her point home until I couldn't hear anymore. Until I was past pain.

I only saw her for who she was the moment before I couldn't see again.

You better listen. If you aren't paying attention, you will think she beat me to shut me up. But at the last, she wanted me to know who she was.

In the end, Florida showed me what I did to that woman—because until then I didn't fucking understand.

She showed me.

And she showed herself to me. Still wanting it both ways—wanting me to know the truth but never to speak it.

She left me for Dios to finish off. Because Florida was always halfway to anywhere and never fully one way or another.

I'm losing steam here. They jabbed me again and my thoughts are flying free.

But Tina's said her piece.

Her story is now part of my story.

Our story, Marta reminds me.

Then we fade to black.

FLORIDA

Even in the dark Florida can tell someone has been here. The pool towels are out of place. The loungers scattered. The glass window in the garage has been shattered. The pedestrian entry door swings loose.

At the far end is her Jag. The dustcover has been pulled back. Florida rushes to the car. The top is up, but it looks as if it has been wrestled or wrenched out of position. She tries the door. Locked. Both locked. She pops the hood. There are fingerprints in the dust on the battery. Next to it a bouquet of loose wires.

The car is useless. The car is done.

There is no leaving. There is no going away. There is only here until someone comes to find her.

Florida leaves the garage and heads for the pool.

It's time to lie down. It's time to close your eyes and relax, let what's coming down the pike pick up speed and do its worst. It's time to rest not quite in your own bed but close. It's time to let the night take you away.

Florida strips, turning away from the stench that rises from her clothes and her body as she removes her filthy garments. Then, naked, she dives into her mother's pool, feeling the grit and grime release. She runs her fingers through her tangled hair, working the chlorinated water through the knots, tugging and pulling until her scalp aches.

She surfaces and floats on her back, naked to the night sky.

And then she submerges.

The only sound is the seashore echo in her ears and the thump of her heart as she forces herself to remain below. Florida's lungs squeeze, her throat tightens, and her head feels pressurized to the point of explosion.

Now is not the time, though. She just wants to know what it might be like to give up, toe toward the other side, to chase oblivion should she need it.

But the ultimate dark does not appeal.

So just swim and forget everything for a moment. Forget the blood she drew from the woman on the street. Forget the blood that same woman had drawn out of her. Forget her fists as they flew into Tina. Forget how good it felt to shut her up. Forget the exquisite pain as her knuckles broke skin and hit bone.

Forget the bus.

Forget her stolen debit card.

Forget Dios.

Forget the woman chasing her.

Forget the roadside chicken.

Forget Carter and the fire. Forget the matches.

Just be here, for as long as this now exists.

It was a lifetime ago that she swam in this pool with Ronna when Ronna's father's double betrayal came to light. That's when the first flush of anger had swamped Florence, blackening her thoughts, storming her heart, drowning her.

It was then she first glimpsed the shadowy nimbus that ringed her soul. And then came another one of those moments—just like the split second when she faced down the lady cop through the conservatory windows a few days ago—a fraction of time with a distinct before and after.

She had broken through the water and seen Ronna on one of the rugby-striped loungers, cradled in Renny's arms, his embrace sheltering her from Florence. Florence, the evergreen sidekick turned enemy. She looked from Renny to Ronna. Renny, desperate to cling to these young girls. Ronna holding on to anyone who wasn't Florence.

And Florence losing control, out of control.

She'd sat on the edge of the pool, chewing a nail, watching the scene in the warbling reflection—Renny and Ronna rippling in their stupid, shared grief.

And in the same brilliant sunshine refracted back at her from the crystal-blue water, she saw her own deformity, her defect. She saw what she had done to Ronna.

She knew an apology was possible. Girls will be girls will be girls. And at sixteen, life has no choice but to go on. But she saw a different path to reparation.

He's an asshole, she said through gritted teeth, loud enough for Ronna to hear. *Look what he did to us.*

Renny was the one who looked over. Always negotiating a path for himself between the girls.

What would he do to remain relevant? How far would he go?

Right here is where it starts. Ronna crying. Renny clinging. And Florence tiptoeing toward Florida.

She hauls herself out of the pool and dries off in a bath

sheet–sized towel. She rinses her clothes in the pool, wrings them out, and puts them down to dry. Florida wraps herself in more towels, turns one into a pillow, another into a blanket, and lies down.

She will sleep and what will come will come. It's too late to escape. The car can't take her anywhere. Anyway, it's nighttime now and there's nowhere to go.

Florida can sense it's creeping up on midday when she opens her eyes and sees that the cloud cover has peeled back, revealing a blue skim coat to the sky. The pool catches the color, glinting and winking as it is meant to. And there's a moment when everything seems just fine—when this is just another day by the pool, the city stunningly quiet and perfectly distant, leaving Florida alone and at peace. Just her and the calm lap of the water as it collides with the smooth concrete. Sinking her so deep inside herself she's untouchable and unreachable by the birdsong and insect noises. A moment when—squint and you can almost see it—Ronna's rounding the end of the conservatory and arriving at the pool without passing through the house, as always.

Ronna. Confident and as at ease in Florida's house as if it were her own. Which is what it became after the attack on her father, when the two girls were bound together in the wake of violence and its aftermath. Ronna's father recovering in the hospital and emerging with a disordered personality, the result of the beatdown Renny had delivered.

Renny, not Florence. It's important to remember that.

All she did was make a suggestion.

Tilt your head, so the sun streaks over the roof of the conservatory, over the roof of your bedroom, shooting a shaft of light straight down onto the cobbled path that rings the house. A literal sunbeam through which Ronna will walk, still filled with her teenage spirit. Giddy to be free from her parents, sent to live with

Florida until her father is well again. The girls' friendship healed in the wake of a secret only one of them fully understands.

How much more fun can they have?

How much more trouble can they cause?

How will they distance themselves from Renny, who did what he did for them, though Ronna will never know why?

Florida tips her head farther, squints her eyes tighter, draws Ronna closer. They will jump into the pool, stupid happy, foolish free. Then they will dry off and prepare for the night's adventure. Because the city is still theirs, a place they can absorb and discard at will. A place that doesn't stick to them. Not yet. That will happen later, to both of them in different ways. The damage from this time, permanent and indelible.

But for now, here is Ronna, silhouetted by the sun's backlight, suffused by a radiant glow. Here she is, carefree, her hair sleek and glossy, like she's ready for what party may come.

She stops in front of Florida's lounger. Florida holds out her hand.

Ronna's fingers lace through Florida's. Florida tightens her grip as if she might pull her through the fucked-up looking glass and back to life. And here is the vision made flesh. So goddamned real Florida can feel it—feel the skin and bone, even the pulse of the other hand in hers.

Florida gasps, her heart thundering into her throat, her eyes widening in shock.

And there, hand in Florida's, holding tight as if she is never going to let go, is Dios.

"Happy to see me?"

Florida jerks her hand free, then tightens her towel around her body.

"Nothing I haven't seen before."

Dios pulls a lounger over toward Florida's and sits, elbows on knees. Examining.

She looks good, of course. Clean, polished, and dressed in new clothes that don't exactly seem her style—unremarkable jeans and a striped T-shirt. The bruises on her face are yellowing. Her busted lip is still swollen. Sunglasses hide her eyes but not the extent of the discoloration.

Florida fumbles for her clothes. "Dios, what the fuck did you do?"

"I've done a lot of things."

"You fucking killed that guy."

"An opportunity presented itself, so I took it." Dios's voice is slippery and slick.

"An opportunity?"

"You know what he did to me. You know what he would have done to us."

"Nothing, if you'd kept your mouth shut. Not a goddamned fucking thing. Instead you fucked me. You made me your accomplice."

"Oh, Florida, always the accomplice and never the perp." Dios sits back, crossing her arms behind her head like nothing at all. "But we know that's not true. And you know that what happened on the bus was only one piece of the puzzle. All of this started with Tina and what *you* did. But you don't hear me complaining." Dios surveys the pool. Her hair is tight up top, loose at the back. Her eyebrows are painted fire. "I know you, Florida. I spent twelve months sheltering with the lies you tell. I know given half the chance you'd have pinned Tina on me just like you dropped those dead hippies on your friend Carter. That's not a chance I'm going to take. You need to own your mess."

"But *you* killed Tina."

"What are you protecting, Florida? Who are you protecting?"

"Me."

"No," Dios says. "You are protecting some phony version of you or a version of you that never existed." She yanks Florida to her feet.

"You have to go, Dios."

"We're both trespassing." .

"This is my house," Florida says.

"I don't see the big welcome home sign. From now on, wherever we go, we go together. You and I aren't just cut from the same cloth, we *are* the cloth. We're a whole fucking tapestry and nothing is going to rip these threads."

"What the fuck does that mean?"

"It means we run with what you started with Tina and I finished on the bus." Dios takes a lock of Florida's frizzled hair and tucks it behind her ear. "I have a plan."

"No."

"There's a bus."

"No."

"Another ghost bus. It will ride us out of town, down to San Diego. Down to the border."

"You're even crazier than I thought to imagine I'd get on another bus with you."

"What else are you going to do? It leaves from Olympic and Western at noon tomorrow."

"I am never going anywhere with you."

"Yes, Florida, you are. Tomorrow." Dios wraps a hand around Florida's wrist.

"Let go and get the fuck out, Dios."

Dios has her tight by the forearm and is pulling her toward the conservatory. "Or? Or what?"

Florida's arm goes limp in Dios's grasp. Or nothing. And that's the truth.

They are next to the French doors. Dios shades her eyes and peers through the gauze curtain. "Nice place. A little boring."

Before Florida can stop her, she slams her elbow through one of the small panes in the doors. The glass falls silent to the heavy carpeting. The only sound is the chopper beating time overhead.

Dios reaches through the glass and fumbles with the lock. The door opens. The house alarm unleashes a jarring screech. "Disarm it."

"I—I."

"A woman like your mother wouldn't even think to change the code even when her only kid turns out to be a murderer."

"You don't know—" Florida says over the noise.

"I know."

Florida breaks free from Dios's grasp and rushes to the front hall. She opens the secret panel and finds the keypad. Her mother's birthday. Easy.

Dios has a satisfied look on her face when Florida returns to the conservatory. "Home sweet home," she says. "Happy?"

The sight of Dios standing in the midst of her mother's cream-and-coral furniture. The sound of Dios's voice bouncing off the bland tropical fabric wallpaper. The idea of Dios invading this place, twisting it and deforming it. The rage comes unbidden and unchecked. Florida picks up a ceramic egg from a wooden stand and hurls it at Dios.

Dios ducks. The egg shatters against the window frame. "That's right, bitch," Dios says. "Tear this motherfucker to the ground."

And then . . .

Dios grabs a lamp, drops it, and stomps it. The shattering bulb pops like a breaking bone. Over to a side table and with a sweep of her arm, cleaning all of Florida's mother's objets to the carpet, where she tramples them. "What?" she says, giving Florida her serpent smile. "You actually like this shit?" She grabs a sea-glass bottle that never touched the sea and forces it into Florida's hand. "Go on. Do it. This isn't your house. It never was. You were never the person your mother pretended lived here."

"Stop it, Dios."

"Stop what? Stop letting you pretend you are going to step back into this shit and act like you didn't kill those fucking drug dealers and nearly beat Tina to death? How long can you keep that charade up? How long can you sip white wine by that pool and make small talk around the truth of the matter? How long can you do that before you explode?"

Florida puts her hands to her ears.

"Just do it," Dios says. "Just let it out. Like you did with Tina." She presses her lips to Florida's ears. "Your mother knows, doesn't she? She knows the real you. She knows who you are and what you did. And you can't take that, can you? She lies for you. She lies to you. You are all a family of liars. And in service of what?" Dios looks around the room. "This?" She knocks over a set of picture frames and shatters the glass with her shoe. "Remember, I know women like your mother. Women like your mother made my life hell by pretending they were making it better. They paid for my fancy schools. They paid for me to turn my back on my friends and family. And then you know what? They landed me in jail for giving their sons what they deserved when they fucked with me. Charity has its limitations. But you already knew that. Throw it."

"No."

"Your mother never visited you. Nearly three years and she kept away. Because she knows. She knows who you are and she doesn't like it. She doesn't want it to rub off on her perfectly manicured life. She stayed away because she knows the real you. And you can't handle that, can you? I know what you do to people who discover what you are really like. You beat Tina to a goddamned bloody fucking pulp. You want us to know, and you can't stand when we do."

It's over before she knows it. Florida hurls the bottle through a window facing the pool. The glass shatter is a release. A relief.

Her mother. So cold. So at a remove. So entirely aware of Florida but unable to acknowledge her. She knew, didn't she, that Florida willingly let a man three times her age take her on a two-week road trip in Mexico? She knew that Florida didn't pay for her jewelry and clothes—that she stole some and accepted the rest. She knew about Renny, about all the time her sixteen-year-old spent hanging with that lowlife. She knew how Florida repaid Renny for access to clubs she was way too young to frequent. She knew about the smaller transgressions and the bigger crimes. She knew about the company Florida kept—the men, the now-expunged juvie record of petty theft and misdemeanor. She knew about the men she introduced Florida to herself, imagining her daughter would be just fine. She knew that at fifteen, Florida didn't know better. She knew and she didn't care. What's more, she knew the score with Carter. She knew exactly what Florida did because she'd seen her grow up. She knew everything, because in order to help Florida hide the truth, she had to know it.

Florida grabs a jade rabbit figurine and hurls it at the pane next to the one she's just broken. She grabs a brass palm tree. She grabs a ceramic coral.

Dios's voice is an incantation as Florida throws object after object through the French doors, at the walls, at the sconces, the hanging fixtures, the moldings.

"Women like your mother patronize you. They pay for you so they can ignore you. That's their right. That's their goal. Instead of pushing you aside, instead of ignoring you, they pay for the right to hate you because it makes them feel better. Yes—even your mother. Even to you. Their money—their phony charity—it justifies their hate. It allows them to excuse it. Because women like your mother aren't allowed to hate. They aren't allowed to have such dirty passions. So they deflect. They lie. They are no better than us. They are worse because they are the ones who make us who we are, then pretend we are our own devils."

Object after object.

Picture frame after picture frame.

Painting after painting.

Window after window.

Room after room.

The conservatory. The formal dining room. The kitchen with its towering cabinets. The library. The sitting room.

Upholstery torn. Glass shattered. Carpet stained. Everything, everywhere. Trampled. Shredded. Toppled. Smashed.

The pool filled with debris—the stupid, broken detritus of her mother's self-important life.

Florida is sweaty. She's breathless. Her heart is in her ears. It's in her fingertips. It's everywhere at once. This is better than the MDMA high that propelled her back to that desert trailer, that made her long to dance around that bonfire with a man she marked for death. Because here she is, in lockstep with Dios as they dismantle the prison of Florida's childhood, as they tear it to the ground so she can be reborn once and for all. Finally.

They are in the kitchen, which opens onto the far end of the pool area from the conservatory. A door swings loose on its hinges. A chair from the kitchen island teeters half in and half out of a broken window.

And then, a voice. A woman's voice from the hall.

Florida reaches out and grabs Dios's arm. "Ssshh."

Hello. Hello.

"It's her," she whispers. "The detective hunting me. Lobos."

Dios narrows her snake eyes. "Detective?" She reaches for a

vintage bottle of port that has sat on the kitchen counter as decoration ever since Florida can remember.

Hello?

Florida cannot concentrate over the noise in her head. She doesn't hear the footsteps coming closer, crunching over everything strewn and scattered and smashed that carpets the already carpeted floor.

Who's there?

Florida is frozen. But Dios is a live wire at her side, ready, eager to ignite.

Hello?

And then, there she is in the kitchen. A moment. A beat.

How many moments will Florida remember forever? How many inflection points is one lifetime allowed?

The moment she saw Ronna in Renny's arms and decided to take control?

The moment she lit the cloth dangling from the pipe bomb?

The moment she saw Detective Lobos tracking her down Rimpau and, instead of turning herself in, kept running.

And here is another. A moment when Florida could let Florence out instead of hiding her away.

"Florence?"

Her mother's face is white with terror despite her perma-tan. Her hand loosens its grip on the suitcase she's wheeling behind her. Her wide eyes pulse as she takes in the damage, takes in the two women in her kitchen—her daughter and the rabid fury at her side.

"Florence."

The look on Dios's face—the pure, twisted joy.

Florida's arms begin to shake. Her knees bend and bow. Her stomach rises.

Her mother has her phone out. She's tapping away.

"Put it down," Dios cautions.

There is no hiding anything anymore. There is no more lying. This is who she is. An intruder. An invader. A murderous hellion rampaging in her mother's house. A criminal.

Her mother knows. Her mother sees. There's no turning back.

There's no warmth in her mother's eyes, not that there ever was. There is only the stone-cold reflection of who Florida is and what she has done.

She takes a step toward her mother. Then another.

With a shriek, her mother retreats into the hall, phone to her ear. "I'm calling the police."

Once more—maybe for the last time—Florida runs, out the broken door, toward the pool, around the far side of the house, out onto the street. The final thread tethering her to a different life snapped.

It is only when she is outside that she realizes Dios hasn't followed.

DIOS

Wait. Hold up.

I know I said this would be your story, Florida. But here I am at the turning point. At the crossroads where you became you. Almost. Before you ran.

And we were so close.

But I'm not giving up.

So I want to take a breath. A beat. I want to look outside before we enter the final act.

See that tree. What is it? A palm? A date palm? A fan palm? The fucking palm from the Bounty Bar?

See that tree watching over this phony English garden. See it bend and sway, always out of reach.

Now hear it. Hear it rustle—the only sound in the nearly silent city. A city holding its breath. A city waiting to explode. A city waiting to be exploded.

Did you watch this tree too, Florida? Did you watch it as you floated faceup in the pool while your old life drifted further and further away? Did you watch it while you hatched plans with Ronna? Did the tree watch you until it knew that this little estate could no longer be your home? Until it knew you were a goner?

The things it must have seen.

I know that there is a depth to your darkness. I just wish you were here with me in this moment as I step toward your mother. It's time that she learn about all the wrong she did in the world to people like me. To people like you. It's time I tell her.

You probably think that my mind is a whirl right now, churning, churning. A blaze of color, lights, and sounds. A flash of red-hot anger, a metallic clash. Rage blind. Fury sickened.

It's the other way around. I'm crystal cool, unblemished, and sailing smooth.

I'm elemental.

Have you ever swum in the ocean, charging headfirst into a wave that was too big? There's that panicked second when you think the wave is going to destroy you, swallow you whole, shatter you on the rocks or back on the beach. That moment when you think you've good and fucked up once and for all.

But then you get inside the wave. You find your place in its rhythm. You let it carry you. You feel weightless, as close to flying as you're ever going to get. You feel the ocean's power. You feel part of that power. It lifts you, making you soar and grounding you in the same moment.

That's how I feel now. Like balance is being restored. Like all the world's energy is my energy and my hands are the right hands, my calm the right calm. And what I'm doing must be done—the only thing that must be done. Right and strong and essential.

In my fury, I am at peace. As it should be. As it's always been.

I know exactly what I am doing.

I have always known.

See the tree as it sees me. As it sees what I am doing. And have done.

LOBOS

Bloated and blue. Sunk to the bottom of her own pool. Been there for a few hours at least. Some dumb accident when we've all been ordered to be safer at home. The bruising on her neck, the popped vessels in her eyes tell a different story.

Ugliness within ugliness. Suffocated and drowned. A double death, as if one wasn't enough.

"Guess we found the mom," Easton says.

Lobos reaches for her mints. Empty. Go fucking figure.

"You think—"

"Do you?" Lobos asks. "You think Baum did her mom? Trashed her place?"

"These days I'm out of guesses."

"I'm guessing no."

"Yeah," Easton says. "But you never know."

He's changed his tune. Suddenly women are capable of anything. And he's not wrong. Look at this scene.

"Fight over money. Refusal to help. Just running through the possibilities."

"And which one fits?" Lobos asks.

Easton cocks his head side to side, like he's trying on the answer. "It's just fucked."

The techs are hauling the body out. A neighbor called it in. What a sight. You think you're all tucked away, safe as houses in your nine-million-dollar mansion. All you've got to do is stay inside, keep the doors shut, and nothing can touch you.

But then you look out of your top floor window and see a woman at the bottom of the pool next door. The house ransacked. The signs of struggle obvious from a distance.

Maybe you saw the fight.

Maybe one of your neighbors did.

Lobos winces at the idea of door-to-door in this climate, where fear is other people. She'll arrive like death on their doorsteps, her masked face on the intercom. Regardless of the badge, she and Easton will be treated like pestilence stopping by for coffee. Like it's their fucking fault they've got a job to do. Like they're putting everyone at risk and not the other way around.

The techs put Florence's mother on the pool deck, then lift her into a waiting stretcher.

The pool ripples tiny waves that smack the concrete sides, the sunset reflected in the water.

Lobos stares into the blue and orange shimmer. It's as if it's pulling her into some other dimension. Those trippy visuals that let you know you're going back in time or sideways into another reality. Because the pool is no longer empty. There's a body, her husband's, floating faceup. His lifeless eyes fixed on the sky. Bruises at his neck. How hard would it be to hold him down, to choke and drown him? What would it feel like to feel that struggle in her palms, the windpipe flexing hard, the last gasp in her grasp? Would she feel the blood vessels pop in his eyes? Would it feel like Bubble Wrap? Would she notice that final burst of life, as it explodes and expires and then—nothing?

How much strength would she need?

"Lobos?"

More than she has, that's for sure. And it's not just her stature. That strength comes from the inside. A superhuman power source. Almost admirable if it weren't so fucked up.

Lobos looks down at her hands. She flexes them, testing their muscle and torque. Then jams them in her pockets.

"You okay?"

Easton at her side, his hand at her back.

"She would have to be pretty strong."

"Let's check the vic before they haul her off," Easton says.

Her neck is the color of bruised fruit—purples, blue, and graying black. You can almost see prints indented into her flesh, pockmarking the discoloration as if whoever held her overdid the job. Her eyes are dotted red and frozen fast.

Lobos puts on a rubber glove and lifts one of the woman's arms—a wet deadweight, her time in the pool making her feel somehow more lifeless.

She turns the hand over. Broken nails, signs of a futile struggle.

How many victims in her career? A hundred? Double that? Twenty years on the force and she only saw through the eyes of the injured and the dead. But now look at it another way. Flip the script. See it from the position of power. How does that feel?

Better. It feels better. Less pain. Easier to see the crime for what it is. It comes with a shiver. An electric shock, like someone's got a finger deep in her brain, messing with the wiring.

———

She replaces the woman's arm on the stretcher.

The other hand—also with broken nails. Something else too, an odd crook in two of her fingers, as if they got broken or sprained as they clung to life. Lobos turns the hand over. And there, twined at the base of her ring finger and palm—a small knot of jet-black hair.

She tweezers it out and holds the small clump up to Easton.

"Sandoval," he says.

Lobos bags the hair.

"What's her game?" Easton asks.

Lobos closes her eyes. She reaches for her mints before she remembers that they are gone.

Where does this start? Sandoval's crime: aggravated assault. Defending herself against an attacker. Broke his eye socket with her cell phone.

But what if that wasn't it? What if there was more to that story? More to that attack?

What if—? What was it that the prison personnel was saying or not saying about Sandoval? What was Lobos hearing between their lines? What was missing?

They didn't get her. They didn't understand her. There was something about Sandoval that defied classification, description.

Trace it back.

When did it start?

How did it happen?

What had she read in the file? Scholarship kid. Some kind of regional chess champion. College scholarship too. One of the fancy branded ones handed out by a tech mogul. What happened to her?

Was it in Queens? At home? In the projects? Was it at school? At college? How did it begin?

Lobos sits on a deck chair, holds up her hand. *I'm thinking.*

She stares into the too-blue pool. Her husband, when did it start? The same question she's been asking herself for years, since it became unbearable at home, since he grew dangerous and she weak.

But what if . . .

Lobos puts her head in her hands.

What if . . .

Now, here of all places—the thing she's been hiding from hauls itself out of the pool and reveals itself in the plain light of day. What if it was there at the start? What if the mistake was hers to begin with and life—the small setbacks and larger conflicts—just drew out her husband's anger?

It's easier to admit that he changed than to confront the fact that he'd been troubled at the start. That way she's only on the hook for one mistake instead of two.

"Lobos?"

She holds up her hand again. In the distance sirens wail.

There's a moment on which she pins her husband's downfall—the car accident that led to him losing his job, that led to him day-trading, to all-night trading, enslaved to his monitors, enslaved to different currencies, enslaved to misinformation and vitriol and the rest of the twenty-four-hour YouTube death spiral. But that accident, wasn't that also his fault, a conflagration of his issues and irritations and shortcomings? And what came before that? And before that? Where is the moment that made him the man who wrapped his hand over her throat and threw her against the wall, who ransacked her loft, who haunted her at work in defiance of her restraining order? In defiance of her job, her rank, and everything she stands for?

For years she's been fixated on this moment instead of on the possibility that maybe it wasn't there and that maybe she's been holding her breath for even longer than she thought.

What if there is no back? What if there just is?

That song—the one about the light leaking in. The one on every therapist's website.

What if there isn't a crack? Or light? What if it's just darkness all the way down? You could have a building that's more cracks than wall and it wouldn't fucking matter at all. It would just be dark. So let the whole building fall. Let it crack and crumble. There's only darkness on the other side and the light is no more than myth.

"There is no game," Lobos says. "This is who she is."

Easton is looking at her as if she's misspoken.

"Why not? Why is that harder to believe that anything else?"

"I'm not disbelieving it. I'm swallowing it," he says.

Easton tilts his head and closes his eyes, as if the answer is somewhere slightly off to the right. "And it's hard to do," he says.

Lobos nods. "Remember our last case," she says.

"Run-of-the-mill homeless-on-homeless stabbing."

"What was the perp's game?"

Easton shrugs. "The usual, I guess."

"That's not much of a motive, Detective." Lobos turns round so she is facing her partner. She barely comes up to his chin. She angles her head up so they are eye to eye. "We look for reasons so we don't go spiraling into the deep end. We need those reasons for ourselves—to make sense of the work we do. They're not a requirement of the job. Some people just like to watch the world burn and others want to set it on fire."

Easton is doing the driving thing that Lobos hates, one hand on the wheel, his head angled toward her in the shotgun seat, half an eye on the road. A careless night driver even when an approaching car careens toward them, its headlights dark.

Two hours of door-to-doors up and down the block. Each

house with forbidding security. Half the interviews done over in-
tercoms or shouting from more than the suggested six feet away.
And a whole bunch of nothing. It will be a relief to go back to
the times of unreliable witnesses and mistaken IDs, which at least
hold the possibility of teasing out some inkling of truth, instead
of this mania for see nothing, say nothing, do nothing. As if looking out the window, paying attention to the street, to your surroundings, to the people on your own damn bus, is what's going
to get you sick.

"At least we have the hair," Easton said as he got into the car.

The lab will do its work. Maybe not as fast as they'd like. But
the confirmation will come.

They take the curve on Sixth and Rimpau too fast. Lobos
clutches the dash.

Easton's eyes widen. "I'm going forty," he says.

"I didn't say anything."

Still, his eyes are on her, not on the road.

"He's my husband, if you want to know."

Easton glances at the street, slows to pass a car making a
left turn.

"The man outside the station."

"I didn't know you're married."

"Separated. In the process of getting divorced. It's complicated. And—"

"I don't need to know," Easton says.

He returns his eyes to the road, changes the whole angle of his
body, releasing Lobos.

"I have a restraining order on him," Lobos says. "He's not
supposed—"

"But he did." Easton crosses Western. The large intersection
is desolate. "And you didn't report it or notify, I'm guessing. And
that's your story. I'm not asking. We all have our reasons."

Now it's Lobos's turn to stare at Easton until he looks over—never mind he's taking his eyes from the road again. "Do you have anything more to say?"

"You're the one who brought it up."

"It's not weakness, you know."

"I'm not saying it is."

Just one more chance at him. That's all she wants. One chance to stand up to her husband. Lobos swears she'll take it this time instead of succumbing to her anxiety, instead of shrinking into herself. The next time she'll let him see the real her, the one who can muscle confessions out of murderers, strong-arm pimps, subdue the lowest of the low.

One more chance and she'll take it. Because she's lucky. She's not like these other women on the streets or even at home who don't get a second grab at the ring—who are killed or beaten so badly they don't get the opportunity to fight back.

She's had her chances to take matters into her own hands with her husband—to stand up to him—and each time her weakness caused them to slip through her fingers. Each time she turned away or made her husband someone else's problem. Each time. But not the next.

They drive in silence through the silent, plywood city—a whole story written and rewritten in graffiti. They pass one of those living murals lit up by flickering streetlights. Koreatown falls away into Pico Union. Pico Union gives way to downtown. The skyscrapers stay dark. Up ahead, the first choppers rise, getting ready for what may or may not come.

But as of yet, no one is out. No one congregating, no one protesting or rioting.

Easton parks in front of the station.

The tents are up. The tents are always up, pressed against the outer walls of Central, holding close to those who crack them down.

Up the steps to their office. Lobos's head darts left and right. Checking. She notes Easton doing the same. On the lookout on her behalf.

No one beyond the undomiciled who've come too close.

They enter the dim interior. The staff sergeant masked. The waiting room empty.

"Easton, hold up."

But Easton is already past the desk.

You can't train yourself out of your old habits that quick. Lobos has to double back. One last look. She opens the door, steps back outside.

"Detective Lobos?"

FLORENCE

The detective is even shorter than Florida imagined. Not like a real cop at all, more like a sidekick—pint-sized, micro. A little toy police.

She'd never have cut it inside, on the line. The women would have eaten her alive. Or maybe she'd have punched above her weight and punched hard, inflicted pointless punishment to distract from her stature.

What would they have called her? Pocket-Pal? Peanut? Snack-Size?

Or worse?

Dick-sucking height.

Blowjob tall.

Something in this woman's eyes tells Florida that she's not down for denigration.

"Detective Lobos, I've been waiting for you. You have something of mine."

The detective comes down the steps and squints at Florida.

She knows how she looks. Her face battered by the woman

outside Renny's. Her hands still bruised from pounding Drew. Her clothes torn from tangles with brush and debris around the city. Her cheeks hunger-hollow. Eyes wild. The chlorine scent of her mother's pool clinging to her hair.

She feels turned inside out.

"Florence?"

Florida blinks blindly at her old name.

"Florence Baum?"

There's a note in Detective Lobos's voice that Florida can't place.

"My debit card?"

"You want to step into the station?"

Florida jams her hands into her pockets and backs down the steps. "I just want my card. I didn't do anything."

"Except break parole," Lobos says. "And there's a chance you're an accessory to murder. Or even guilty of murder."

"I wasn't even on that bus when it happened. I read about it in the paper."

"That's hard to swallow. But let's just say I believe you."

The lady detective is lying. Her whole job is not to believe women like Florida.

"Then give me the card and I'll be back in Arizona before I need to check in with my PO."

"I'm not sure that's how this is going to work."

Florida looks over Lobos's shoulder for the backup that doesn't seem to be coming, for the reinforcements to handcuff her and lead her away. For an unceremonious end to this whole mess Dios created.

Weak, Dios would say. *Down without a fight. Surrendered your own goddamn self like that's all you deserve.*

"Would you like to sit?" Lobos says.

"Here?" Florida looks at the station steps.

Lobos comes closer, then sits on the low wall that runs along Sixth. "You're in some trouble."

"The man on the bus—I didn't. I told you." But how many things has she told to officers in the past? How many were lies? How many truths that weren't believed? What does it matter anymore what she did and didn't do? What does it matter what she says? You are who they say you are, and at the end of the day you do what they tell you to do.

Dios was right about that. They remake you.

Lobos takes out an empty Tic Tac canister and taps it on the wall. "Have you been home?"

"It's not my home."

"When were you there last?"

"Earlier today."

"See anyone?"

Florida side-eyes the detective. She knows. "Dios."

"Anyone else?"

"No."

"Did you leave her at the house?"

"Yes."

"How come?"

"Because Dios is— Because Dios wants . . ." Florida pauses. "She wants to destroy me."

"Why?"

"Because she thinks we are the same."

"Are you?"

Florida looks down at her battered hands. "She's crazy. I'm just fucked up. She can't tell the difference and she will hunt me until I see it her way."

"And your mother? Did you see her?"

The shame—that's what this strange sensation is—feels unfamiliar. Like a passing glance at a world she barely recognizes.

"She called us in, right. I ran before she finished." She glances over Lobos's shoulder into the station. "Is she in there?"

Lobos rubs her hands on the thighs of her pants. "We got a call a few hours ago from one of your mother's neighbors."

You think you've hit rock bottom, that you've been scraped raw, brought low, emptied out of emotion. You think you've lost the ability to care what happens to you or to anyone else. And then . . .

Florida doesn't really hear Lobos's next words as much as she feels them with a nauseating disorientation, like falling off a cliff and never hitting the bottom. Falling and falling in a sickening descent that stretches eternal.

For the rest of her life she will fall through this space in purgatorial suspension.

You think there's nothing left, no you in you. No there in there. You think you are empty and calcified, nothing soft left to bruise or damage.

Then someone reaches in and finds a lingering weakness, something intact and fragile. And they trample it to shit—mutilate and destroy it, which hurts worse than anything that came before because you thought you were done with pain. You thought you were harder than pain. You thought you were less than human and more than tough.

Lobos has finished talking and is staring at Florida with a look of concern, like she's worried Florida's going to rage or going to pop off. Or worse—fall to pieces.

What Florida will remember from this moment is the smell of the streets. The tang of the unwashed. The antiseptic the city sprays to mask it. She will remember the scent of herself—her sweat and the chlorine odor from her mother's pool, the same water where Dios strangled her mother and left her to drown.

She smells of her own mother's death.

That's what she is going to remember most of all. It's funny how in an instant you recognize what you will carry forever.

"I know where she is," Florida says.

"Tell me."

"I know where she will be. I can find her. I can bring her to you."

"No," Lobos says. "That's not how this is going to play out."

Florida stands. "I have nothing left. I have no game. This is all I've got. Let me go and I'll tell you where I'll meet her. Otherwise, nothing doing."

"Florence—"

"My name is Florida."

"You know I can't let you go."

"If you don't, you'll lose Dios forever. She'll be gone tomorrow. Let me go and I will help you find her."

Now Lobos stands and places her hands on her hips. There's a strange look in her eyes that Florida can't quite figure. "We don't all get the chance to fight our own battles. Sometimes the fight comes to us before we can react and other times it's out of our hands before it's begun. But too often we run from our own fight." Lobos holds up the debit card. "If you give me the info, I'll give you this free and clear. I'll get you on that bus back to Arizona if possible."

"I don't believe you."

"This could go easy or it could go badly. Come inside."

"No," Florida says, taking a single step backward. "If you take me in there, I won't tell you anything. Then Dios will disappear."

"When it goes wrong, it's going to go very wrong," Lobos says. "And I can't protect you."

"Do you want Dios or not?"

"Do you?" Lobos holds Florida's gaze, a challenge lingering in the question.

"We want the same thing."

"Now, I don't necessarily believe that," Lobos says. "Maybe we want the same outcome."

Florida takes another step back and another, waiting for a takedown that doesn't come.

"Where will I find Dios?"

Florida backs across Sixth, her eyes never leaving Lobos's, who hasn't moved from the station steps. She's blind to whatever cars may come. Her only focus is on the tiny detective.

On the far side of the street, she cups her hands over her mouth. "Where Olympic hits Western. At noon tomorrow."

"Where exactly?"

"That's all I know and that's all I'm giving you."

In the dark the choppers circle like vultures, waiting for the carnage below.

On Figueroa, Florida runs into a melee of protesters, their numbers not yet strong enough for a march. Where there are protesters, there will be police.

Florida picks up her pace, turning south until she comes to the ramp where the 110 meets the 10.

She continues alongside and underneath the freeway in the miles-long shanty city of cobbled-together communities and shooting-gallery hideaways.

A trade.

A bargain.

A barter.

How do you exchange nothing for something? She hurries, keeping an eye on the camps she passes, looking for discard, scrap, anything of value. Something no one will miss but someone wants.

But everything is already claimed, repurposed, or stashed. It's hard to steal from people who already have nothing.

Here's a gas station, though. An off-brand one. No credit card machines at the pumps. No quickie mart. No customers.

Florida glances through the smudged and scratched window. The sole attendant is sequestered behind bulletproof glass. He's hidden behind his own mask and scooted way back from the counter. A sign on the door reads PLEASE PAY THROUGH OUT-SIDE WINDOW.

Florida sees a window that's been carved out so customers can slide their credit cards through without having to enter the store. She tries the door. The attendant bangs on the glass, furiously shooing her away.

But the door isn't locked. The sign is the only thing keeping people out. She will have to be fast, use whatever legs she's got left.

Florida steps inside. Next to the door is a display of red plastic jerricans. Before the attendant can burst from behind the safety of his hermetically sealed counter, she's grabbed two of the cans and is back outside.

Her legs are numb. The cans slap-bang her thighs as she hurtles to the on-ramp for the 10. The attendant was shouting after her and then he wasn't, giving up the chase before it started.

Florida is on the freeway now. Like last time, the few cars are wide-spaced.

The sky is flat black under cloud cover that has blown in.

Here's a brush fire on the far side of the freeway—a loose blaze that leaps from tree to tree.

Here's a man sitting on the guardrail, sipping something from a champagne coupe.

Here's a shrine.

Here's a tent in the breakdown lane.

Fireworks explode in the smothered sky. Dogs howl. Sirens wail—their alarm rising and rising and getting nowhere, like a barbershop pole.

The man is standing in front of his encampment. The ribbons, mirrors, and wind chimes sway in the slight breeze. He's wearing a dirty silk robe open over a pair of shorts that look made out of burlap. He's not alone. A large woman seated on an overturned bucket is weaving torn strips of fabric together.

"You've returned," the man said.

"I brought these," Florida says, holding out the jerricans. "A barter."

"Set those down," the man says.

"I want to trade."

"Set 'em."

Florida lowers the cans.

The woman looks up from her weaving. "I can smell the trouble on you," she says.

"I've got something to do," Florida says. "And there's something I need to do it."

"Trouble is what you've got," the woman says. "Trouble is what you'll get." Her hands are swift and deft. Her nails hard, black claws. "Sometimes trouble is the only destination and you might as well take the shortest path."

"Sit," the man says, indicating a camp chair that's missing a leg. It sinks to the ground under Florida's weight, tips her back until she finds her balance. "Take off your shoes," the man says.

"I'm fine. I just need—"

"She already told you we'll get you where you need to go," the man says. "And that we will give you what you need."

"I haven't told you."

Before Florida can object, the man is at her feet, unlacing her boots. "I told you before. It's the feet they check first. Whatever's coming for you, the feet come first."

"I don't need—"

The woman considers Florida top to toe. "You hardly have anything, so don't get started on the list of things it seems you need. There's a list that goes on."

Florida's feet breathe. The wind brushes her toes.

"Tell me where it is you're going," the woman says.

"Nowhere good," Florida says.

"Don't tell me what I already know. There's no magic in this world. Nothing but the need to put one foot in front of the other until you come to what's next. No point in explaining the past or guessing what's waiting ahead. The only thing that matters is what's right in front of us."

The man hands Florida a soda bottle filled with water. She tips it to drink. Then he hands her a rag. "Wash," he says.

She soaks the rag, crosses one leg, and begins to clean her blistered foot.

"We are nothing more than our own scars," the woman says. "But they don't tell the future. They only remind us of the past."

Coyotes cry, a frenzied fever song. Behind the camp, Florida can hear the chickens tut their panicked response.

There's food in cans—sausage and beans eaten cold with plastic forks that are bent and weak with use. The man cranks a radio and plays a station somewhere between Spanish and static.

The food is electric in Florida's stomach, sparking her nerves, reviving her head to toe.

Fireworks take to the night—blossoming yellow and purple, white and blue.

A caravan of cars streams down the 10, honking and flying homemade banners bearing the names of the brutalized Black.

"All these rich folks fleeing their homes," the woman says. "Always imagining they can outrun their problems instead of figuring out they themselves are the problem."

The caravan passes, its noise melting away.

Now cars stalk the freeway at distant intervals. Their headlights twinned eyes, searching the dark.

"They leave the city for us to do as we please," the woman says. She stands. She takes Florida's hands and leads her in a dance round and round the encampment.

Coyotes come to the far edge of the camp, their eyes glowing green. They stare, unblinking, then pace the perimeter, before the hunt calls them off.

Florida knows that when she lets go of the woman's hands she will have spun into a new world. She will have shed her old skin and be reborn under a violent moon. When she lets go, she will step into a moment from which there will be no release.

The man makes her a bed again, this time in the shelter of two oleander shrubs. She camps on an old sleeping bag, her jeans for a pillow. She can hear the radio crackle. She can hear the murmur of the man and the woman conversing. She stares into the knot of branches that protect her from the city.

She doesn't dream of the freeway, of prison, of her mother or her mother's house. She dreams of the ocean as it was when she was nine years old. She dreams of the rocky outcrop where the tides were trapped and the waves churned and spat. Where the lifeguard told her not to swim. Where she went anyway. Where she felt the ocean pull her in two directions before returning her safely to shore.

Her parents somewhere else. Not watching.

The lifeguard paled at her daring. Cautioning her. Warning her.

And yet she went again, diving back. Letting the current pull her toward the rocks. Letting the waves churn and buffet. Feeling in control of the dangerous slip of ocean. Taming it. Overpowering it with her spirit. Small and mighty. The world, the ocean, no match for her.

Until it broke her. Knocked her out. Cracked her skull and somehow, mercifully, returned her to the beach, half-dead, half-drowned, but suddenly alive to destruction.

She wakes having slept hard. Her body sleep-strengthened.

The man and woman are already up. They've fixed her a breakfast of beans. When Florida has eaten, they prepare her with fresh socks and a clean T-shirt. The woman combs her hair until it flies up and out from her head—a burned, yellow halo. Then pulls it back.

The man is holding a small case, which he hands to Florida. It's not what she came for, but she takes it anyway. Inside are a few small paint palettes and brushes. He dips a brush into a cup of water, dabs on black paint, then sweeps two lines beneath each of Florida's eyes. He rinses the black and switches to red, defining the curve of her cheekbones.

Then he puts the paints away.

The jerricans are where Florida left them when she arrived. The man picks them up and disappears into the cluster of bushes where he makes his bed.

He emerges with the gun and hands it to Florida. She checks the chamber. Full. She tucks it into the waistband of her state-issued pants.

Now is the time for endings.

Florida crosses Pico just before midday by the sun, although it's hard to tell under the marine layer. She can't be sure of the exact time, but time barely matters now and won't for much longer. She will be early. She will be waiting for Dios.

She checks the street signs to make sure this is the place. Like the time, this place isn't anywhere in particular. It's a street crossing another street, emptied out like the rest of the city—soaped-over windows, vacant parking lots, vanished businesses. A world up and gone.

Behind her, Western rises slightly, blocking the southern reach of the city from view—an expanse of lost consequence. To the north, the road is a deep cut running toward the hills and the distant Hollywood sign, which hovers like a dream that overstayed its welcome.

The storefronts and restaurants that line the avenue are boarded with plywood that's layered with graffiti that's been graffitied over already. Stories on top of stories that will be erased and forgotten.

Western dips before a gentle incline toward Olympic. There's a slight wind, the air free of exhaust but also tanged with the trash stockpiled on the sidewalks and the stench of outdoor living.

The wind gathers masks and gloves, sending them swirling south over the cracked sidewalks, where trash and weeds have made their stand.

Florida walks through it, blind to the disorder, her focus past the disarray. At what point does the disarray become the norm—when does it settle in, ushering a twisted sense of order?

In prison, things made sense. The chaos had its own sort of calm.

Here the calm itself is chaos.

She doesn't hear the few city sounds. Her ears are filled with her boot strikes—the measure of time between life and death.

There are a few pedestrians on the sidewalks, scattered and guilty-stepping, in violation of the new world disorder. They stop to watch her pass, tracking her passage, aware that they are in the presence of a force that must not be disturbed. Something determined and determining, a decider of fates.

Florida takes no notice of those who see her. They are no more or less important than the empty buildings and peeling posters from an obsolete world.

She passes a shuttered Mexican restaurant built in the style of a Spanish mission. She passes a white two-story shopping plaza, spectral and abandoned.

She begins the final ascent to Olympic, past a piano store with smashed windows, past a bank where the plywood did its job, past a four-story shuttered shopping mall with LED displays and electronic billboards flashing in Korean and English for the forbidden customers.

She has arrived first.

But she is not alone. Two men are drinking on a bench outside the boarded-up bank. Someone has made camp in a tent in front of the gas station opposite. Six people keep their distance near a makeshift bus stop, leaning on the soaped-over windows of a defunct storefront.

Up ahead, a rattle. Florida's eyes track the sound. On the wall behind the gas station a young man with tufted dreads has begun a mural, streaks of paint flying from his spray can.

Florida thought rage would flow in her and that her heart would beat hard and fast. But she is ready. She keeps her eyes focused to the north.

A loose board taps against the bank's window, beating a

countdown of hollow seconds, marking time in a place where time has paused.

Now she waits.

The people on the sidelines watch, wanting none of her business. They know bad when it comes. After it happens, they will have borne no witness.

Rattle, rattle. The hiss of the paint exaggerated by the silence. A streak of gray appearing on the wall.

A gust of wind summons a trash funnel, sending it diagonally across the intersection. It breaks across the tip of Florida's boot, a mask settling like a steel cap. She shakes her foot free and resumes her watch.

Eight lanes of no traffic. This is not the city she dreamt of for the past three years. But she is no longer the person who inhabited those dreams.

The board taps.

The sun hides.

The moment stretches and spreads.

There's a shift, a change in the air. The drinkers, the people at the bus stop, and the tent dweller reposition themselves to make room for a brand-new noise coming down Western from the north.

The artist keeps painting.

Florida stands, hand on hip, another on the makeshift holster of her waistband. Feet planted hard to the asphalt. Tree-solid and rooted firm.

The noise isn't footsteps or a war cry, but a creak of wheels. Florida stiffens. The watchers on their corners gauge her tension. They brace and step or slide back as if what's coming will be on them at once.

Florida checks her palms with her fingertips. Her hands are dry.

The wheels are coming closer—like Florida, down the middle of Western. It's a woman pushing a shopping cart filled with four blue beverage coolers, her face swaddled in a cloth, revealing only her eyes. She calls out in Spanish as she draws near Olympic. *Champorado*.

The word sounds as if it has arrived after decades of transmission—a missive from another universe.

The woman halts her cart in the northern crosswalk of the intersection. She has stepped out of a different world, a pre-apocalyptic vision.

Champorado.

The woman lurches the cart to the left and heads for the sidewalk, leaving the street to Florida.

The people waiting for the bus crowd around her, forgetting to keep their distance as she fills cups from the coolers' plastic taps. When she is done serving them, she wheels her cart into the painted crosswalk. Soon she has disappeared to the south, the creak of her cart's wheels and her one-note cry swallowed and subsumed.

The loose board on the bank tap-taps away the seconds.

The wind rises, scuttling more trash—cups and paper bags, Styrofoam and plastic clamshells. The city is disgorging itself.

Behind Florida one of the men on the bench tosses his empty into the street, where it shatters, the shards skipping into silence.

Florida waits, a watcher at the crossroads. Her body has absorbed the beat of the board and she shuffles the toe of one of her boots in time, willing time itself forward.

There is action on Olympic—movement to Florida's right. She cuts her eyes to see a bus, no signage, no decals. It stops on the corner. The passengers toss their champorado cups to the ground and file on.

The bus waits for the light, then continues west. The driver stops in front of Florida and rolls down his window. Seven sets of eyes try to meet hers. Seven sets of eyes try to break her stare.

The driver leans out.

¡Muevelo!

The board taps. The bus idles.

Move.

Florida stares at the bus as if she can see through it.

She moves her hand to her hip, where her gun is visible.

The bus screeches off, filling the air with a burned-rubber scorch and a cloud of criminal exhaust.

The smoke settles and there is Dios. Her black curls are braided in two plaits tight to her skull that fall halfway down her back. There are fresh scratches on her cheeks. The cut in her lip has reopened.

Still, she is beautiful like a fucking cobra is beautiful.

She's wearing a tight black T-shirt with a pink ringer, gray skinny jeans torn at one knee, and flat red boots. Her clothes once belonged to Florida. A badge is hung around her neck. The name, of course, is not her own.

"Pero nunca se fijaron / En tan humilde señora." Dios smiles. "You weren't paying attention. I wasn't saying that I was the humble woman. She was always you, Florida. No one saw *you* coming. Except for me."

The time for talk is short. Words are a distraction. They are Dios's trap. Their time is almost over. Their time was never meant to be but was inevitable.

Florida pulls out the gun.

It's heavy. Her arm shakes with its weight as she extends it toward Dios, sighting her.

What does it feel like? A toy? An appendage that is not her own? A prop from a different story?

The wind rises.

Tap-tap.

Tap-tap.

The board beats faster.

Florida is aware of someone on the sidewalk scuttling away, someone for whom this is too much to witness. But others will watch, drawn like vultures to the promise of someone else's pain. Sustained by it.

She coils her finger.

Think. Think back to all the moments that led up to this moment. The hundreds of thousands of seconds that made you you.

Look to the left and you might see Ronna's ghost on Olympic, here to bear witness to the last stand of your ruinous course, understanding, at last, that she was simply an accidental obstacle to be knocked down. Collateral damage on your journey.

Feel the slight wind.

Imagine your foot on the gas, accelerating to your own destruction.

Press harder.

Drive blind.

It will be over soon.

Florida feels the gun's weight. The cool metal. The nubbled grip worn smooth. She feels the weight of a decision already taken. Her life has moved on, past this point. She just has to do one small thing to cut the line to the present.

The woman by the freeway was right. There is no magic in the world, no point wasting time detangling patterns and problems, in rationalizing yourself for others, in explaining yourself away and prophesying your next move. No sense in saying because you handed Carter those matches you wound up in the here and now. There's no reasoning about who and why we are. No point in puzzling it out. It's time to take the next step on the journey. Make yourself solid.

Like the tree, for instance, the one outside the jail. It didn't represent freedom. Everyone had that wrong. It was steadfast. It stuck it out against nature's odds.

But it knew.

It understood.

It acknowledged its outrageous claim, its unholy state, and stood there until lightning took it down.

So see the tree. See it in your mind's eye one last time. See it as it withstood and stood fast. See it proud even when bare. See it prouder in bloom.

See it.

See it as you pull the trigger.

They are calling to her, summoning her.

Florida hears her old name.

KACE

What will you remember? What will you take with you?

Feel the kickback, the reverb.

Feel the difference half an inch can make, an insignificant movement that contains everything.

Feel yourself explode into that negligible space.

Because there is no hiding in this heartbeat's worth of time. No way to deceive or lie.

And before everything changes—everything ends—let the world know who you are.

FLORIDA

It's not a lot—a simple coil of the finger, like scratching your forehead, picking a scab, flicking a piece of lint.

But in that space is a decision.

In that space there is room.

In that space there blossoms a whole world in which you can scream—*this is me*.

LOBOS

"Florence!"

How many things can happen in a single moment?

A second ago, Lobos and Easton screeched to a stop crosswise on Olympic and Western, zigzagging the intersection.

The bus was early.

She saw it pulling away as they raced up Olympic.

She understands that the bus was beside the point.

Her eye catches something in the distance. A young man painting a graffiti mural. No time for that now.

Together she and Easton spring from the car, their doors as shields, their guns drawn. Her fault that they are late in the first place. Her fault for being unable to speak openly to her partner about how she'd let Florida go. Her fault for trying to handle this on her own, to admit her weakness, her need for help until Easton wrangled it out of her.

And now . . . Baum and Sandoval stand off a few feet ahead. Neither turns at their arrival.

Sandoval is unarmed.

Baum is sighting her over a pistol that's approaching antique.

Lobos hears Easton cock his weapon.

She hears herself do the same.

"Florence."

Her eyes are on Baum's trigger finger, willing it to be still, to stay the course.

Her neck prickles, alive to each and every movement in the intersection.

And then . . .

Baum's finger coils.

It's time or it's too late.

"Florence," Lobos calls again.

Florence turns to face Lobos as her gun goes off. Their eyes meet. Her shot flies low, burying itself in Sandoval's upper thigh near her groin.

But Lobos's shot is bang on the money, right in the dead-heart center of Baum's chest.

She hears Easton exhale next to her. She knows what he'd been thinking. She wouldn't take the shot. She'd fail at the last minute. She'd make her mess his problem.

She rushes to Florence Baum, whose blood is painting Western.

But it's too late—the leak of life like the leak of light. In the end, darkness all the way down.

Lobos jumps in the ambulance with Sandoval. Through the back window she glimpses the artist still at work on his mural, showing the intersection of Western and Olympic. Why paint what's right in front of you? Lobos wonders as the siren screams and the bus hurtles away.

Sandoval's eyes are glassy with pain. Her voice fever-pitched.

"Shattered hip bone," the EMT tells Lobos.

Sandoval tosses her head from side to side. She pulls off her oxygen. "Water."

The EMT helps her sip. The water streams down her face. Sandoval clears her throat.

"They'll be telling our story for generations. Yours, mine, and Florida's. A tale of violent women. A song for the ages with a surprise ending."

"I've had enough of stories," Lobos says.

"How dark is the darkness in you, Detective?" Sandoval's voice is tight with pain. "Was it always there, or did it grow when they started telling you how weak you were?" The ambulance hits a bump. Her eyes roll. "Do you want to hurt them? Do you want to hurt us?"

Lobos sets her jaw.

"How fucking good does it feel? Tell me, Detective."

"Quiet," Lobos says.

She signals to the EMT. He puts the oxygen mask over Sandoval, silencing her.

There is only the moment that something happens. Everything up until that point dwells in the haze of conjecture. A puzzle that tempts you with the promise of relief, only to confound you once more.

She looks down at Sandoval, furious in her oxygen muzzle. She knows there will be those who will read too deep into Sandoval's deluded reasonings and make her crimes more important than they were. They will analyze and examine, making the unreasonable reasonable until they've found a palatable excuse for her violence. Leave it to the shadowland practitioners who moonlight in Lobos's field to figure this woman out. Let them find every excuse for what she did except the simple fact of who she is. A violent woman. No different from a violent man.

In the end, what's done is done and there will be no undoing.

Let others make a story out of it, if they will.

Let them sing their songs.

The siren screams, clearing the cleared streets.

Sandoval thrashes on her stretcher.

She has more to say.

Lobos had thought she'd ridden along to listen—to crack Sandoval's code, to solve the puzzle. But it turns out she prefers the silence.

Easton is waiting by the desk sergeant when Lobos returns to Central. She knows what awaits—the protocols and procedures that follow the discharging of a weapon in the line of duty. The interviews and counseling sessions after killing a suspect. She knows that she will have to live with Easton knowing that she chose to let Baum go.

It will be months before she is officially free of this.

And a lifetime before she is free of it at all.

Except, he's holding out a bottle of whiskey. "You were right. She came to us."

"You're kidding," Lobos says.

"A bet's a bet."

She takes the bottle, knowing she won't enjoy a single sip.

She'd given Florence Baum a choice. She'd explained the stakes.

One way to look at it is that she put Florence in death's path.

Another is that she allowed her to finish her own story.

A grace we are not all granted.

She looks at her hand, flexes her fingers. If she hadn't fired, Easton would have, and the outcome would have been the same.

"Lobos, you coming?"

She's stopped midway to the desk sergeant.

"Got someone for you in interrogation."

Already it's starting. The bureaucratic tangle of the messiest cases. The interviews and paperwork, the protocols and conferences set in motion by the slight motion of a finger.

But it's not one motion, is it? It's all of those that came before added together. Right?

Wrong.

Lobos empties the last of her mints into her mouth.

There is only the now. Everything else is a trick of the light.

She follows Easton into the station. He leads her to the interview room, then stands back and lets her go in first.

The shades are drawn.

The lights are low.

Easton steps away, closing the door, leaving Lobos alone with her husband.

He is wild-haired and wild-faced, shaggy and spectral all at once. He is her husband and he isn't. The stranger she always failed to see before her.

They face off over the table. The heavy two-way glass is dark. No one is watching. The station is silent behind the soundproof walls. Whatever happens in here is hers alone to do and know.

The anger rushes from her brain, coursing through her chest, down her arms, and ending in her hands. Lobos clenches her fists.

She squeezes hard, forcing her nails into her palms.

She pulls out a chair, ready to sit, ready to begin this, to end it, to drive the final nail into their splintered tale.

Where to begin?

What to say?

What—with all eyes shut and ears deaf to this room—to do?

She looks at the man across the table. The streets worn into his face. The smell not his own. His disorganized thoughts playing in his eyes, curling his lips. Who the fuck is he? And . . . and why does she care?

There is only one thing to do.

Her hands relax. She rolls her shoulders, closes her eyes, exhales a breath she's held too long.

Nothing.

What's done is done. This story too is over. However Easton found her husband is his matter. This is just another case. Another perp. Another stalker violating a restraining order.

There are protocols in place for this and Easton can handle them.

Lobos isn't going to say a word.

It's not weakness to walk away—to stay quiet and to do nothing. It's not shame or disgrace. It's not lack of confidence in herself or in her badge.

It's time to close this book in silence.

KACE

Not even Marta believed me. They always come back, except the ones hauled away sick. The rest, they come back one way or another.

Even the ones who think they are special. Especially the ones who think they are special.

And here they are again.

Here's Dios in her cage, watching me from her jail within a jail in the yard. Watching me like she knows something I don't. Like there's something superior about solitary.

I know what she's mouthing but I don't have time to listen. And I don't need to. I know she's trying to tell me that Florida didn't make it back—that she's flying free, finally able to be herself. I know Dios wants to tell me Florida grew her wings, blossomed into some twisted beauty. That she became.

I've heard it all before. And it's still a fucking lie.

Because she's here, Dios. She's with you always. You brought her back to us. And here she'll stay, summoning you home. A rubber band you can never snap. Pulling and pulling.

Do you hear her voice? Is it inside your head? Or are you plugging your ears to her as you did to Tina? Are you abandoning her now that you've finished her story? Are you already on to the next thing?

Soon enough I'll hear her. No matter that you weren't the one who pulled the trigger. We all knew who brought her down.

Look at you in that cage, your one hour of recreation and you're watching us living our limited freedom, which is still greater than yours. Watching like you know something we don't.

But there's nothing to know.

You're one of us. Always been one of us. Nothing above or beyond.

They always come back.

And here you are.

The sun sets every day. Some of these ladies think it sets for them alone. Like the sun plays favorites.

And tomorrow it will rise. And rise again. Always on the come-up. Always returning to make a great circle of our days. Nothing special. Just a great burning orb that lights our path for a while until we have to begin again.

Except I'm starting a new journey. I'm going. Getting out. I did my time and came out ahead.

They're letting me go not because I played their game, but because I played mine. I listened to the voices in my head. And they guided me, they guide me still—everyone else's story smoothing my edges and carrying me on.

I got it all worked out. There's a car waiting to take me to a friend's for a spell. Then an apartment. Maybe a job one day. I'm happy to hang in this desert if that's the place that will have me. I don't need much. I only want what's given. And maybe I too will come back. We are who we are.

But first, a journey.

A pale winter sun hangs in the sky, this day no different from the days that came before and will follow.

The streets are busy, cars and pedestrians, coming and going, moving who knows where.

I approach like Florida did, heading north on Western. I stick to the sidewalk. I won't own the streets like she did. I am a spectator, a watcher. Not the main event.

I pass shops and strip malls and shopping plazas.

Korean restaurants and cafés.

Buses and banks. A city coming back to life.

I don't know Los Angeles. I don't know normal from not. I suspect it's only half in action, but then again, I don't really care.

Marta is quiet. She's been quieter since we got out. Her work is nearly done, she tells me. She knows I understand what I've done and that there's no undoing it, only carrying it. And that is how we will move forward. Together.

The intersection is busy. It's wide, four lanes in either direction. A Friday-afternoon line stretches around the bank. Opposite it, the neon lights on the shopping plaza's sign dance dully in the sunshine.

There's the gas station. It's filled with cars every which way along the pumps.

There are cars backed up along Western, waiting out the long light.

What do they see?

Are they aware? Or is the mural unnoticed in the rush to be elsewhere?

I see it immediately, the movement.

I see Florida striding up Western. I see her approaching the end of her story.

It's a gun in her hand. You can't see it in the painting, but I know.

I know how this will play out.

I cross the street to get a better look.

The city falls away. The cars and buses, the voices. The whir of traffic and the whip-whip of the light wind.

Dios stands firm. Mistaken in her confidence. Trying to dominate until the end.

Except there's a choice that's been made—a magic the artist hasn't granted her. Except for a loose strand of hair, Dios is stagnant, frozen.

But the mural's beauty is in its movement. And that's all Florida. Florida on the move. Florida taking control. Florida walking up Western, in motion eternal.

Mostly they blow past the mural—the cars and pedestrians, the customers coming and going from the gas station's quickie mart.

But I can't take my eyes off it. I stand there until the sun slips away to the west, over the ocean I'm still hoping to see.

A man steps out from the store to smoke.

"That thing," he says, exhaling toward the mural. "It moves, right?"

We watch.

"You see," he says. He tosses his butt. "There's a story there. I'm certain."

True enough there is. But I don't have to tell it anymore.

"Come on," I say to Marta. "Let's go."

"Who are you talking to?" the man asks.

"Everyone," I reply.

ACKNOWLEDGMENTS

Thanks to my wonderful agent and remarkable friend Kim Wither-spoon, who got this from the get-go, and to my exceptional editor, Daphne Durham, who took it to the next level. As always to Jessica Mileo and Lyndsey Blessing at Inkwell, as well as William Callahan, whose edits were savage but mostly necessary. Thanks to Brianna Fairman, Sarita Varma, Claire Tobin, Sheila O'Shea, Bri Panzica, Daniel del Valle, and everyone at MCD and Farrar, Straus and Giroux. Gratitude to Smith Henderson. Extra special thanks to Jonathan Lethem for taking me to Upland and Baldy and letting me borrow them, and to Susan Straight for giving me advice and confidence when I needed them most. Ongoing gratitude to the one and only Gary Frenkel, who has designed and maintained my website for so many years. My thanks to Justin and Loretta. And finally to my parents, Philip and Elizabeth Pochoda, who remain, as always, my first and best readers and without whom I would be . . . well, who knows?